I0593517

THE HEALER

BROWN MOHAMED

Cedar&Oak
PUBLISHING HOUSE

To the one reading this, just know that
I wrote this story specifically for you.

...but it goes both ways, so in turn,
thank you for the motivation!

I

The last two months had been a blur, but Mark remembers the nightmares beginning only a few weeks ago.

Rachel was furious—he didn't recognise her. During his dreams, she'd turned into a man-slaying demon with only one objective: kill Mark. She was angry—vengeance and death emitting from her core. Her long blonde hair was now jet black, curled like rearing snakes, and her eyes—her soft and bright hazel-green eyes—were folded into dark narrow slits. A demon ready to devour its prey.

He feared her. At times, he swore that he'd seen it during his waking hours, the beast slipping out from his subconscious. One time, he was sure he saw it looking at him with those threatening eyes as he pulled into his driveway, but maybe it was a sign he was beginning to lose his mind.

"Mark? Mark!"

Eyes blinking, he snapped out of his reverie.

Right. Board meeting.

He must have zoned out—the general topic was regarding the direction of the company based on the last quarter's performance. He'd been in countless meetings like this. He enjoyed the post-meeting chatter. It allowed him to interact with some of the company's most senior teams.

Mark had proven himself as a programmer, single-handedly (for the most part, although his close work friend

Brad would probably disagree!) developing the CyberGuard Security Solution the company still uses to this day. It was twelve years ago. He'd completed his degree in computer science and IT and was one of the lucky few to be granted an internship working on Varion's (the company's) security system and coding for cutting-edge software. It was a crucial step at the time—Mark was young and full of enthusiasm—and it didn't take long to prove himself to his bosses.

From a young age, Mark focused on his career. His thirst had led him to become the general manager of Varion, a company boasting some of the globe's greatest minds in tech, VR and AI. It employed just shy of one thousand people with sixteen offices worldwide.

With relentless passion, each day was a new and exciting challenge. He was smart; articulate and intellectual—something many said about him—but things at Varion quickly went from bad to worse.

Mark tilted his head, a quick gaze to his left before scanning the room. They all wore the same expensive suits—Briony, most likely.

"...Mark, after our last two meetings, we haven't seen a change in your behaviour and performance and the board feels you're no longer an asset. Out of good faith, we feel it's appropriate to let you finish the last three months of your current project. But following that, we'll have no choice but to—"

A pause.

"—to let you go."

Mark squinted, simultaneously scrunching his face. He wiped it with his right hand before springing his head up, attempting to survey the space. He had no idea who'd given the speech—just that it was someone on the opposite end of the room. It didn't matter though.

It took him a few moments to realise what was happening, but once it sunk in, red and black smudged across his vision.

"What, me?"

Silence.

What the fuck? All those hours—the sleepless nights working on proposals, plans and apps. All the challenges and effort. He'd given this company everything. And those first two "meetings" about his behaviour and performance (or lack of)? Bullshit.

And not to mention Mark's contribution to Varion. His CyberGuard system had implemented a strategy that ensured the company's data was secure—it filtered spam, prevented viruses and its AI was complex enough to update itself by attempting to hack Varion's system, the one it was designed to protect. CyberGuard had gained industry-wide recognition as the most secure software available. It made Mark famous as the Corporate Security Genius. And now they were sacking him. Bastards.

And Rachel—

"Anything you want to say?"

Mark snickered. "No." What was the point?

"We know how hard it's been, especially with your loss."

Mark's palms began to sweat. The nerve they had to bring her into this. Crimson filled his mind. He balled his fists at his sides, rage blurring his thoughts.

I can't blow up now. I have to calm down.

His heart pounded, threatening to burst through his chest. His shirt felt uncomfortably tight, the air around him oppressive and heavy. Fury rose, a tangled, throbbing knot of rage demanding to take over.

He took a few deep breaths before muttering, "I've been nothing but committed to this—to the *company*."

"We might be able to shuffle things around but for now, it's not the best look. Your lack of professionalism and attention to detail has given the board no other choice."

It was difficult to understand why they were so calm. *Can't they see what I've been through?*

Mark wanted to grab each one of them and shake them—shake some sense into their heads.

"I was willing to focus on this company more now than ever—and it's come to *this*?" His anger dissipated, but the frustration didn't. Despite his efforts to keep from exploding, his voice quivered like a wounded child, betraying his feelings to the boardroom.

"Mark, we're with you. If there's anything you need—"

He scoffed, wiping his face again, this time with a little more vigour. "No, don't give me that!"

"Well, that concludes our meeting. Business as usual."

They all hurried out. Mark rose from his chair last and walked over to the window that stretched from the floor to the ceiling. He stared out over the city skyline and the Brisbane River below. It felt like a rock was tethered to him—to his guts, to his chest, to his heart—and he feared he'd fall through the floor.

He'd miss the view. His eyes trailed a vessel that floated on murky, brown water. It calmed him, but not by much. Not the most pristine view, but magical in its own way. It brought a distinct flavour to the city he had enjoyed calling home. A culture that locals and visitors appreciated about a town that screamed progress, but deep down, was as laid back as they come.

He'd always wanted a corporate job, working in IT and software development.

What was all that for?

All those years. He'd lost Rachel, and the same had just happened to his career. He couldn't understand the board's decision to dismiss him. Had he been that bad at work? Sure, he probably could have worked a little more efficiently, but that calls for more conversation, not a sever.

II

It had been two months, but Mark could remember as though it happened just yesterday. She was gone. Rachel.

He'd always struggled with the truth—and so he considered himself responsible.

She was five and a half feet but had made a tall impression on Mark's life. It had been impossible to imagine a life without her. Especially one where things would turn out the way they did.

When not haunted by the thought of what happened, he was often lost in the fantasies of the joyous, lustful and romantic moments they'd spent together.

Her perfume. He smelt it everywhere—and his heart would jolt every time. A racing pulse that made it difficult to focus. Sometimes on the way to work if she crossed his mind. At the grocery store if he noticed her favourite ice cream. And other times for no reason at all.

He couldn't forget the day they met.

He was in the café near work, rushing toward his usual, hurried-morning coffee. A petite blonde had stepped into view. Mark's eyes widened. Curves in all the right places. But those eyes... magnetic, green eyes. And they stared right through him as she moved toward him. Her smile glowed when her eyes met Mark's, crinkling at the corners.

Everything went silent.

The room (and his day) had felt brighter. But that was after Mark collided into a table where some people sat.

He'd apologised, but he didn't care to see whether they'd responded.

Running into her there became a regular thing—until he'd decided to shoot his shot. She had a bubbly voice. A sparkle in her eye. And eventually it led to ice cream, the first step in a string of memories—lots of them. Getaways. Sun and sand. Also mountains, nature and bushwalks. Their date nights often involved more ice cream. Other times, a restaurant for the two self-proclaimed foodies. In fact, they'd created an Instagram account to highlight some gourmet adventures.

Our delicious encounters. Yum. That was the bio—and they'd amassed hundreds of followers.

Over the last two months Mark had scrolled through the profile so many times it was anyone's guess how his thumb still worked.

And now she was gone.

Toward the latter stages of their time together, he barely knew her—and he'd let her down. The train that was their relationship derailed along the way. And by the time Mark realised, it was too late. Now he was left to pick up the pieces, wondering how he'd let it happen.

It was ten years since they'd met. Today was their second wedding anniversary.

And what made things worse was that every time he started to heal, an invisible hand would grip him. Suffocate him. And remind him that it wasn't '*right*' for him to move on.

"Not easy, is it?"

Jerking up on the spot, Mark flinched. There was still someone in the room. Mark spun around. A man sat at the table, looking his way.

His persona differed from the rest of them. It was positive—calming. Possibly it was the way he held himself; no slouch, back straight and chin up. A weak, yet genuine smile. Confident, but not arrogant. Unlike the faceless members of the boardroom that just let him go.

"Didn't mean to scare you," he began. His voice was soft but simultaneously powerful. The cadence was reassuring to Mark's ears.

He rose to his feet. He wore a classy navy suit. No crinkles in sight. Mark was six foot—but even then, the man towered over him by at least some inches. Maybe in his thirties—around Mark's age. He had well-groomed facial hair. A short, contoured beard and hair that was shaped to one side.

It would probably have been more fitting to see him on a men's fashion feature.

"I know what you're thinking, but I'm Henry—Henry Frayne," he said, thrusting his hand forward. "I was hired as a contractor, but they offered me a permanent position— and a seat at the table."

Mark went to shake his hand, then snatched it back once realisation popped in his head.

"You're replacing me? You knew?" The red haze of rage began to descend once more.

"I didn't know their intentions. And I heard a lot about you—mostly praise. So when your wife... well, I suggested they give you time. But now, based on your... *recent performance.*"

Henry paused before the last bit.

"You think it's your fault, and you feel bad?" Mark said, folding his arms. "I'm not looking for sympathy, and I won't give you what you're looking for. Leave me alone."

II

"I know. I do feel bad and I wanted you to hear the truth from me."

"Oh well."

"This isn't fair," Henry protested.

Was Henry pitying him? A crude joke? Who knows?

"How long have you been with Varion?" Mark asked. He relaxed his arms by his side.

"About two years—kept extending my contract. Then they offered me the permanent position. Must've liked my work."

Mark glared at Henry but before he could say anything, Henry continued. "Are you okay? You coping?"

How, and why, has this turned into a therapy session? Who is he? How does he know so much? Why did he tell Varion to give me time?

Mark barely knew Henry—and here he was, more invested in his life than Mark was himself.

Henry quickly added, shaking his head, "You don't have to answer that," after Mark stayed quiet. "You at least talking to someone about it?"

"What?"

"Everyone can benefit from it. Especially after something traumatic. You have family you talk to?"

How had the conversation taken such a tangent? Even worse, Mark wondered why he felt so open and willing to reply.

"No, we barely speak."

"Sorry to hear that."

"Doesn't matter."

An uncomfortable pause lulled in the conversation. For a moment they were stuck staring into each other's eyes. The chatter of employees outside the room drifted through and the only other sound was Mark's heavy breathing. He was tempted to turn back around and face the window. Henry spoke, beating him to it.

"There's someone I know. He's great. You should see him."

Mark was both surprised and annoyed by the persistence. "I don't need your help," he snapped, folding his arms again.

"He'll tell you what you need to hear—his name's Apollo," Henry insisted.

"Sounds like a waste of time."

"You may see it as a sign of weakness, but it isn't."

Mark shook his head before muttering, "I can't believe this," to himself.

"I can't make you do anything, but you're struggling. Everyone knows it—and if you're not willing to do anything to help yourself, maybe they were right to let you go."

"Are you serious?" growled Mark. "Who do you think you are?"

"Just telling you the truth. Take his card. Do it for Rachel."

Henry's words hit home. Mark bowed his head, eyes darting across the floor. He uncrossed his arms.

He calmed down, then met Henry's gaze.

Mark sighed. He snatched the business card from Henry's outstretched hand.

"You're a good man. I can sense that. But you need to be careful and treasure your gift. Sometimes good men turn because they can't channel their energy properly."

Energy?

To hide his confusion, Mark nodded and rolled his eyes. If taking the card meant Henry would leave him alone, he was more than willing to go down that path.

FLASHBACK #1

"A little pretentious, don't you think?" Rachel teased through a grin.

"Maybe a little," Mark replied. He raised his eyebrows. "Wait, are you saying I'm not that important?"

"You're very important to *me*."

She stared, her face glowing, wide-eyed, unblinking, with a broad smile. Mark couldn't help but adore her. He eyed the freckles on her upper cheekbone leading to dimples on the sides of her mouth.

They both burst out laughing.

"I think it's too big." She was whispering now—the footsteps of the real estate agent were getting louder.

She was right. Extravagance and status were things Rachel had never cared about. She'd be happy living in a shack if it meant they were together. The thing with Rachel is that when she'd said that, some months ago when they began their house hunt, Mark knew she meant it. He'd said a similar thing too once, but he didn't mean it. To him, it was just one of those things people say when they love each other.

They'd moved in together at Mark's place, two years after they'd met—where Mark was renting. But Mark wanted to buy a house by the bay. Luckily, when he started moving up the ranks at work, money came with it. It turns out Varion was willing to give him bonuses on CyberGuard's success. And with more clients now adopting it due to its reliability, speed and security came even more money. Rachel, a graduate design engineer made reasonable money and so, with both their incomes, it didn't take long to save.

It was a modern two-storey overlooking the bay. The five bedrooms were far too many according to Rachel. It represented Mark—slick, new and edgy, a contrast of dark and white shades on steel and concrete with large windows wrapping most of the house. The bay views and afternoon breeze were a bonus that could be experienced on the open-plan of the lower level. The connected outdoor space led to a pool and the flat roofing finished off the aggressively progressive design. They'd spoken about their dream home plenty of times. Mark knew what they both wanted and it ticked all the boxes.

Mark had already made up his mind.

Earlier that morning Mark left Rachel a note on the kitchen counter. They enjoyed riddles and leaving clues. To them, it kept the relationship interesting. And hand-written notes may be outdated but as much as Mark loved technology (seriously, you'd think he possessed every gadget made—he was obsessed!), he enjoyed the authenticity of a handwritten piece. It felt real in a world full of plastic, acrylic, screens, buttons, codes and metal sheets.

On the note were clues to finding the house. Noon sharp, the note insisted—7 Kay Avenue, he couldn't have made it any more obvious:

The one you love has found us the perfect home.
The one I love needs to see to believe.
What do you find at the end of the clock? That's the avenue
you'll find me. Don't make me say the suburb again. At a time

that is spelt the same forward and backward. The house is an
odd number but take away a letter and it becomes even.
Don't be late...
Btw I'm sure you'll figure this out but if you don't, text me and
I might give you a clue (wink emoji). x

He knew she'd be disappointed he'd chosen to go to work on a Saturday morning but it would only be a few hours. He had to oversee a major system update. Weekends were best because, well, no one was in the office.

He had his own office now as head of AI, data and web-based application development. He'd only had it two weeks but wasted no time in making it his own. Which began with clearing out the room, then a thorough clean, which led to meticulously placing items where they belonged. A sturdy, wooden desk occupied the centre of the room with his laptop sitting directly in the middle. Behind him stood a bookshelf with books organised by author and name. Cords were kept to a minimum and so was clutter. He was on the same open plan floor. He could see his old desk through the glass, but it felt good to have his own space.

He could see Brad's desk. They'd been in the same internship program and had spent some time working on the system that Mark became renowned for. Brad wasn't as ambitious. He had the brains, but he lacked the drive. Mark couldn't help but feel that Brad would be where he was if he hadn't chosen the nightlife over his career. Many people, Brad included, never understood why Mark turned down every invitation to *party* on weekends, but maybe they would eventually. Mark shook the thoughts of his colleagues and entered his office.

Once inside, he got to work. Mainly checking the status of the update on the laptop screen, replying to emails and organising workflows and tasks for the following week.

An hour later he heard a notification on his phone. For a second he thought Rachel hadn't figured out the riddle when he saw her name fill the centre of the screen. His reflexes kicked in and he snatched the phone without thinking which lay perfectly straight on his desk about thirty centimetres away from the computer.

I love you and I already love our new home. 7 Kay Avenue. See you at 12 handsome.

Several red-heart emojis followed.

III

Driving home later that day and with the low sun dominating his rear-view mirror, Mark wondered why Henry would want to help him. It wasn't Henry's fault that the company was discarding him. Henry had taken a personal interest.

But they didn't know each other.

He appreciated living away from the hustle and bustle of the city. 7 Kay Avenue had hardly any traffic, only the occasional barking of dogs down the street and he didn't suffocate from cigarette smoke. Even years after having worked in the city, he'd never gotten used to it.

Rachel had suggested moving closer, but to him the distance was perfect. So by the bayside it was. Right near the boat harbour so when they had any free time and felt like exploring the waterfront, they were able to.

He pulled into his driveway and pressed a button on his keychain to open the garage door. He lowered his window, the scent of freshly cut grass filling his nostrils and the sound of a whirring blade invading his ears. The neighbours must be mowing their lawn.

Even though the garage was dimly lit, he could still clearly make out the same demonic entity that had appeared here before.

Rachel.

She stood, holding what looked like a broomstick, her eyes wide and teeth showing in a menacing glare. Mark knew who she planned to use the weapon on.

She vanished as quickly as she had appeared, but she was there.

"I'm losing my mind," he muttered. He shook his head, trying to get her out of his head. *Maybe I do need help.* He was reminded of Henry when he poked into his pocket and felt the business card.

Inside, he pulled it out. It was plain. Only two words— Apollo and Therapist—and a number. The back was blank. No address, no website, not even an email address.

Interesting.

He pulled out his phone and called the number.

It had barely rung for a second before someone picked it up.

"Mark, I knew you'd call!" A high-pitched voice. A little too lively for Mark. Too perky.

Mark cringed.

How do they know my name?

"Is this some sort of joke? Because I don't have time—"

Between everything going on, Mark didn't have the energy, or patience to deal with some joke Henry wanted to pull. He had jobs to look for, and with bills to pay, he had more important things to worry about.

"It's not a joke. My name's Apollo. Can we meet tonight?"

Mark was taken aback. There was an awkward silence. His rapid breathing led to dryness in his throat. Not realising the appointment would be scheduled so soon. "Um, I-I guess so."

"Excellent. West End, 14 Hickory Lane. Let's say, one hour?"

"Um, sure—one hour."

He slipped into something comfortable and climbed back into his car.

* * *

Thirty minutes later, he arrived at his destination. He walked up the first few stairs of a small house and had barely knocked when the door swung open. He was relieved he didn't see Henry, laughing. He relaxed a little.

He was greeted with a smile. That had to be Apollo— a beaming smile on a small figure with a strong posture, hidden by an overly baggy t-shirt and overalls. Mark felt at ease staring at pearl-white teeth that enjoyed being on display.

"I've heard a lot about you. Come in, make yourself at home."

Apollo ushered him into an unkempt bungalow and through to the living room. Books were everywhere, ranging from nonfiction self-help books to high fantasy novels. They spilled off the shelves onto every available surface, piled up around the twin burgundy leather armchairs and matching sofa. Several lamps were crammed into the gaps and some cushions and bean bags were spread across the floor.

"Please, take a seat."

Mark sat in one of the armchairs, instantly chipper from how comfortable it was.

"Okay, let's get into it. Some of what I'll tell you, you'll find strange—but bear with me."

Mark rubbed his chin. Intriguing.

"I used to be like you. Lost, angry at the world, angry at *myself*."

Mark's nostril's flared. His jaws clenched.

"I sense an interesting energy," Apollo muttered.

"What do you mean?" Mark replied. His jaw relaxed.

"Do you believe in fate?"

Mark rolled his eyes. "No, I don't like the idea of not having control over my life."

"Good," Apollo said, his white teeth still showing. "You have potential, like most people. But it's only potential unless you do something—"

"What?" Mark replied, with an exaggerated swallow.

Apollo spoke to the floor. "It's sad, most don't realise their full potential. We live our lives with an itch we can't scratch. And you know why?" He brought his head up. His eyes met Mark's.

Apollo stroked his chin, head perched, then stared at the ceiling, talking to himself again.

"It's because we've trapped our minds. Focusing on things that don't serve our purpose—"

"What—purpose?"

"We're completely oblivious. Doing the same thing day in, day out. Like drones."

Mark started thinking about his job—his old job. Confusion filled his mind as he tried to follow Apollo's ramblings.

"We've been turned into zombies—robots—whatever you want to call it. And no one questions anything—"

"I don't understand."

"—I started questioning things, and it changed my life. We're more than what you believe; we're just limited by our minds."

Mark's head spun. Dizziness set in.

"I know why you can't sleep at night. You see her, don't you? She haunts you—"

Mark froze in his seat. Breath held. Eyes wide.

"H-how do you..." he began, only for the words to die on his tongue.

How could he know about her?

"Doesn't matter how I know—but like you said, you're in control of your life."

"I don't understand."

"You blame yourself. You're filled with self-loathing because of what happened."

Mark twisted his face into an angry, confused scowl. His chest felt warm and tension was mounting in his upper back. He couldn't prevent his fists from clenching, the stiffness riding up to his shoulders and causing them to hunch. It was getting too much. Too close to home, too close to Mark. *How does he know all of this?*

"You have no idea what I'm going through—"

Cutting Mark off, Apollo applied pressure on Mark's forehead with two fingers. Instantly, the room began to spin and morph, thick ashy smoke clouding Mark's vision. Mark waved his arms in front of him, frantically flailing his arms to clear the fog, but couldn't dissipate it at all.

In moments, it cleared.

He was in the same armchair, but Apollo's living room had disappeared. Like they had transported somewhere else. *But how?*

He couldn't tell *where* he was. The room had transformed into a bright canvas, his view a blinding white wherever he looked.

Apollo's voice behind him made him jump in his seat.

"What is this?" Mark asked.

"Endless possibility," Apollo said, grinning.

The white started to take shape. The canvas bled away, and a board room took shape, with large floor-to-ceiling windows. Outside, an odd pinkish glow emanated from the sky.

After several minutes of convincing himself that it was nothing more than an illusion, he had no choice but to accept his fate.

"You need to face some of your fears. It'll help you to heal," Apollo whispered.

Mark remained silent, digesting the room around them.

Aside from the pinkish glow, it was similar to the board room he'd been in that morning. He recognised the large table in the centre and the chairs surrounding it. He stared at the seat he was in not even twelve hours ago. It made no sense. *Why would he bring me here?* It was true. He felt resentment toward the place—but it didn't represent any fears.

"You notice anything?"

"No," Mark replied.

His eyes panned across the walls. Then he saw it. The art on the walls. He couldn't remember art being there. But if it was, it wouldn't have been what he saw before him now. It disturbed him. Made his stomach turn. The sadistic themes. And it was moving—like horrifying, framed gifs.

It had to be hypnosis. But why would art like this be in a board room in the first place?

Mark found it difficult to make sense of it. The blood, death and gore sprawled across the walls caused his nausea to worsen. His knees started shaking.

He gasped at one painting. It portrayed a man swinging a bat embedded with nails toward the head of a woman. The man cackled. He'd brought the bat high above his head, eyes locked onto the woman.

Why was he laughing?

When he analysed the man, Mark held his breath. There was no denying it. It was him. Slightly taller, some scars, but obvious similarities. The same sky-blue, long-sleeved shirt. Less obvious were the light-brown eyes and the lean, muscular build. Their facial features were identical—a narrow face with contoured cheekbones and some facial hair.

His eyes darted to the woman. It was Rachel. She cowered. Her mouth gaped. She held up both arms, attempting to shield her face from the swinging bat.

"W-what is this?!" Mark demanded, pointing at the painting with a shaky finger. "Get me out of here. *Now!*"

His heart felt like it was about to burst through his chest cavity. An oppressive heaviness weighed on him, an iron band wrapped around his lungs, squeezing the breath out of him.

There was no reply from Apollo. It didn't matter though, for now.

Mark became distracted by a full-length mirror. What he saw instead of his reflection made his stomach clench. It was the same man. The man from the art.

And he moved by himself.

He slid his index finger across his neck and pointed at Mark. Mark knew what the man was thinking: you know what you did.

Sweat breaking across his brow, Mark looked across to Apollo, searching for comfort. None was given. Apollo's teeth had disappeared inside a tightly sealed mouth.

"Why does this feel so real?" he asked, keeping his eyes on the mirror.

"You're making it real."

His attention shifted.

21

He saw her, at the edge of the room. Rachel. Unsure how long she'd been standing there. She swayed a little, her expression blank, mouth slightly open.

She muttered to herself. She looked human. Long blonde hair hung down her back. Her eyes were wide and she blinked slowly.

As Mark's breathing steadied, Apollo snapped his fingers. She froze for a second. Within seconds she changed. Her eyes narrowed and turned from their hazel green into a murky black. Her skin morphed from attractive olive to a drained, pale white. Mark's skin pricked as the air snapped to freezing, and the pinkish glow of the sunset vanished, replaced by a darkness that seeped into the room.

She picked up a laptop on the table and threw it at him. She screamed. Mark recoiled, then shouted, but before the computer slammed into him, the setting began rippling and undulating again, the device vanishing right before his eyes.

He couldn't find an escape to the hypnotic trance, or whatever it was.

The transformation stopped. It didn't take long to realise where he was—home. He recognised the fruity-tropical scent of the diffuser sitting on his glass coffee table. It was well past due for replacing, but it reminded him of Rachel. For a moment he pondered buying a new one and hiding that one in his bedroom.

"That didn't go so well, so—here we are," Apollo said, his voice stained with disappointment.

"Why are you doing this?"

"It's all you," he replied.

Growing frustrated at all the cryptic answers, Mark balled his fists at the sides of his body, clenching his jaw. "What do you *mean*?"

"You control your life, remember? So you control this reality. I'm just trying to help with insight."

Mark was starting to believe that maybe Apollo was a psychopath with the ability to hypnotise people.

"It's nice," Apollo said, nodding his head at the walls. "I can see you've worked hard."

Mark rolled his eyes.

"Realising anything?" he asked.

"What is there to realise?" Mark spat, and Apollo shook his head.

"Guilt and self-loathing—suppressed—are now show-ing up because you think they should—and you've turned these things into something ugly."

Apollo sat opposite Mark, in an armchair.

Mark's confusion turned to irritation.

He thought about Rachel. Then she appeared, down the hallway. Rocking on her feet, as though in another trance.

Must be Apollo.

But Mark knew she still hated him.

"She doesn't hate you—"

Mark could hardly make out what Apollo had said— he couldn't pull his eyes away. He wanted to remember her like this.

His irritation turned to aggravation. The lack of control the main culprit. With fists still tightly clenched, he lashed out. "I don't know what this is, but I've had enough. You need to get me out of here, now!" Mark raised his voice.

"Sure, but give me a few more minutes, we're making progress."

It was difficult to see how this could be *'progress'*. Mark's frustration lingered but he reluctantly nodded. He barely blinked, staring at Rachel.

"She hasn't attacked you. It's not her, it's you."

Mark shook his head. He wanted to yell. The muscles of his jaw tightened, the veins in his neck throbbing. He raised his hand, feeling the tension that was there.

"You know what I think?" Apollo continued.

Mark rolled his eyes again. Apollo's words escalated the emotion he'd tried containing. The sides of his face became hot. The ball of fury grew inside him. It was a rapid realisation. If it came down to what Apollo *'thought'* without hard facts or logical reasoning, Mark couldn't take him seriously.

Mark squeezed in his fists—but remained silent, predominantly out of fear. *What if Apollo leaves me in this hypnotic trance?* It was new to Mark—but it felt real. He caught a whiff of his neighbour's freshly cut lawn trimmings as well as made out the distinct roar of the lawnmower. Birds chirped and the occasional car sped past. The air-con nipped at his skin.

Apollo shrugged. "I think you can direct this energy into something more productive."

Mark's hands trembled and his head grew hotter—to the point of near explosion. Rachel moved. She was coming out of her daze, in perfect sync with his rage.

"I want to get out of here!" he growled.

Rachel jerked her head up. Her eyes on him. They began to mutate.

"Just get me out of here!" He was shouting now. He stood from the sofa, arms crossed. It felt as though flames were licking against his skin, his blood boiling in his veins.

Her skin morphed.

"I've figured you out, and it's—well fascinating! Now I know why we met!" Apollo said, unapparent to the danger brewing behind him.

He just doesn't get it.

They'd barely known each other. Outrageous.

He has to be insane.

The temperature dropped. Mark braced himself. Any minute now and she would charge at him, but—she'd disappeared.

"You're a healer."

It was clear why she had disappeared. She stepped toward him now with a chef's knife. He wanted to warn Apollo, but he was so furious with him that he couldn't bring himself to. Apollo sat with his back to her.

Maybe we'll both be butchered.

"What?" Mark asked, maintaining his gaze on her.

"You're a healer. That's what tonight's been about. It was no accident." Apollo chuckled.

She was still at the other end of the room.

Why is he laughing? Doesn't he realise the danger we're in?

"Let it go. She won't attack."

She was halfway now. She tiptoed, creeping closer.

"Take a deep breath, Mark."

He could almost see the tendrils in her eyes.

"Relax. Mark!"

She leapt into the air.

"*Mark!*"

He saw it as though it happened in slow motion. Then he felt it. The cold, sharp blade sinking into his chest.

Then another hack. Then a slash. The pain was excruciating. Apollo shouted something, but he couldn't make it out. Everything became blurry, and every part of his body screamed in agony. Everything was coated in red. Blood sprayed from his chest.

This must be what it feels like to die.

Through heavy gasps of air, he tried fighting through the pain. As he closed his eyes, a part of him felt comfort in that she was the last person he would see.

FLASHBACK #2

The house was perfect. It was all they'd been thinking about for weeks. Mark hadn't slept last night. Rachel neither. The anticipation that filled both of them was rightfully so. Today was move in day.

It had been months in the works (and it felt like time had been going backward!).

"I'll only be gone a few hours," he started, yawning. His eyes felt puffy.

"Every Saturday you have an excuse to go to work. Even today?"

Rachel attempted to laugh it off but Mark could tell she was annoyed. Knowing her, she probably had something extravagant planned in celebration. It was true, Mark was excited, but it wasn't that big of a deal. It was only a small part of the bigger picture.

There was no point lying in bed awake, both hearts racing, so there they were. 6AM and both eating a plain breakfast—toast with raspberry jam. Not even a coffee, or tea (there weren't many options—the house had been mostly packed and the fridge was almost empty at this point).

"It's not that big of a deal," he responded. "I'll head there around one."

"Okay."

"Love you."

"Love you too babe! I'm so excited!"

Mark paused and grinned as he looked at her. It reminded him of a child when she got excited. Made him feel young.

It was still early but Mark figured he could get a head start, so he pecked her on the cheek and he was off.

No traffic. Perfect. But that early, and on a Saturday—there was no chance.

A podcast filled the cabin of Mark's car (something about free speech and cruelty) but their house filled his mind. Momentarily, he scrunched his face with guilt thinking about Rachel picking up the keys and going herself. *It'll be fine, I'll be there as soon as I can.*

They could've gone together, later, but they told the real estate agency they'd pick up the keys before they closed at 12PM. Not to mention it was already bad enough working on the weekend, making Rachel wait around as a result wouldn't have been fair.

With a team of eight, he'd been working on NetFlow, a networking application for Varion and its clients. It would allow members of the network to rapidly get feedback, set workflows and tasks, assign staff, send information, pay invoices and communicate at a fraction of the time it took now to individually complete those tasks. It was exciting but bugs needed fixing.

He appreciated his team; however, he appreciated working by himself even more—after all, it was his initiative—and Saturday was the perfect day to work in peace.

The app's beta launch was in three months and nothing would get in his way. Efficiency, transparency, security and speed were the principles in which the app would exist. Faultless. Streamlined and perfect—he could already see it.

The vibration of his phone swiftly brought him back to reality. It was sat perfectly halfway between his computer and the edge of the desk.

Rachel sent you a picture.

He swore when he realised the time.

He pressed the notification, thinking it would be a photo of the house, and was instantly relieved no one else was in the office as his eyes widened. He blamed the pink negligee barely concealing a white, floral lingerie set with a choker of the same shade.

She knew how to get his attention.

In the background was the interior of their house, but who cared about that?

He left right away. In the car he wondered if he'd shut off the computer but he wasn't going back.

IV

Mark was drenched in sweat. He was disoriented. His chest was in agonising pain—*how*? *It wasn't real.*

A few minutes passed and the dizziness wore off. He recognised Apollo—they were back in his living room. He recognised the books, the chairs and the dim lighting.

"What happened?" Mark gasped for air, pain still lancing through his chest.

"It didn't work," Apollo began.

"What didn't work? And why does my chest hurt?!" he asked, seething with a mix of anger and confusion. What had he been thinking—coming out here, meeting with someone he didn't know, just to feel this pain?

"She wasn't supposed to attack you. It's good you're still alive. You kept telling yourself it wasn't real—so I guess there's that." Apollo was shaking. "Not sure how that went so wrong."

"I know it wasn't real."

"Your mind made it real. It's why your chest hurts. We failed."

"I'm done here," Mark snapped, raising himself from the seat. Shards of ice stabbed through his chest and he fell back into it, wincing with pain. He pawed at his chest, trying to find the wound, but nothing was there.

"It doesn't matter—I can't help anyway. I've never failed anyone before, and I'm sorry. I'm glad you're still alive."

Alive?

How could I have died?

Mark was lost. There was no logical reasoning to explain how he could have died—but then again, the pain. It felt like he'd been speared through the chest.

"Get some rest. Take some days off work. Let your chest heal."

He didn't need another invitation to leave. After battling through the throbbing pain, he got up and hobbled to the door.

"Remember, it's all in your mind."

"Sure," Mark muttered under his breath as he left through the front door, still struggling for air.

He squinted at the sun in the sky—adding to further confusion.

He staggered to his car.

On the way home, thoughts ran through his head. *Had it been a dream? If evil Rachel was just a figment of his imagination did that mean he was clinically insane—suffering from hallucinations? Maybe what Apollo should have done was refer him to a clinic.*

His swirling, tangled and messy thoughts gave him a headache and he clamped his jaw, anxiety settling into his muscles.

Through the pain, he made it home. He stumbled over to the sofa and fell down, collapsing onto the soft surface.

* * *

His eyes popped open. He reached for his phone and tapped the screen. It had been almost twenty-four hours. His chest still hurt, but not nearly as much.

Several missed calls from work. *Who cares?* Shaking his head, he tossed his phone aside. It bounced off the sofa and onto the floor. Mark ignored it.

Am I feeling a little better today? Strange. He felt relaxed. He took some deep breaths. The usual dull headache that often persisted when he woke up had vanished.

He stood and admired the wedding photos on the wall near the sofa. He wanted to smile but his face failed him. He wanted to hold her like that again—horizontally, gazing into her eyes.

Remorse filled his heart, replacing the anger that had been following him for so long.

Hot, salty tears began to roll down his face. He didn't even notice at first, not until they reached his chin and fell, landing on his shirt. Exhaling slowly, he unhunched his back and corrected his posture. A weight lifted off his shoulders. Then he felt it. The comfort forming in his chest as he stared into her eyes. It was a warm kind of love without the pain of losing her. But it felt rough around the edges, like it was laced with hurt hiding underneath, threatening to burst through at any second.

He put on some of her favourite RnB classics and for a moment, as Mary J. Blige resonated in the living room, he listened and the corners of his lips finally curved up— just slightly—reminiscing when the song had filled the room on their wedding day.

He stayed home that day.

He didn't bother with the voice messages. He'd lost count of how many there were. The encounter with Apollo was at the forefront of his mind, torn between whether it had been a dream or hypnosis. Regardless, he'd rather waste his time looking into what he'd been told, dream or no dream—*but then again, the chest pain*? It would serve as a good distraction from Apollo, the pain and most of all, *her*.

A Google search on healing ended in disappointment—nothing of interest appeared. Aside from a few dictionary definitions and hospital jargon, it was, for the most part, useless. Although, he did see something about Reiki Healing. If he wanted to learn more, he would need to find a library, or worse, Apollo. The thought of having to spend more time with that man made him shiver.

* * *

Over several days, the chest pain faded.

The strange experience had been shoved to the back of Mark's mind. The unexplained chest pain would remain that way—there was no way he was willing to try and get answers from Apollo. Maybe he'd fallen during hypnosis and landed on the edge of one of Apollo's fancy, leather sofas. It seemed the more logical explanation.

Fortunately (although, Mark wouldn't dare consider it a correlation), he had fewer nightmares and no longer saw Demon Rachel while awake. It was clear she was still out for vengeance, but she resorted to appearing only in his dreams. Last night she'd tried running him over while he crossed his street. She'd driven the Toyota Hilux she'd disliked so much when they'd first met. Even his subconscious version of her still resented it.

With the chest pain continuing to mend, Mark remembered his conversation with Henry. He'd mentioned his family. He hadn't visited since moving away, but he feared forgetting who they were. Apart from the funeral, he'd last seen his family two years ago, at their wedding.

As a child, it wasn't easy. Mark appreciated that his mum, Alice, did the best she could.

His dad's suicide, however, had never been easy for Mark to accept.

For years, he'd tried escaping the reality of it all. Mark convinced himself everything was okay and that Dad was on a business trip. When Dad never came home, he told himself that he'd moved. Left them. He didn't dare entertain the fact that somehow his dad had died. But then the surface lies embedded themselves deeply into who he was, and what he believed—and for some years it made life somewhat bearable.

Mark was ten at the time and as a child, didn't understand how difficult it was for those around him too—his mum and his three siblings. Even worse, he didn't know his dad was suffering.

Were all of them too much for him?

Dad always seemed so happy. He took Mark to soccer practice, they went fishing—all that normal dad stuff. He'd bought Mark runners that he'd won his first cross country race in. Dad had been so proud, hugging Mark so tightly that he crushed his ribs and Mark's feet came off the ground. He went on to wear the same shoes daily until they fell off his feet. His dad laughed when Mark had brought the busted shoes to him.

Mark remembers when *it* happened—it was a Saturday afternoon. His mum had gone to a netball game with his sisters. Michael, Mark's younger brother, was at his friend's. He'd shouted to Dad that he was going to the neighbour, Ryan's, place. No reply. It was unlike him to nap during the day. He went upstairs to say bye—maybe he hadn't heard him.

Vividly, Mark recalls walking in to find him on his bedroom floor, surrounded by pills. It looked like he'd been sitting on the floor, at the base of the bed just prior. It was hard to tell if it was sweat or tears that had rolled down his face. He looked pale and rigid, slumped to one side.

The regret of trying to wake him, then calling Mum (who didn't answer) instead of calling an ambulance kept Mark awake at night for years. *What had he been thinking? Maybe Dad would still be around.*

When the ambulance eventually came it was too late.

Rachel had often tried to convince him to reach out, but he would insist he was too busy with work. The reality was that he feared those memories—the ones attached to his family.

Mark clenched his jaw, picked up the phone and dialled the number.

His mum answered right away, her hoarse voice tinny through the speaker. Her persistent coughs interrupted the line. She'd been having regular colds. Mark suggested visiting another time but she insisted that weekend was fine.

They organised the trip. He'd stay with Michael and his family: wife Sarah and two kids; Ollie, who was seven and Laura, nine.

Mark had wanted children with Rachel. She joked about what their names would be. Their features.

He scowled thinking about how work had taken him to Melbourne more than his family had in the fourteen years since he'd left. But at the time he needed to get away. He'd needed the fresh start.

And so he accepted the offer from the university in Brisbane. It was a good reason to relocate—and he never really looked back.

Over the years they'd reached out, more than Mark himself had. Phone calls, invitations and the like—but they were met with refusal at nearly every instance.

But Mark missed home. He booked the next flight before he'd even ended the call.

After hanging up, he packed some things into a suitcase and made his way to the airport.

At the airport Mark was worried they'd be angry with him for being gone so long and considered that they wouldn't want to see him—but despite the overwhelming fear, he shook the thought of turning around.

Once his flight landed, he made his way to Michael's house. His niece and nephew greeted him with giggles and tight hugs, even though they barely knew him. Everyone was there. Mark's siblings, Ally, Beth and Michael, and their families.

His anxiety instantly turned to relief.

Mark got settled. They exchanged hugs and told stories. They talked for hours, until teacups ran dry and all that remained of biscuits and snacks were crumbs on saucers. The conversations followed a comfortable and natural trajectory, like they'd regularly caught up.

They spoke about what they'd wanted to be growing up. Beth, in a rock band, Michael had wanted to be a firefighter and Ally, a teacher.

Mark had wanted to be a superhero—specifically, Spider-Man—after being obsessed with the movies. But then he realised it was impossible. He needed to pay bills, and vigilante work doesn't provide an income. So, the corporate, IT life it was.

Rachel needed a hero.

The conversations died down. Nervous glances now directed his way.

Do they know what I'm thinking?

Ollie didn't receive the memo.

"What did you want to be?" he chirped at Mark.

"Let's give uncle a break," replied Sarah.

"No, it's okay. I wanted to be a superhero. Spider-Man."

"I want to be a superhero too—Iron Man!"

"I'm not a superhero, but apparently, I'm a healer," Mark laughed before sharing his encounter with Apollo.

"Sounds like hypnosis," Michael said, after the story.

"Can you stop Grandma's cough?" Ollie asked.

"I wish I could."

"Just try—"

"No, Ollie, enough," snapped Sarah.

Ollie whined, folding his arms. Mark decided to play along—there'd be no harm.

"Okay, I'll try. You ready?" Mark asked, walking over to his mum. She'd slumped into her armchair. She coughed as Mark approached.

"Yes!" Ollie replied.

"Okay," Mark said. He winked at the rest of his family. "You have to put your hand here, take a deep breath and focus." He grinned at his mum. She smiled, going along with it.

With two fingers, he applied pressure to her forehead. Mark inhaled deeply. Followed by a slow exhale.

The floor vanished underneath him. It only lasted a few seconds. The house faded away, transforming into an empty canvas. He stood next to his mum, who was still in the armchair.

Then everything snapped back, as quickly as it had transformed. Ollie said something but his ears felt weird, like he was on a plane. Mark couldn't make out what anyone was saying. He stared at his mum's unfocused gaze. She cocked her head, blinking rapidly. Mark felt disoriented, and flustered—a haze in his brain.

V

What had occurred had been all Mark could think about for the remainder of the weekend. And during that time, there were no answers. No logical explanation.

He had to contact Apollo.

Mark shuddered.

His family had made the trip to the airport to see him off. A grin replaced his confused frown as he shook his head, in appreciation of them.

As he walked up the tarmac, he glanced back.

He tried swallowing his developing guilt but it was difficult. It felt as though his throat was being squeezed at the sides. They had no idea what had happened between him and Rachel—and how he'd...

He shook the thought, turned toward the plane and made his way to it.

On the plane he was tormented by similar thoughts. Guilt weighed heavy on him, pushing him down until he slumped in his seat, his poor posture causing soreness in his lower back—and soon the rest of his body was aching.

Chills danced across his skin, and he raised his arm to switch off the air-con. The person next to him flashed a disgruntled look. But he spun his head back when Mark peered across.

The Uber ride home was cold too. "Can you switch the air conditioning off?" Mark asked, moments after the driver pulled out.

"Sure," was the friendly response. Mark wriggled and massaged his aching lower back and applied pressure to his chest.

Back home, it didn't take long for sickness to set in. He'd felt 'off' on the plane, dismissing his sore throat as something that would pass. Now he swore his entire body was on fire. Cold and hot sweats alternated in rapid succession, leaving his skin clammy and uncomfortable.

He'd barely been home two hours. But he struggled to his local doctor, who prescribed antibiotics and told him to get plenty of rest.

It only worsened, to the point where he hadn't eaten a proper meal in at least a few days.

He scratched his chin and pondered. He wasn't getting any better. His body ached. He'd had recurrent fevers.

He tried Apollo's number.

No answer.

He tried again. Same thing. Then again. He gritted his teeth.

He drove to the house. It was deserted. No lights on inside. Blinds closed. Mark knocked and waited but it was useless.

He must have moved, but why? And why is his number disconnected?

Mark clenched his jaw.

Had it been a dream?

He had no choice. Head drooped, muscles aching, he got back into his car and drove back home.

Once he was back, he was barely able to stay upright and crumpled onto the sofa.

* * *

There was a pounding on his door. Checking his phone, he saw that hours had passed—it was midday the following day.

"Come... in..." he croaked, barely having the energy to call out.

He heard the door open, and pounding footsteps filled his eardrums.

"You look terrible."

Mark was instantly relieved. Apollo leaned on the arm-rest of his couch, overlooking Mark. A heavy bag landed on the floor next to him.

"I experienced something similar—but psychological. I became depressed, irritable and anxious. Here, drink this."

Apollo passed Mark a flask, the container warm to the touch.

He brought the drink to his lips. It was sweet Aloe Vera. His headache subsided in minutes—and he was able to think.

"Henry mentioned that you weren't well." Mark bobbed his head, although confusion flooded his mind.

Where had he been?

He filled Apollo in on what had happened with his mum. Apollo's face contorted into a wide smile, he skipped and waved his hands in the air.

"I knew it!"

"I did nothing, and now I'm sick."

"Because you didn't know what you were doing. What made you try?"

Mark explained that he was pretending for his nephew.

"You've got a lot to learn then!" Apollo had barely let Mark finish the story and had sat across from Mark and begun reaching into his bag, handing over books. Mark briefly made out the titles: *Healing through the Ages*, *The Sacred Art of Healing*, *A Peaceful Healer: The Hidden School*, *The Sacred Human Abilities - Healing* and *The Universal Laws of Healing*.

"We have psychic abilities. We can manipulate energy around us."

Mark blinked at Apollo. "Something happened—everything disappeared. And we went somewhere."

"Mm, it's complicated."

Apollo drummed his fingers on his chin.

"It's a place of unlimited potential—a medium place. Help them realise they can get better... Then they do half the work."

"A medium place?"

"It can be anything you need it to be. Just think—use your mind. Understand that person."

"How do I know—"

"Let them lead you," Apollo cut him off. "They have to decide to change—and believe it too."

"So, anyone can be a healer?"

"Like you? No. But there are other types who are more accepted—like Reiki."

"More accepted?" His heart thumped. He was unsure if it was his illness or sudden intrigue.

"Not the economy's best friend."

Apollo's head dipped to the floor, staring at the rug. His lips squeezed shut. A slight shake of the head.

"It's how you control the masses—have them depend on an inadequate system for power and financial gain."

"I don't get it," Mark said. Apollo jerked his head, like he'd come out of a daze. He raised his eyebrows, looking at Mark once more.

"Imagine if everyone knew—what would happen to healthcare?"

Mark's head spun.

Apollo continued, "Things can go wrong, though—getting unwell, for instance." Apollo nodded at Mark. "It's rare, but the healer can take on a disease."

"Why?" Mark responded.

"Inexperience. Sometimes a personal choice—but other times, maybe the only option."

Mark's fingers twitched.

"You're struggling to heal a loved one—and you're running out of time. Might be more bearable to take on the disease than see them die, I'm sure."

Mark shivered. His heart palpitated.

"It doesn't work all the time?"

"Depends but if you're good, usually works all the time."

"And when it doesn't?"

"I don't know. Don't have all the answers—but maybe some illnesses must be served."

Mark scoffed.

"Well," Apollo continued. "Energy can't be created or destroyed, but—"

"—transferred from one form to another. I know," Mark added.

"Well...."

"I'm not destroying anything. I'm channelling, right? I saw something online."

"Yes, but sometimes all you can do is transfer."

Mark gulped. His throat didn't feel as scratchy anymore.

"But I'm no expert on healing. I just know it's similar to what I do—and sometimes you can't just eliminate the issue," Apollo said.

"Why would it be the only option?"

"Who knows? Maybe to keep balance. Maybe a sick joke, a game—or even punishment. We may never know, but do we need to? What is knowing, and will knowing really change anything at all?"

Mark stared, his mouth dropping open as he absorbed Apollo's words. Mark accepted that Apollo was a little crazy—possibly a lot crazy.

"Anyway, I have to leave." Apollo snatched up his bag and stood from the sofa.

"Wait, what?" Mark responded, trying to stand.

"I have to go. Good to see you—all the best," he replied, heading toward the door, empty bag clutched in his right hand.

"How do I reach you?"

"You know what you need to do. If not, it'll come to you. Use the books as a guide.

"Where are you going?"

"It's not relevant. I just came to help. You'll be okay."

Apollo had reached the door. He opened it. Some sun shone in onto the tiles. A cool breeze reached Mark. The racketing of birds outside was now more prevalent.

Before leaving, he turned back and said, "Oh, and be careful. Don't make too much noise."

Mark went to say something, but Apollo had disappeared.

FLASHBACK #3

Boxes filled the house, though Mark couldn't bring himself to care. Rachel's lingerie lay on the vinyl floor, while both of them now laid on the living-room sofa. It had started at the front door and somehow they'd ended up in the kitchen and now, the living room.

"This is so cliché," Rachel whispered.

"Why are you whispering?" Mark asked.

"I don't know."

Mark laughed softly. Rachel giggled.

"What's cliché?" he asked.

"The first thing we did was have sex."

"It's what people do, I think," Mark replied. "We kind of did a tour at the same time though."

"You know what we should do?" Rachel sprung up from his chest, now sitting upright. "We should organise a housewarming. Invite your family—"

"No."

"No to a housewarming or no to your family?"

He ignored her question, got up and completed the tour on his own.

VI

Invisible hands wrapped themselves around Mark's neck. He felt like he was underwater, the anxiety manifesting itself each time he reconsidered his options.

He'd been on autopilot for the last thirty minutes. He'd made the trip hundreds, possibly thousands of times. He couldn't recall how he'd gotten there—but he'd reached his destination.

After days of contemplation, this was going to be the final time he entered the building. Making his way to his office, he reminisced about the years. His outlook had changed. There was no sense of comfort. Nausea rolled in his stomach, as tiny things that would previously not have bothered him caused him to grit his teeth. The phony smiles pointed his way as he walked through the foyer. The complete disregard for the fellow employee's wellbeing. Hell, even the smell of coffee from his previously favourite café rankled. He glanced over as he passed, catching the eye of Alexia who'd worked there for years.

It all frustrated him.

She beamed, then waved. Mark attempted a smile. He snapped his head forward.

Regardless of his relentless efforts, they'd had no qualms when it came to disposing of him. But even then, he felt free. Free of needing them.

Rachel must've felt so alone.

"Mark, good to see you."

He broke out of his daydream. It was Henry.

He'd been preoccupied. Not even the usual 'hello' to Fred at security. None of that mattered.

Seeing Henry relaxed him a little.

"I know why you're here, I think it's a great choice."

"What? How do you...?" Mark began but trailed off when he didn't know what to say. *A great choice? How could he know?*

"I had a hunch. Mr Millman's Academy always brings out the best in people." With a sly smirk, he waved goodbye and left Mark confused in the hallway.

Mark hadn't been able to figure him out. He always left Mark wondering. And who was Mr Millman, and his academy? What an odd thing to say.

Oh well, after today, none of that would matter anyway.

As he approached his office, he pondered the injustice of leaving without any sort of grand announcement. His position was well regarded. Other general managers hadn't drifted away, quietly—there was usually a farewell party that went well into the night. But Mark hoped that his silent departure would remain just that—modest, and not a big deal. There'd be less fallout that way.

He walked into his office and was met with familiar comfort. It had remained unchanged except for the cards and neglected flowers co-workers had left. For a brief moment, he felt an attachment to the space.

The sun's rays filled most of the room, the heat forcing him to remove his blazer and sling it over his arm. His shoes squeaked on the polished tiles as he made his way to the opposite end of the room—to the large window. The river below captured his attention. Much like the boats he watched, he drifted to the right until he sat on the edge of a three-seater, thumbing the leather as he reminisced. A black, glass coffee table sat in front of the sofa. Near the coffee table sat a single, black, leather armchair. The brown of the river below, the white floor, and the light-brown walls were balanced by the greenery of the indoor palm in the corner.

Deep in thought, his eyes drifted to the wooden desk in the middle of the room—there was a laptop in the middle and a photo in the corner, while everything else was in the drawers below. He sat in his chair, the sun's rays warming up his left arm. He wiped his forehead with his palm, opened up Word, and started typing.

As soon as he was done, he felt the tightness in his neck muscles. But it was too late. Glancing at the wedding photo adorning his desk, Rachel freed him of his nostalgic attachment and he regained clarity.

He made his way to the CEO's office, his now former colleagues looking the other way as he passed. He could hear his footsteps—and even his own breaths—as he neared.

Andrew was the face of Varion, and it comforted Mark, slightly, remembering how close they had been for years. Mark admired him—the way he cared about his employees and stood up for them. He used to get the best out of them. He'd improved the morale and efficiency of staff, working with HR before becoming CEO. But things changed when he became CEO, two years ago. It was most likely the pressure, but he had turned into a lifeless zombie, and an arrogant one at that. The board had let him go and Andrew sat there, saying nothing.

He took a deep breath and knocked.

VI

"Come in."

Mark stepped into the office and closed the door behind him. "I've come to give my notice, effective immediately."

Andrew winced and took off his glasses, grabbing the letter Mark handed over.

"Mark, are you sure about this? You still have your entitled three months."

Mark turned to leave, but Andrew was able to stop him. "Meet us in the board room, for... a proper farewell."

"Don't—" Mark could feel himself getting hot.

"Mark, it's the least we can do, especially the number of years you've been here. Meet us there in half an hour?"

Andrew cared more about how the company looked. A farewell would be an activity the board felt they *had* to do. Mark acknowledged the suggestion by nodding, a hint of a frown crossing his face.

* * *

Grabbing the handles of the boardroom doors, Mark inhaled deeply and shoved them open, surprised to see board members in the middle of a meeting. Whispers circulated, but Mark was unable to understand a word.

He didn't have a plan.

But he wanted to get away. He figured he'd know what to say when the time came but for now, his mind was blank.

"Mark has undoubtedly been one of our best," he faintly heard someone say over his thoughts.

Why were they putting in the effort?

Cakes were brought in. Sodas and snacks. There were even gifts.

What a joke.

Some people came to him and thanked him, but he made no effort to engage in conversation.

"A few words, Mark?" Mark looked up and saw who'd asked. It was difficult to recognise Steve, the COO, now. Years ago, they got along, working alongside each other. They'd pitched CyberGuard to emerging tech companies. They had travelled the country, and often overseas together. Travelling salesmen, as it were.

Now, Steve was a traitor, having thrown Mark under the bus, along with the rest of them.

Mark made his way to the front of the group.

"I've enjoyed being a part of this company. I wish you all the best."

Mark dipped his head and headed to the side of the room.

His short speech left them murmuring among themselves but Mark didn't care. Steve came to pat him on the back but Mark evaded him, just, drifting into the crowd of faceless board members.

Several minutes later the crowd shrunk. And with that, he gathered his belongings and left the building for what was to be the last time, leaving the gifts, unopened.

VII

His alarm went off—5AM as per his usual routine. Gym, then breakfast.

At 7AM, he took to the books Apollo gave him.

His pupils dilated as theories and concepts assembled themselves in his mind.

He read the books. He re-read them. He meditated, as per their recommendation. His inner ear vibrated and there was a slight pressure on his forehead—*weird*.

He dismissed it.

By then it was late morning. A thought occupied his mind as to where he'd find others like him—where he could learn.

He hadn't found anything in the books, as per Apollo's suggestion.

His frustration lingered. He'd been reading for hours. He had been reading *A Peaceful Healer: The Hidden School*. For a split second, he grew annoyed with Apollo and then Henry for being so encouraging of whatever this was, and his frustration got the better of him. With a wrinkled nose, he shook his head and tossed the book. It hit the floor with a loud thud.

"Sorry, Dan Millman," he muttered, almost immediately, staring at the cover which now lay spread on his rug. He felt guilt. Someone had worked hard to create the book.

I need to get a grip.

He picked it up and placed it on his coffee table.

He looked at the cover again, and his heart jolted. *Millman*. He'd heard that name before—from Henry. He had mentioned something about an academy, come to think of it.

Mark grabbed his laptop and searched for Mr Millman's Academy. Nothing. He snatched up the book and went over every word, again. Nothing.

On the last page, he lowered his eyebrows and nearly tossed the book again. But stopped himself when he saw a faint, red mark he hadn't noticed earlier. It was similar to a library stamp. It was too faint to see clearly, and he had to squint to make it out. He found his magnifying glass, camera, superglue and lamp and sat at the dining table.

First, he scanned the page, but the text was still mostly undetectable. Next, he carefully tilted it toward the bright light and took an infrared photo with his camera. He played around with the contrast until the words became more visible. He was glad there was no need to burn the superglue and risk damaging the book. Now, he saw the words '*Property of*' and the numbers '*4101*'. He also saw '*Taraby Ln*'. It was difficult to make out the rest, as though it had been permanently erased through years of use but could also make out one final word—'*Academy*'.

He figured it would be enough to set him on the right path.

It was an address. The number suggested it was the same suburb he'd met Apollo. A quick Google search didn't show anything relating to an 'Academy' but, with adrenaline rushing through his veins, he grabbed his keys and got into his Mercedes.

* * *

The coloured graffiti of contrasting reds, blues and greens coating the brickwork of houses and cafés tightly arranged in rows gave the lane a hipster feel. For a second Mark wondered how anyone could make out the writing, the way it twisted and coiled the way it did. Teenagers in overalls, others in skinny jeans and cargo pants walked through the street. He glanced at a man around his age sporting a long, reddish beard and couldn't help but feel out of place.

He found a spot to park, grabbed the book, and got out of the car. He found himself at the beginning of an alleyway. It was a short street, probably about one hundred metres.

To his left was a café. People crowded near the front, but now was not the time for a coffee. Something told him he was close and simultaneously he felt a wind of emotion as though electrified. Struggling to walk casually, he made his way to a door just beyond the café. He knocked and waited. No answer. He fidgeted, alternating his weight on each foot.

"Hello?"

No answer.

Must be the wrong door.

There were fewer people as he walked further down the lane, away from the café. It didn't take long to have tried all the doors and gates. He asked a young couple if they knew anything about a Healing Academy but they just looked at him like he was crazy, puzzlement and confusion crossing their faces.

Maybe a coffee is a good idea after all.

Disappointed, he made his way to the café. He felt strange—the insides of his ears didn't usually vibrate. And the heat on his forehead. It wasn't normal.

"Hi! Can I get you a coffee?" The barista had to raise her voice.

He'd made his way inside and was submerged in a sea of voices and other sounds. There was laughter from a group near the back. Three people near the front were huddled, possibly in an attempt to maintain discretion. Or maybe, like Mark, they thought the café was too loud. Throughout the space, cups knocked on wooden tables and cutlery chinked on ceramic plates. Mark focused on the question.

"I'll get a regular flat white, thanks. To have here."

She nodded, then grinned. "One flat white coming right up." Mark paid and squeezed his way through the cafe.

His drink arrived and he took a sip. He'd managed to secure a seat when he noticed a couple leaving. He scratched his head, wondering how he would find the academy. The address had led him to the street, but that was all.

He pulled out his phone and searched again. *Academy, Taraby Ln*, but nothing. He also tried *Millman's Healing Academy, Taraby Ln* to no avail. He shook his head and gulped down the rest of his beverage.

Maybe it wasn't real—a wild goose chase that was turning out to be a huge waste of time.

He shook his head as he thumped the empty mug onto the table in front of him. Shoulders slumped, narrow-eyed and top teeth clamped on his bottom lip, he made his way toward the entrance where he overheard one of the baristas talking to a customer.

"Where's Apollo?"

"No idea. No one at the school has seen him."

"If you see him, tell him to come in for coffee. It's not the same without him."

Mark couldn't help himself. "Excuse me, you two know Apollo?"

"Apollo? Yes, everyone here knows Apollo. Right, Aaron?"

"True. Anyway, I have to go, I'm running late—bye, Susan."

Mark momentarily locked eyes with Susan and for some seconds considered questioning her. Eventually, he decided he might have more luck with Aaron.

He dashed toward the door.

Outside, the balloon of hope, which had inflated inside him only moments ago, deflated. Aaron had disappeared. Possibly through one of the alleyways, leading off the lane. He ran down one, searching, but soon had to accept he'd lost him. He stood for a few minutes, searching the book again, looking for another clue.

"Apollo said you'd turn up one day."

Mark propped his head up, squinting, and saw a man who looked slightly younger than him, with short brown hair, wearing glasses. He stared at Mark, his face shifting into a friendly smile.

"I thought years, instead of weeks, based on what he said. I'm Dan by the way," he said, thrusting his hand toward Mark. "I assume you're here for The Academy?"

Mark nodded.

"Follow me," Dan said.

He led Mark through an alleyway which led to a dilapidated red door, the paint peeling at the edges.

Inside, the low-ambient lighting made it difficult to make sense right away—but once it set in, it was easy to make out the high-tech, futuristic interior, with generous amounts of plants hanging from the ceiling and walls. Strips of warm lights lined the ceiling and floors and to one side was a reception desk with ambient lighting of its own—a hypnotising shade of slightly pulsating blue. Covering the entirety of the back wall was a screen with low-brightness videos of waterfalls, rain and sunsets—it almost looked like a window. The shiny floor reflected the ambient lighting and ceiling.

"It's good to have a powerful healer here," Dan said, bringing Mark back to reality. "The low lighting helps healers focus," he continued.

He followed Dan through the reception and into an office down the back. They walked past closed doors where soothing melodies resonated through the walls.

In contrast, Dan's office was well lit. There was a slight arch in the roof. Half of the office ceiling was clear glass, allowing natural light to seep through. Similar strips of lights lined the ceiling, but this time arched and with high brightness. A desktop computer sat on a large, wooden desk—similar to his own. Other devices were scattered across the table. A phone, tablet, a smartwatch and others with screens Mark didn't recognise.

"Welcome to The Academy," Dan began, once inside the room.

"How did you know I was here?"

"Aaron."

Mark nodded slowly.

"This is a school for healers but you might need to teach us!" Dan chuckled.

"I doubt that. I don't know how to heal yet."

"I guess that's why you're here," Dan said, winking. "You'll be a natural. What you have—it's rare."

"Is it?"

"Yeah. When Apollo said he knew a *real* healer, I asked him to bring you here straight away. We need more healers in this world, wouldn't you agree?"

"Sure," Mark said.

"Well, let's go meet the others."

VIII

After only a few classes, Mark was told by Dan that he'd need private lessons.

A bit of a shame really—Mark appreciated that the other students supported him. If he failed a technique, they would still say "nice try" and tell him to just "try again."

According to Dan, the reason for the private classes was Mark's inability to heal. But Mark felt Dan's expectations hadn't made it easy—and maybe the expectations of the other students too.

Mark's third private class was today, and it might as well be his first. He knew what he had to do—and he could often feel energy pulsating through his body. His ears would vibrate and his head and hands would burn but that was it. A total buzzkill.

Even then, Mark was empathetic. He felt Dan's excitement—often patting Mark on the back—was palpable, but then only to be continuously let down. At the same time, Mark felt pressured. Especially when he considered that at the beginning they had all acted like he was something special. Now, not so much.

Despite all this, he enjoyed the classes with Dan— energy manipulation had been the topic yesterday. Dan's patience was godly, often repeating himself with not as much as a raised voice. Dan's effort in not allowing his disappointment, or frustration to show was commendable—

but Mark knew. The corner of his eye would twitch. Sometimes even the edge of his lips. Other times there was a soft sigh.

Also, Mark still saw Demonic Rachel. Nothing explicit, like the hallucination with Apollo. More like passing glances, like her figure would appear when he passed an empty room, or she'd hover in the corners of his eyes whenever he'd screw up a healing technique.

He sat in the main hallway, waiting for Dan, mesmerised by the blue ambient light dancing throughout the space. Dan didn't want to begin class in the main dojo, as usual.

But it didn't take long for him to appear.

"Can you come to my office?"

Mark followed him. Once inside, Dan pushed the door slowly so it wouldn't slam, a solemn look on his face.

"I don't think you belong here."

Dan was right. It was all out of Mark's depth.

"Do you think you're a healer?"

Mark had been excited in the beginning. He'd been bubbly. Animated in conversations with the others—but the constant failure had made him dull.

Mark had even considered insanity on his part— maybe a psychotic manifestation by his mind. *I need to heal from Rachel, not create fantasies in my mind.*

"Do you think you're a healer?" Dan asked again.

Mark cleared his mind and inhaled.

"I don't know anymore."

"Maybe that's your problem, or maybe you're not. Either way, I feel like we're wasting each other's time."

Mark shuddered. His heart sank.

"If I said you were a healer. What would you say?"

"I'd say you're wrong," Mark replied.

"See, that's your problem."

"What do you mean?"

"Thoughts create universes, Mark, remember that."

"I don't understand," Mark objected.

"It might not matter. But I'll give you this chance. Prove me wrong, right here."

Mark's hands were clammy. He felt dehydrated. He closed his eyes, held his breath, and attempted to clear his mind.

"Focus," he heard Dan say.

Mark softly grabbed Dan's wrist and felt a massive gust of wind. Next, the floorboards and room disappeared. Moments later, they were surrounded by a bright white. A canvas. He hadn't made it that far with Dan yet. He couldn't help the slow, delighted smile that formed. He looked across at Dan, who responded with the same.

"Halfway. The rest should be easy—"

Dan had barely finished his sentence when the white switched into a gloomy grey. The temperature was harsh. Bitterly cold.

Is this a test?

"You doing this?" Dan asked. He'd folded his arms, wrapping his palms across his upper arms.

"No—"

That's when he saw her. Demonic Rachel. And she was sprinting toward them. Her screams filled the grey, refrigerated void. She raced across the plain, but before she could get too close, Mark opened his eyes.

They were back in Dan's office.

Dan sighed. His head moved abruptly from side to side. "Spoke too soon."

"I was wrong," Mark said, turning to leave.

"Maybe Apollo was," Dan replied. And with that, Mark glanced at Dan and left his office, out through the foyer and out of the building. The "hi's", "hey's" and "bye's" from other students were ignored. He kept his head angled down. The ambient lights seemed dull.

He made it out onto the street. He raised his posture as he neared his car.

He'd barely started the car when he called his mum. Her voice was husky. She filled Mark in. How it had started with the flu but the doctor said it had progressed to pneumonia.

"I might be contagious," she said. But Mark didn't care, he booked a flight as soon as he got home.

He'd gritted his teeth as he packed some belongings into a backpack. Hours later, he headed to the airport.

He'd made it to Melbourne while golden hour was in full effect. As the plane hovered above the city, Mark tilted his head out toward the golden orb. He'd nearly pulled out his phone to take a photo of the sun lying on the horizon, inspiring shades of vibrant orange but he lacked the energy to care.

Bag slung over one shoulder, he had made his way out of the airport, then took some time to find the Uber—the driver claiming he'd done some loops because Mark wasn't where he thought he would be.

Thirty minutes later and he arrived.

And now he sat opposite his mum in the living room. Ollie lay on the floor on his stomach, feet up in the air. A slight sway. Fight scenes appeared and diegetic sounds boomed from the TV. Ollie's eyes were glued to it as he watched *The Avengers*.

Mark turned his head away from the TV and tuned out the heavy combat that tried to overwhelm his senses. He locked eyes with his mum. She grinned.

He placed his palm on her wrist. A deep breath.

The room snapped into something blurry and multi-coloured. Like a candy store. The walls fell away and the colours began taking shape. It was a field, flowers filling the plain. Sweet scents invaded Mark's nose. It was hard to know how many types of flowers surrounded them— but Mark spotted daffodils, roses, sunflowers, tulips, lilies, gardenias, lavender and jasmine. And that was just a brief scan because he was quickly distracted by what he saw nearby.

His mum was trapped in a glass, transparent box, separated from the flower-filled terrain. The box was the same size as a shipping container. The thickness of its glass stretched over several inches. Mark couldn't hear a word she said but it was easy enough to decipher, even if it were soundproof. *Mark, what is this?*

"You need to come out. Through the door!" Mark tried acting it out like Charades!. He pointed to the door and made a motion as though pulling the handle and walking through.

She reached the door and tried the handle. Although she tried forcing it down, it wouldn't budge. It had been locked. She tried twisting and turning the handle.

Her arms collapsed by her side.

"There must be a way of unlocking it!" Mark shouted.

She shook her head. Pacing back and forth, she gazed around and scoped the interior, but it was empty. Some scattered light bounced off the glass, reflecting some of the sun. Heat coated Mark's skin. Mark screwed up his face, then closed his eyes. He tried taking them somewhere else, but it didn't work. They were stuck. He kept his eyes shut. Focused. But he wasn't even able to modify the transparent container.

Fuming, he marched to the door and tried the handle. It turned—smooth—and the door swung open. Mark formed a fist with his hand. Then a slight punch of the air. The muscles in his face relaxed.

"Finally," she said, coming out to meet Mark. "What is this?"

Mark was lost for words. He went with the first thing that came to mind. "Healing."

"It's beautiful out here—and the smell. Wow," she replied, twisting her head across the landscape.

It was like waking from a lucid dream. Back in the lounge, Mark fixed his gaze on his mum, stroking his chin and monitoring her.

The only noise came from the blaring TV.

Over several seconds her eyes narrowed, then widened. Finally, her face lit up. It had been a while since Mark had seen that bright smile. In response, his chest glowed with a warmth that brought on an uncontrollable and affectionate, yet apologetic smile.

"What did you do?" she asked.

Mark's grin broadened. "Healed you."

"What do you mean?"

"You're cured. Should've done it a long time ago."

"How long have you been able to do this?"

"Since just now."

Mark knew it had worked.

She hopped up off the sofa, springing off the balls of her feet through the lounge.

"Sorry I left," Mark said after some moments. She stepped in front of Mark, then stopped, her eyes narrowing as she turned to face him.

"Sorry?"

"All those years ago. Sorry I left and made no contact with anyone."

"You're here now. That's what matters," she replied, coming in for a hug. Mark stood and wrapped his arms around her.

Mark looked over at Ollie, whose eyes were still glued to the TV. Spider-Man was going head-to-head with Thanos.

Healing. It wasn't a form of insanity. He'd just proved it, and now he planned to show it to the world—but first, Dan.

IX

White everywhere. So far so good. A small and deserted sandy island had occupied Mark's mind. So he'd gone with it. Their surroundings began taking shape, and it only took seconds for Mark's feet to start sinking into white sand. The unforgiving sun blared on his back.

Dan was still right there in front of him. The other side of the island could be seen in the distance, beyond sandy hills. It wasn't far, about the length of a football field. Birds flocked above the lush, green shrubs and ferns, swaying delicately in the breeze coming off the water.

What mattered the most was that he had just proved to Dan he could do it. He'd been nervous on the way over. Even now, he'd avoided eye contact, but finally, he looked Dan in the eye. Dan responded with a slight nod—his smile barely visible, but it was there.

With a blink, they were back in his office. Dan placed his hand on Mark's shoulder.

"Wish I could say I knew all along, but—nice work."

It was all the validation Mark needed.

Dan reassured Mark that he'd passed the test and he now considered him a *competent healer*.

Mark went to say bye, turning to leave. He had work to do and didn't want to waste time.

Reiki. He had thought about it on the plane. Apollo had mentioned Reiki Healing, and Mark remembered reading about it. He'd found online courses. And it was just what he needed on his way to becoming legitimate. *Heal Yourself, Family, Friends, Clients and More*—perfect.

* * *

In the main lobby, as he said "bye" to the other students, Mark heard Dan's voice. Dan called his name. Mark spun. Dan held a certificate.

"You'll need this."

"Oh, I had no idea," Mark replied.

"You passed, congratulations," Dan said, handing it over.

On thick khaki paper, Mark's name was written in black ink over a certificate of accreditation.

Association of Natural Practitioners
Commission of Accreditation
This is to certify that Mark Pierce has met the requirements of the Natural Practitioners Board as a Natural Energy Healer with all the applicable rights, privileges and responsibilities.

It had been signed by Dan and dated.

He wouldn't need the online course after all.

"Didn't think I'd just send you off did you?"

Mark chuckled.

"Actually I did," he replied going in for a firm handshake before making his way out.

X

Mark was thirty minutes early. He sat opposite a woman named Julia in a small office. She owned the wellness centre—Spring Wellness.

It was close to home, about a five-minute drive. They advertised that it was *wholesome*, offering massage, nutrition and dietetics, physiotherapy, counselling and health and fitness. So far, Mark had been given a tour of the gym, filled with workout equipment and a personal trainer here and there. There were also private rooms dedicated to various allied health services.

Mark had called earlier and Julia had agreed to meet. And so here he was. In an office barely big enough to house a third person, pitching what he could offer them.

"What is it that you do again?" Julia asked, scanning her eyes over the certificate Mark handed over.

"I'm a healer."

"And what does a healer do?"

"I help people recover from health-related issues, mostly common illnesses."

An awkward silence filled the room. Mark eyed a dying plant in the corner. The outer edges of its leaves were browning.

Julia beat Mark in breaking the silence. "Reiki?"

"Similar," Mark replied.

"We've never had a healer before but I'm willing to give it a go."

Mark tilted his head forward. He smirked.

"My goal is to diversify our options. How soon can you start?"

"As soon as you need."

Mark would start the following day.

He spent the remainder of the day preparing. Insurance, going over the terms of engagement and the like.

When he met Julia for the second time, she showed him to his office.

"People will often be referred to you," she said, leading him there. "But it's based on their needs."

They walked past a massage room. "Kiara is our masseuse," Julia said, pointing at the door with Kiara's name on it. "Your business cards will arrive in a few days, I only just ordered them."

"That's fine," Mark replied.

"Let me know if there's anything you need." They'd made it to his workspace. She unlocked the door and gave Mark some keys. "Feel free to make it your own. I'll touch base soon."

Julia left.

His office was smaller than the one at Varion—about half the size. But it didn't matter. With the door shut it was quiet, and that was all he needed.

Over the next few days Mark fashioned the room to his liking.

An anthurium sat on a tiny glass table by the door, bright red flowers contrasting with the vivid-green leaves. A Black Cat resided in a pot plant in the corner. Inspired by The Academy, and through the conscious effort to make the space less formal, the work desk and office chairs were removed, making way for cushions, beanbags and a couch. String lights were mounted to the walls that could be dimmed at any time. Gentle, ambient tunes came from a small, portable speaker.

It helped him focus.

His first client, Molly, suffered from persistent stomach ulcers and heart complications. She clutched her chest when Mark asked where her pain originated. Doctors had prescribed her medication.

"What do you do in your spare time?" Mark asked. Molly responded—and then he knew what to do.

He guided her to close her eyes and placed his palm on the top of her hand. He showed Molly a representation of her body using a classical symphony. They sat in the audience a few aisles from the stage. Around them, people clapped and cheered. Some whistled. Mark found himself joining in.

Each artist on stage represented a vital organ. A banner hung on the top of the stage was titled *All Heart.*

"What is this?" Molly asked, eyes toward the front. "Where are we?

Mark nearly responded, but was cut off by the Maestro on stage. He wore a shiny tailcoat tuxedo and addressed the audience. "Ladies and gentlemen, I'm sorry. There will be no show tonight—our star performer, the violinist, has not shown up."

"What a waste," Mark began, glancing over at Molly. She stared at him with a blank expression.

"Imagine not even showing up. Talk about being unreliable," Molly said, now giggling to herself.

The Maestro spoke again, "Ladies and gentlemen, I'm hearing there's one of you who can fill in for Kardi. Would you care to step up, please?"

The audience murmured, glances in every direction.

"Anyone at all?" the Maestro continued.

Molly had joined the crowd, twisting her head in every direction. But only minutes ago she'd mentioned playing the violin in her spare time.

"Why are they all looking at me?" she began. It was true, they'd all turned their heads. Some even twisted their bodies to look directly at her—both the audience and performers. Someone coughed toward the back. The only other sound was a rustling of what sounded like a foil bag. Possibly filled with chips or other snacks.

Mark pursed his lips. *Come on Molly.*

He gave her a hint.

"Don't *you* play the violin?"

"Wait, what?" she asked, eyebrows lowered.

She glanced down, eyes taking in the bright red costume she now wore.

"You'd better get up there," Mark urged with an encouraging grin.

She hesitated.

"No... it's embarrassing? And I don't know how to play that well!"

"They need you," Mark said.

"I don't want to get up there," she argued.

"Really? Okay," Mark replied.

By this point, the characters were pointing and waving at her to join them. But it looked like his plan would fail.

But eventually she stood and made her way up to the stage, nervously glancing at the audience.

On stage, she hugged the Maestro before taking her seat. It didn't take long before she picked up her violin and bow, slotting in seamlessly with the rest of the orchestra.

The crowd roared. Mark cheered and shouted until he feared losing his voice—and moments later, they were back in his office.

She thanked him and paid.

"Nice work," Mark said, as she left.

But she returned after some days.

"Mark, I feel great!" she said, with just one foot inside the door. Her pain had faded. She explained having some tests booked and hoped she no longer had to rely on the medication. "I'm going to tell everyone about you!" she said, as she went to leave, only for Mark to stop her to hand over a stack of business cards.

Over the coming days Mark received multiple phone calls. Some had been referred by Molly. As he healed more people, word spread.

Rachel occasionally crept into his mind, but it had become more of a fleeting thought and it was easier to blow it away. He recognised her dislike, but he could shut her out.

But things changed when he met Robert.

Robert had been diagnosed a quadriplegic after a surfing accident—he'd insisted on meeting Mark after speaking with his sister, Lucy. Mark had healed her fractured ulna a week prior. They had gone to a lake where the two of them had gone fishing and the bone healed within days.

Mark agreed and made his way to the hospital where the healing went well. He sat next to Robert, arm raised onto the bed. He'd gently touched Robert on his forehead and they immediately teleported into an animated version of Robert's body. They were inside his brain. There were two Roberts. The miniature one, with Mark, and the giant one, who lay dormant—hibernating. Miniature Robert was the real, conscious Robert, the one that had been injured. Their mission was to wake up the dormant Robert who lay motionless.

They travelled through the body of the giant who lay in a coma. It hadn't taken Robert long to understand that he needed to become one with the giant to be successful.

Moments after they were back in the hospital, Robert had moved his foot. But it was Robert's reaction. He slammed his fists into the mattress and threw a pillow at the wall.

"You can do this and you let people suffer here!" he barked, his face turning red.

Mark understood. But he couldn't just march into a hospital and do what he wanted with their patients. Not to mention trying to explain to the doctors and nurses. It was easier to avoid altogether.

But nausea bubbled in his body, the feeling so unsettling it set in a headache. Was it guilt? It was hard to know but he couldn't explain why his hands were shaking, nor the anxiety that nestled in the back of his head.

"Are you listening to me!?"

Robert's fists were practically white as they hung at his sides, the veins in his arms and forehead threatening to burst at any second.

Mark was too lost in his thoughts and could barely hear Robert's shouting. *No wonder she still hates me. Have I not changed at all?*

People still suffered.

He had to get out of there but he could feel *her* again, all around him, coating him like coarse cement. His skin grew cold, prickling uncomfortably, and he could hear her faint hiss in the air around him. The migraine worsened. Mark's eyes blurred, and he struggled to stay upright.

A faint shriek rang in his ears.

The walls began to close in.

Bursting out of the room, he began running through the hospital, hoping to find an exit—only to be trapped, twisting and turning through a complicated maze. As his anxiety peaked, he began seeing her more vividly with each passing second, in reflections, in windowpanes or through cracks in doorways.

Running into a dead-ended corridor, he collapsed to the floor, breath ragged from the running. Just as his heartbeat began to slow, he looked up and saw her, cornering him in the corridor. Rabid with rage, she started dead sprinting toward him. He didn't know what to do— he was rooted to the spot, eyes wide open in terror.

"Mark?"

Mark heard the aggressive stomps of her feet as she sprinted across the tiled floor.

"Mark, are you okay!?"

She was metres from him. The last thing he saw was her tendrils of hair swirling around her face, her banshee screech filling his ears, and her bloodshot eyes.

FLASHBACK #4

It was 4AM on a Saturday—why was he getting a phone call? Even half-asleep, he recognised the number—it was an overseas number. The New York office.

As though on autopilot, he popped in his Bluetooth earbuds, answered the phone and headed to his office downstairs. He didn't want to wake Rachel.

"Hello?"

"Mark, I know it's not good timing—"

"It's fine, what's up?"

"It's CyberGuard, we think it's been hacked. And because NetFlow uses the same security system, we're worried about client data."

"Who's on it?"

"No one, you're the first person I've told."

Mark paused. Collin, who headed the New York office, was smart enough and should have consulted his local security team before calling him. Mark sighed, then clenched his jaw.

"You still there?" Collin asked.

"Yeah. Leave it with me. I've got remote access," Mark replied.

"Let me know how you go—"

Mark hung up, shaking his head. There was a reason he'd chosen to stay away from the first-responders and twenty-four-hour security teams. To avoid phone calls like these at the worst possible times.

He booted up his computer and connected it remotely to Varion's mainframe. He suspected a Trojan, which CyberGuard should've identified with its inbuilt monitoring safeguard. What the hell was going on?

To protect client data in the interim, he dissociated all client files from NetFlow. Hopefully, the hacker hadn't been able to retrieve anything yet. It was time-consuming. Client data took up several thousand gigabytes.

"You're up early."

He'd barely heard Rachel. He looked behind him, briefly toward the door then let the computer screen regain his attention.

"Well, good morning."

"Morning," he replied, not taking his eyes off the screen.

"Would you like a coffee?"

"Babe, just. No."

Mark heard a faint sigh as she left him to work. He looked back toward the door for a second, nearly apologised but shook his head and turned toward the screen instead.

"Would you like some brekky?" She was back—Mark shook his head. He needed to focus on fixing the security issue. Not breakfast.

"Oh, by the way, are you still coming to Lauren's birthday? I told her you were—"

"Rach, I can't think about that right now. I have to do this." It was a little more forceful than Mark would have liked and he felt more heated than he ought to. Being tired and frustrated didn't help.

Lauren was Rachel's best friend. Mark knew it was important to Rachel for him to go but he had more urgent matters. Mark turned to say something to ease the tension but Rachel had disappeared. He shut off his computer and grabbed his laptop. He didn't look for her. Instead, he headed for his car. On the way he saw their digital clock on the kitchen counter—it was 7AM. Next to the clock, a plastic cover shielded some toast, scrambled eggs and bacon on a ceramic plate. And a note by its side:

Don't starve.

XI

Mark opened his eyes, his skin covered in sweat.

"W-what happened?" He looked around. A nurse hovered above him.

"It looked like you blacked out. You were standing in the middle of the hallway. Next thing I know you're on the ground, convulsing. Are you feeling okay? Maybe we should run some tests."

"No, I'm fine, I had a migraine and probably should've sat down, but I'm okay now."

In truth, Mark had no idea what happened—a hallucination, maybe? She only ever really appeared in his dreams, not like this. The nurse continued to try to convince Mark to admit himself for medical issues but after his constant refusal, she had no choice but to let him go.

His temperature was still raised and Mark felt lightheaded as he made his way to his car. He sat in his car until his hands stopped shaking on the steering wheel—and finally the dizziness faded away.

He drove home. He'd have the rest of the day off.

But the nightmares that night were the worst he'd had in months. In one dream, Rachel contorted into the demon. She got down on her hands and knees and crawled toward him. The dream ended right before she reached him. In others, she attempted to possess him, beat him with a metal rod and tried to stab him with a recognisable chef's knife.

He woke numerous times, covered in sweat, only to fall back to sleep and experience another nightmare.

When morning came, she was cemented in his mind, clouding his judgement. But that wasn't the worst of it.

Work was absolute hell. Oliver, his first client, had been complaining of recurrent headaches. When the room snapped away, a chill swept over Mark, sinking into his bones. His mouth turned down at the corners, his breath catching in his throat as he surveyed the scene before him. He'd been dreading something like this happening—and now the time had finally come.

They'd arrived at a cemetery.

He looked down and immediately wished he hadn't. It was a tombstone and it had a name. Her name. Rachel Pierce.

He apologised to Oliver and said they needed to get out of there. But as he caught sight of her in the distance, he felt invisible hands wrap themselves around his neck. At the same time, his feet began to sink into the ground.

"Wh-what is this!?"

Mark couldn't reply to Oliver. His mind said only one thing, to get the hell out of there, but his body wouldn't respond. And although his pulse raced, his body had stiffened—either unwilling, or unable to escape.

"Why Mark, why?"

It started as a whisper, but then her voice grew and grew until it reverberated throughout the cemetery. She started chanting. But still, he was rooted to the spot, his feet cemented to the ground.

Oliver shouted.

Their darkened surroundings drifted away just as she came within touching distance of them. Cool gusts of wind blew on his face just as he opened his eyes.

They were back. And Oliver left with a confused gaze—and unhealed.

Every other person that day was taken to the same hellish graveyard. Most left showcasing disappointment.

He cancelled the remaining appointments.

At home, his mind drifted back to the graveyard. Relaxation exercises and his attempt to exercise were useless. His mind gravitated to the tombstone.

Even worse, the nightmares weren't a one-off. And they were vivid.

He tried fighting through it for days but demonic thoughts invaded his mind. And he wasn't able to heal.

Just the other day, he had looked behind him as he reversed out of the driveway, only to see her in the back seat, staring at him. His heart had nearly stopped altogether and he'd sworn loudly before slamming on the brakes. She'd disappeared straight away.

His absence hadn't gone unnoticed either. Julia had called several times. People wanted to book in with him. But he kept using the excuse that he was unwell.

But eventually he had to terminate his contract. "I'll need to consider my options elsewhere," he said to Julia over the phone.

"You just started and things were going well. Everything okay?" Julia asked.

"I'm fine," he replied. He kept the phone call short and hung up soon after.

He received phone calls but Mark ignored them.

When the vivid hallucinations persisted during the day, he made an appointment with a regular psychologist.

No Apollo but adequate for Mark's needs. A balding, middle-aged man named Laurence. He didn't smile much and spoke in a soft tone. At times it was difficult to hear him.

Mark recapped his story.

Laurence helped Mark identify things he already knew—from Apollo—but it helped getting it off his chest.

"Grief," Lawrence said, "can take some time to process."

The reminder made Mark sink further into the chair, the tension leaving him. It was the confirmation he needed that he wasn't insane.

But when Mark described his hallucinations Lawrence suggested a referral—to investigate the likelihood of psychosis. Laurence had smiled for the first time as he said it—but Mark didn't take it so well. He sat up in his chair. The thought of being labelled psychotic brought back the tension he'd felt relax just moments ago. *I'm not insane.*

Silence followed. Laurence stared. Mark glared back.

"Have you apologised?"

"What do you mean?"

"If you're to blame, why not apologise?"

Why would he support things my brain's been making up? Am I a joke to him?

Mark remained silent. Then muttered, "I haven't apologised." He stared at his hands. His fingers trembled.

"It's often hard to forgive ourselves." Laurence had said this a few times. "You're not a bad person, even if you feel you did something bad—and do you know what that makes you? Human."

Mark raised his head. He tried saying something but his voice was weak. He opened his mouth but nothing came out. He saw the time. It had been forty-five minutes already.

On the way home Mark stopped to get some groceries. He'd filled his trolley and was heading to the checkout when he noticed some cereal Rachel liked. Nostalgia followed. Mark never understood how she was so cheery all the time. Especially in the morning. He wasn't a morning person

As he picked up the packet, his body grew hot, a now familiar sensation. The walls blurred. Without warning, the demon appeared at the far end of the aisle. His grip squashed the cardboard in his hand. There were no other shoppers or staff in sight.

His skin prickled and he held his breath. Simultaneously, there was a drop in temperature. Dizziness overtook him and the aisle appeared to lengthen and stretch. Her shadowy figure was mind-numbing and Mark was powerless, frozen in place and unable to move.

She screamed, speeding toward him, the soulless entity shrieking louder with each step.

As she neared, Mark forced himself to stare directly into her dark eyes. He mumbled, "I'm sorry."

She sped up. The temperature dropped to sub-zero.

"I'm sorry." It was a little louder.

She was unaffected by the apology and continued to drag her grotesque figure toward him. She was metres away.

He shouted.

"Rachel, I'm sorry!"

She stopped as though she'd hit a barricade. She continued to snarl and punched her fists at the air.

"I'm sorry for everything."

She began to fade away. Parts of her body evaporated into the air.

Mark's eyes stung.

He abandoned his trolley. Instead, he went to the place they had gone to on their first date: Darcy's.

His classic hazelnut and coconut combo took him right back.

FLASHBACK #5

He sat, motionless, in his car in the Varion staff carpark letting out slow, steady breaths as he processed the severity of the hack. He contemplated texting Rachel to apologise for being a dick earlier.

Instead, another call came from Collin.

"I don't have any updates." He basically blurted it out as soon as he answered—and Collin had barely said "okay" before Mark hung up.

He rushed into the building. Files still needed to be secured.

On NetFlow, client activity was typically low on a Saturday but Mark still got phone calls—clients asking why the platform was offline. "What's with the user error? Why can't I log in?" they demanded.

Mark spent the better part of an hour explaining to clients that they were working on a solution as quickly as possible and that Varion had a team capable of handling a minor system crash (for their sake, he referred to it as that).

"Should I be worried about our data?"

It was the question Mark had been dreading. John from Alliance Accounting was a long-standing client and he wasn't stupid. He'd clued in that the issue involved a security breach. Mark assured him that all client data had been secured.

"We might have to consider an alternative." After a moment's awkward silence, Mark convinced John that NetFlow and CyberGuard would be back in no time.

He was reminded of the time when Rachel called. The party started in an hour. Voicemail took care of it.

An hour later he pulled himself from the screen and diverted his attention to his phone.

Sorry, stuck at work. Won't be able to make it. Have fun x

No response.

XII

Mark took to transforming one of the rooms—he'd decided to work from home. He dragged furniture out, vacuumed and instead replaced it with cushions and pillows, mood lighting, plants and chairs. He'd taken inspiration from bohemian-themed healing rooms he'd found online. Momentarily, he stood at the door, arms aching slightly and admired the browns, whites and oranges throughout the space.

Next, he created a website, social media accounts and notified his old clients. Business cards followed, but they'd take some days to arrive.

He called some hospitals—maybe Robert was right— but they didn't understand and, frustrated by his attempts, he realised he needed another plan. They didn't want some random person meddling with their patients.

He came to an alternative, realising it would be better to apologise than to ask for permission—but he wouldn't need to apologise. If it worked.

He called the major hospital in Brisbane and asked about their visiting protocols—they allowed visitors provided they weren't unwell. Perfect.

He investigated some maps online then headed to *The Royal Brisbane and Women's Hospital.* He found his way through the maze of a carpark and finally he was inside.

He briskly made his way through the foyer trying to recall the map he'd studied—but it was different now, not so straightforward. Straight ahead, a large sign occupied the wall. It had arrows and directions for infectious diseases, oncology, cardiology and emergency.

He'd have to just choose one at random—though not oncology. It was too soon.

"Can I help you?"

Mark's head rotated, and his body followed as he turned to face the voice.

"Sorry?" he replied.

"Are you lost? I can give you directions." He was security—as stamped on his navy polo—about Mark's height. No sign of suspicion.

Mark lifted his posture and locked eyes. Then replied, "Yes, I'm looking for infectious diseases—visiting a friend."

"Go down this way and take a left at the end." He'd pointed toward Mark's right.

Mark thanked him and made his way down the hall and veered left. Before long, there he was. Infectious diseases.

There were other visitors. He walked down further and peered into a room. Someone was in there—and they were alone.

"You're here to visit Megan?"

Mark spun around. "Yes."

"Bacterial infections can be contagious through food and water. Are you family?"

"Close friend." He held the nurse's gaze, trying not to bring attention to his fake bravado.

The nurse led Mark into the room.

Then he felt it, his chest swelling with anticipation, a nervous excitement buzzing through his fingertips. It only lasted seconds before dissipating having been replaced by a quiet confidence in his abilities.

Megan's eyes opened as Mark entered. She wiped her eyes and face.

"I'll be back later," the nurse said, going to leave him with Megan.

"Sorry," Megan said, eyes fluttering open.

"No, it's fine," replied the nurse. "You have a visitor." She pulled the door behind her and headed out.

"Hi, Megan, I'm Mark. I'm a healer," Mark began.

"What?"

Mark sat down next to her. She was young, maybe in her twenties. Her youth was only highlighted by the roundness of her cheeks, but the dark circles under her eyes, stark against her pale skin, gave away how awful she had to be feeling. Strands of long brown hair had escaped her bun, hanging limp and straggly around her face.

"I promote alternative medicine," he said.

Her voice was raspy.

"Really? I study medicine—just started my PhD."

Mark nodded.

"Are you open to alternative medicine?"

"I don't know," she replied. "I'm open to learning."

Mark gently cupped his hand on her wrist, and the room vanished.

In a lucid transformation, they were taken into a virtual world representing a robotically-immortal urban city set in the future. The futuristic skyline consisted of fast-paced, well-oiled machines—all components of the city linked together flawlessly. It was complex, yet sophisticated. There were cars arranged on the highways in rows, perfectly spaced out from each other, with traffic flowing smoothly, like a jacket zipper. Over in the distance were high-rises and homes that were precisely arranged in square-shaped suburbs—like hashtags, linked together like grid paper. Grasses had been consistently cut and flowers were intricately maintained and arranged. The vast landscape was filled with robots carrying out human tasks. They drove airborne and land-based vehicles, attended to stores and walked dogs. To any observing human, it was bizarre.

"What is this?"

"Year three thousand. Robots have taken over the world and have enslaved, imprisoned, or killed the humans."

"Why does this feel so real? Must've fallen asleep."

"This is what I do."

"I must be asleep, or maybe hypnosis? Or a lucid dream?"

"It's not a dream," Mark replied. "This is real, well, sort of—it's as real as you make it."

"I've seen some videos on lucid dreams—never thought I'd have one. I'm aware I'm dreaming."

Megan crouched to pick up some metal devices on the ground and inspected them. She glanced over at Mark.

"Okay, you win," she said after some moments. "It's the most exciting thing that's happened to me in weeks."

She snatched at a large, shimmery hunk of metal, shaped like a gun that levitated off the ground close to where she stood. It made a noise like it was charging up.

"Quite intuitive. You've got weapons. This is your health," she said, pointing at green stick holograms hovering above their heads. "And, you've got the bad guys."

She pointed to some robots in the distance.

Megan pressed a button on the side of the gun, and it glowed for a moment, tiny green lights pulsating.

"Megan," Mark began, but she focused on her gun.

"It has my name on it too."

Metallic grinding and whining rang through the air as robots closed in on them.

"Megan!" he shouted. Mark grabbed at a rifle-shaped weapon hovering near him. The coolness of the gun in his hands quickly turned to warmth when it automatically charged up and some lights appeared. Mark wasted no time and started shooting. Few robots exploded into a million metallic pieces.

Nice.

Megan glanced up at the horde of silver marching toward them.

"We need to get out of here!" Mark shouted. The tall, anthropomorphic robotic beings were regrouping and had formed a circle around them. The ground shook with the weight of their stomps as they edged in. He couldn't shoot quickly enough and his arms were beginning to ache.

"Get away from them and shoot!" he yelled.

Megan pulled the trigger but her weapon didn't fire.

"Run, there's too many of them!" Mark shouted.

As they escaped, the robotic barrage was difficult to evade—parts of whole buildings had now been destroyed, and a blast from one of their rays was enough to disintegrate the both of them.

"This isn't looking good!" she shouted, and she was right. They were outnumbered. Nowhere to run among the mindless, metal-encased, eight-foot beings.

Their running led them away from the central city district. Navigating turns and sharp corners of streets, the pair ran into extensive, dilapidated ruins—a vast, futuristic wasteland. Human skulls littered the ground and Mark flinched when a bone crunched beneath his shoes. Nearby laid long-range rifles. The thick rust coating them ensured they were no longer salvageable.

Exhausted from running, the pair stopped. Mark held a bent-out-of-shape light pole as he leant forward to catch his breath.

The remains of the destructive war were now exposed. Large chunks of metal, debris and robotic limbs filled the landscape among the bones and weapons. Mark hid behind a dumpster while Megan crouched behind a nearby pillar, both temporarily sheltering themselves from gunfire. They were still out of breath and Megan's loud panting echoed in Mark's ears. But they had to act. Quickly.

Megan shook her head as she glared at her weapon.

"Believe in yourself!" Mark yelled over the sound of gunfire. She looked over at him then her head drooped toward the ground. "Come here."

Megan darted toward him, barely avoiding the barrage of bullets slicing through the virtual air above her. He squeezed her wrist and they teleported inside a darkened warehouse. Light seeped in through large windows and Mark could make out the large steel walls separating them from the outside world.

"How'd you *do* that?" Megan asked once inside.

He ignored her.

"We win by defeating the boss. Understand?"

"And if we die...?" Megan began.

Again, he ignored her question. She'd get the gist.

"You need to learn how to use your gun. And your special ability."

"Special ability?"

"I can teleport anywhere in this city."

Megan had confusion written all over her face.

"My special... ability? What is it?"

"You're the main character so you're a creator. You'll need full health though."

Megan smiled. "This is a great dream. Where do we go now?"

"You tell me."

With eyes squinted nearly shut, she aimed at a giant nearby roller door and blasted her gun. It exploded, chunks of corrugated roller metal flying out of the warehouse.

"Let's go," she commanded.

Mark followed. She shot and killed the metallic villains with merciless precision, taking each of them down with a single shot. She upgraded her weapon at service stations and stocked up on health. Mark didn't refuse when she handed him a health bar and immediately he felt more energy pulsating through him. At the same time, a digital screen appeared in front of him and he saw the numbers go up to one hundred. Megan handed him armour. They were now even more combat savvy.

They (mostly Megan) continued their pursuit, destroying one robot at a time. With Mark's minimal assistance, she had essentially, single-handedly taken on the entire army. And the robots were no slouches either, with their own bags of tricks and state of the art weaponry. They would attack in heavy groups but she was too strong, too skilful, and too smart.

XIII

The landscape was filled with lifeless chunks of metal—thanks to Megan.

Megan pounced on a robot who was rolling in pain on the ground and began an interrogation.

"Who's your boss?" she asked, menacingly. She turned around and raised her eyebrows at Mark, grinning.

The robot said nothing.

She grabbed a metal rod that lay nearby and shoved it through the robot's midsection. It wailed.

"Who's your boss? I won't stop until you tell me." She pierced the robot with the metal rod and twisted it into parts of its body.

With its dying breath, the robot responded. "Steph. Aregon." It then drooped its head to its side, all signs of life vanishing.

"Steph Aregon. Why does that name ring a bell?" she asked. "Oh, wait! I know—follow me!"

They made their way to an abandoned laboratory. She blew down the door to reveal a shadow of a half-human, half-machine lingering on the other side of the room. He stood impassively. His bright white suit struggled to hold in his overweight midsection. His limbs were a combination of metal, wires, buttons and LEDs but his head and torso were flesh and humanlike. On the front of his suit was his name; *Mr Steph Aregon*. They'd found their boss.

"You found me, but this is where you die!" he shrieked, with a high-pitched voice.

"I don't think so," Megan replied.

Steph was agile for someone so overweight. He waved his arm and objects in the laboratory hurtled toward Megan and Mark. There was no warning and they were lucky to evade the random, flying items. He waved his arm again and their weapons were yanked from their grip.

"Let's do this the old-fashioned way," he snarled, pointing toward a large sword gravitating off the ground, close to Megan. It gleamed in the low-lit laboratory, the writing on it just about visible. *VANCO* had been written in large, bold letters that complemented its grand design. It was long and the metal was too bright to stare at for too long. Mark wanted to touch it, to feel its power but it was Megan's fight. It was her time to defeat the boss—Mark would have to stand by and watch.

"Take your weapon. You'll need all the help you can get," sneered Steph.

She sprang into action, yanked the sword from the air and faced him—the battle had started. Megan and the sword were rhythmic and perfectly in sync, although Mark could've sworn the sword had a mind of its own. It gave Megan determination and confidence but it was clear she'd met her match.

As the battle wore on, Steph didn't showcase any signs of losing stamina. But it didn't take long for Megan to be drenched in sweat, her hair hanging limply in front of her face. The boss had a response to each and every one of her acrobatic slashes of the sword, easily deflecting from every angle. It didn't take long. Her arms looked heavy and the frequency of her attacks slowed as she began favouring her right side.

"I don't know how much longer I can go on!" she shouted.

"Your special ability!" Mark reminded her.

The slow and gruelling battle dragged on. Steph was beginning to overwhelm her, raining down blows in an effort to destroy her as she stumbled backward. As a final demonstration of superiority, he yanked the sword from her grip and snapped it in two. Megan cowered when the broken sword hit the ground, her eyes filled with fear and confusion. Megan, now panting and struggling to stay upright, slowly walked backward toward the wall. Steph flung her across the lab using a form of ergokinesis from his metallic hands.

"You're too weak, that's why you'll never defeat me," he snarled, looking over at her. He kicked her in the stomach, and then a final blow to the head, rendering her unconscious. Next, he shoved her inside a cage, one barely large enough to fit a human.

"She's pathetic," Steph addressed Mark. "I'm going to kill her, then you. But I'm disappointed, I heard great things."

There was only one thing Mark could try now—but he'd never done it before. They weren't back so Megan wasn't dead. He ran over to her, who lay in the cage, seemingly all but dead. It was too small—and the sadistic display disturbed him.

"There's nothing you can do. You're in my domain now. You're both going to die here." Steph's voice echoed.

Mark had lost control. It should have been challenging, but not this challenging—*it was his fault*. He didn't have much time.

He closed his eyes and gently cupped her wrist.

They found themselves in an all-white landscape—an endless view of light as far as the eye could see.

"What happened? Am I dead?" she asked, hesitation in her voice at the question, as if she didn't want to know the answer.

Mark knew how she could win.

"What's going on? What is this place?"

"Your subconscious," Mark began. "Your special ability. You're a creator. You're responsible for everything that happened."

"What?"

She looked baffled but Mark knew he was right. She was the creator and had generated their sequence of events. From meeting the robots, the battle, even how it ended. The reason why Mark had become second in charge—why it had been easy for her to lead. Megan's subconscious had known what would occur even before it happened.

"That... That can't be right. I—I wouldn't have created a plotline like that. It doesn't make sense," she stammered.

"You made it that way—your subconscious. You're the most powerful person here."

"I lost. I'm going to wake up, right?" Her voice quivered and trailed off.

"You know I'm right. You've shown potential, and you can still beat this thing."

Mark gave her some moments to process, staring out at the ivory landscape.

"So, I have absolute control? Even more than you, the one that brought me here?"

Mark turned his head and chuckled. "The only thing I can do is take us back to the hospital. Everything else is up to you."

She nodded. A smirk appeared on the corner of her mouth. "How do I know what you're saying is true?"

95

"You don't. We're in your subconscious, remember? Reality is what you've made it."

Without warning, she jumped up and gripped his shoulder. They teleported back to the laboratory.

How did she do that?

It didn't matter.

Megan was back at war with Steph.

If he'd blinked he would have missed the finale. With pulsating energy from her hand, Megan destroyed the cage with some kind of force—the cage exploded, a blue-purple force field blasting it as the air crackled with static electricity. Pure energy shot from her hands, glowing as it snapped through the sound barrier, striking through Steph and vaporising him. Steph wasn't even given the chance to flinch. His ashes now lay in front of them, smelling of smoke and death.

She smirked the entire time and moments later they were back at the hospital.

"That was. Wow, I feel great!"

Mark smiled. He left her a business card and went on to find another patient.

FLASHBACK #6

The brightness of Mark's screen stole his attention—a text from Rachel. He titled it slightly and it only took a second for an uncontrollable smile to form.

Let's go to Darcy's? xxxx

It wasn't even lunchtime but a deal was a deal. He'd left her a note.

They'd been together four years (as boyfriend and girlfriend)—and if Rachel decided what they would do today, he'd leave work early and take her.

Morning gorgeous x
No riddle today but a challenge nonetheless. If you decide what we do today before I do, I'll leave work and come pick you up! xx

Darcy's. They went on their first date, and a few others followed. Creamy ice cream. The nostalgic, multi-coloured wooden chairs with soft cushions and shades of bright blue across the walls made it special—and it hadn't changed in the last four years.

Mark would have to come back to NetFlow another day. He signed out of his computer, said bye to the others who had decided to be there on a Saturday (mostly the twenty-four-hour tech support crew) and made his way to his car. He'd stop and get Rachel her favourite flowers on the way home—bright red roses.

XIV

The hospital stunt had been successful; Mark had to use a waiting list now, and was often forced to work late into the night.

The media soon requested an interview. Finding the time would have been difficult, if he hadn't had a last-minute cancellation. Mark nearly hung up when Diane called. He thought it was fake—but she held his attention long enough to explain that she wanted to include him in a short digital segment regarding his work. It would be televised in two weeks as well as a snippet in the national newspaper at around the same time.

The news team weren't turned off by the short notice and confirmed that the thirty minutes was enough—they would be ready for the interview at his house the following day.

The interviewer was a high-spirited lady, with a colourful, rainbow dress and a similar personality. She admitted to being a fan.

"I heard about you through friends!" she exclaimed when Mark opened the door.

Mark looked across the street as he held the door. A black SUV he'd seen parked there for the last few days. Dark tinted windows that made it difficult to see through. The vehicle gleamed in the sun but the shadows inside stole his attention. One, maybe two, sat so perfectly still he was convinced they were statues.

He shook the thought and smiled at the woman in front of him.

She introduced herself as Diane and presented her small team. The first one, Stan, was responsible for notetaking. The other—Ben—was to record the interview on a camera with a large, expensive-looking lens.

Mark led them to his living room where Stan took some time to set up the video camera.

"If you don't feel comfortable with any of the questions, let me know and I'll skip over," Diane reassured Mark.

Once the two men were ready, Diane gave the cue and they began.

Diane started by asking about his journey, and so Mark started with Apollo. Ben scribbled intensely in his notepad the entire time. By the end, he had told his entire story—even about Rachel.

The next thing Mark knew, it was over. Diane thanked him for his time and Mark walked the small team to his front door. He was surprised to see three people across the street, taking photos as the interview team left. They weren't with Diane and her crew.

"Looks like you're famous," Diane said, glancing back over her shoulder with a smile.

It was difficult to make out their faces, but after a few minutes, the three men—wearing long, black clothing—got back into their dark SUV and drove off.

The ringing of his phone reminded him that he had work to do and clients to get back to so he stepped inside, closing the door behind him. His phone rarely stopped ringing now.

He needed help.

* * *

As the days passed, word spread. People knocked at his door. Some said they'd pay whatever it took—it was getting out of control. He wasn't available—and he wasn't prepared.

Not only that, other media teams called, inviting him to shows and interviews—and he had to turn them down.

It didn't take long for the *letters* to arrive. First, through email but soon they appeared in his mailbox. Typically from local clinics and medical centres and so, he wasn't bothered, even by their confrontation and aggressive demands. They demanded to have their patients referred back. Mark ignored them.

Weeks later, he received letters from an international audience. His initial reaction was motivation. There was the letter from the *International Pharmaceutical Federation*, then, the *World Medical Association*, then finally, the *Medical Research Council*.

He barely had to read them to know what was inside.

In short, they weren't pleased. They ordered that he stop due to laws regarding the authority of practice—under the conspiracy to practice without a provisional certification.

But in his mind, he hadn't done anything wrong. Even so, the letters were increasingly threatening. Most warned of legal repercussions but among them, one letter stated: *this is your last warning, you will be stopped by any means necessary*, but Mark disregarded all of them.

And so, he stopped opening them altogether. It was always the same message, after all: to stop, or else.

Besides, he had a lot more to worry about than the threatening mail. People queued, and the media were relentless for his time.

* * *

He was travelling to heal now—and he'd gone to several countries. In Japan, a group of people had met him outside of a hospital for him to sign autographs.

In Mexico, he met with members of congress who thanked him for healing a member of their parliament.

Interviews occurred—some he needed a translator for. In Germany, the translator described his work to the audience in a popular sit-down talk show.

He enjoyed travelling but Mark was exhausted, and he missed home—and so he decided to return. Travel would be put on hold for the time being.

It was mid-morning as Mark hopped out of his rideshare to find two shadows in a black SUV again, opposite his house—but he was too fatigued to care. They didn't move. Even by the time Mark had pulled his front door shut, they still hadn't moved.

But they stared at him the entire time.

He napped. Only for a few hours, but then it was back to work.

As he led a client to the door to say bye, he noticed the men across the street again, but this time, no cameras. They'd gotten out of their car and were heading toward the house—and there were three of them. One must have been in the back. Were they from the media? Or the mail? He hadn't responded to any—he'd ignored all threats that lay in unopened envelopes.

He shook the paranoia off and held the door.

They walked with purpose, their postures ramrod straight and arms swinging rigidly by their sides. Their black suits hugged their figures, the white shirts beneath their jackets practically gleaming under the sun. Their leader was broad and barrel chested, possibly capable of inflicting immense brutality with his bare hands. The other two were tall and slender.

Mark squinted, raising his gaze to look at them. They now towered above him at the front door, making him feel small. Mark shot his hand out but the gesture was ignored.

"Can I help you?" Mark began. No response. Familiar frustration set in, his cheeks flushing red as his efforts at politeness were ignored.

They stood in a tight triangle, one directly in front of Mark with the other two flanking him. The one in front led the team of three into Mark's living room. They hadn't waited for an invitation to step inside. Jaw clenched, Mark dug his nails into his palms and followed them into the lounge.

"I'm assuming you know why we're here?" the leader asked.

Mark had a pretty good idea but he didn't want to play their games. His fingers were still rolled in, like balls of fury—the thought of their audacious invasion still fresh in his mind.

"You tell me," he replied sarcastically.

"You're playing a dangerous game, Mark. We need balance and what you're doing—" He spoke in a soft voice, but each word was anything but. They were warnings. Daggers to Mark's chest—and he'd been doing too much. This was their final *letter*.

"This is a first, and final warning."

"And after that?" Mark couldn't help but blurt out.

The men stared at him—then the leader lost his composure, his face twisting into a scowl. "Do we have to remind you who we are?" he snarled, a vein throbbing in his jaw.

Mark nearly responded that there were no introductions in the first place, but bit his tongue.

"If we have to come back here, you're coming with us. Understand?" One of the other men spoke up.

Mark asked no further questions. The message was loud and clear—not that he wanted to be bullied into submission.

They turned, almost in perfect sync, walked out of the house and back to their vehicle. They didn't pull the door shut behind them.

* * *

Mark had more clients that day but briefly, he considered his options—submit to their threats or assume they were bluffing.

Maybe a break will help.

He blocked off a month, set up auto-replies on his digital accounts, and prepared a voicemail.

Thanks for contacting me. I will be away for the next four weeks. This inbox will not be monitored during this time and I will reply when I return.

He called his mum to arrange a visit. Days later, another flight to Melbourne. He'd stay with her this time.

Mark, his mum, and Michael were in the living room when Mark found the newspaper article.

"You guys still read the newspaper?" he asked, mockingly.

"We got it because you're in it," replied Michael.

He'd completely forgotten. He snatched up the paper and turned pages and soon, there it was. He quickly digested the article.

"How can they write this?" Mark said, fury running through his veins as he clenched his fists. He showed his mum.

Michael chuckled. "There's no such thing as bad publicity. You'll be famous after this. Well, you already are, aren't you? How many countries have you gone to?"

"But have you seen *this*?" complained Mark.

At least the photo was reasonable. His lazy, but polite, half-smile. The picture was cut off at the waist and you could see the top half of his green suit.

But the article? Not so good.

Starting with the headline: *The Healer: A man of past delusions heals the sick?*

It was a translation of an interview in Germany. It described him as a hallucinating man, angry and grieving, who had decided to leave his normal life, confident in what someone—whom he didn't even know—had said.

Actually, that part was true.

But, that aside—he wasn't delusional. The journalist had twisted his words.

"You're misinterpreting it," Michael said. "I don't see anything wrong with it."

Despite his frustration, Mark slowly nodded.

"I think it's good you opened up, it'll help," Michael added.

"Sure," Mark replied, this time shaking his head and rolling his eyes.

Mark stopped worrying about the article and instead focused on spending time with his family.

It was obvious they pitied him—because of Rachel. They went to a park—a family picnic but even then it was undeniable. The nervous glances when he was quiet, the constant checking in on him, the special treatment—but he had to accept that they cared.

I wonder if they were telling the truth about the article?

He enjoyed his stay—he went and watched Ollie's soccer games (Ollie was a speedy winger as it turned out) and also took him to practice, he'd listen to Michael play the guitar and the family dinners were great. But after a few weeks, it was time to go home, to a life where people had no issues telling him what they thought.

FLASHBACK #7

Rachel had on a bright pink, plaid-print, pleated skirt with a white, long-sleeve crop top and black leather combat boots—and she fit right in. Darcy's had its fair share of contrasting colours. The pink floor, red ceiling and blue walls popped like multi-coloured confetti, littered with nostalgic posters commemorating ice cream in the 1900s.

Mark wasn't as bold, with his black jeans and a navy-blue polo on top of brown, leather boots.

As they waited behind two kids, Mark glanced up at a nearby poster and couldn't help but smile. It was titled, *1948: Date night*. For a moment he mirrored the emotion of the New York couple who, while displaying affectionate smiles, fed each other sundae in the black and white photo.

Mark's head veered back to the front where a clear glass left nothing to the visual imagination. Still, they waited but it didn't matter—they knew what they wanted.

When it was their turn, Mark ordered his classic hazelnut and coconut combo—Rachel went with her familiar cookies and cream and cookie dough.

"Thanks for the flowers," she said as they sat in one of the booths.

"No problem."

He grinned at her then glanced outside through the window. One of the kids who had been in front of them toppled and fell on the bitumen. Her wails invaded the parlour. The boy tried pulling her from the ground but she tore her hand away and continued sobbing.

Mark glanced at Rachel then ran outside to them. The afternoon sun was still high in the sky and nearby fumes filled Mark's nose.

"Hey, are you okay?" He crouched down next to her. Directly to her left, her ice cream had already started melting.

"I don't have money for more ice cream," the boy began. Mark put his hand up to his face to shield the sun as he looked up at the boy.

"Are you her brother?"

"Yes."

'What's her name?"

"Stella."

Mark turned toward her.

"Hey, Stella, are you hurt?"

She nodded.

Out of the corner of his eye, Mark saw Rachel come outside with their ice creams.

"Where does it hurt?"

"Here on my arm. It hurts." She'd grazed it but not too bad, it wasn't bleeding—but it looked raw, the skin red and scratched.

"You'll be okay," Mark replied.

"But my ice cream—"

"I'll get you another one, how does that sound?"

Her head bobbed up and down. Her loud, convulsive gasps had stopped.

"What ice cream did you have?"

"Chocolate, in a cone." She'd stopped crying, but her voice trembled.

Mark left them and went and ordered. Minutes later he was back, handing her the cone and a couple of Band-Aids he'd gotten from staff inside.

"Thank you," her brother said as they walked away.

Mark looked across at Rachel. He had felt her eyes on him. She stared—and now her eyes sparkled with an adoring gaze and the corners of her mouth slid upward, followed by a grin.

"What?"

"Nothing," she responded, handing him his melted ice cream. But she couldn't hide her smile.

XV

As Mark entered the house, he inhaled deeply, thinking about his workload. The emails. The messages. The adrenaline was an instant reminder of what he'd left behind.

He rolled his bag into the living room, tossing his backpack onto the sofa before taking a few deep breaths and sitting beside it. Eyes closed, he cleared his thoughts.

He sank into the leather. For some seconds he sunk, further and further, the comfort feeling like he was cradled inside a hammock.

Then the pressure changed.

He was floating. He kept his eyes closed and allowed the feeling to spread through his body—like he was suspended in mid-air. His ears vibrated while he felt a warm pressure on his forehead.

He was reminded of the leather beneath him when a tapping reached his ears. Frowning, his eyes shot open. Why did no one ever want to use the doorbell?

Loud bangs now reverberated from the front. It couldn't be that important, surely?

"Coming!" he groaned, as he heaved himself off the lounge and toward the door.

He opened the door and instantly his heart sank. Two rigid, muscular men wore suits of a dark shade of navy. Mark remained silent and the men stood and did the same. They had hawkish eyes and unwavering, and robust demeanours.

Mark didn't recognise them and for a second, the memory of how *the other ones* had allowed themselves in, intruded his mind. The muscles on his arms twitched and the tension on the back of his neck mounted.

"Can I help you?"

"We need you to come with us," the man to Mark's right said while the other nodded slightly. Authoritative. There was no deviation from demeanour. No movement of the limbs. Hardly a sway, despite the blowing of thin branches nearby. Cool as anything, the man demanded with a voice so terrifyingly calm that Mark nearly went along.

Instead, Mark frowned and scanned the one who had just spoken—wide shoulders and a few inches taller.

"I haven't done anything. When the other three left, I stopped. For weeks."

The men briefly looked at each other, narrow-eyed, before facing Mark again.

"I'm not asking you again, you need to come with us," the same man spoke and took a step toward Mark.

Mark's adrenaline surged.

"And if I don't?"

"Enough." This time the other one spoke. His voice was bearish—more of a growl than anything. He was slimmer than the other, but not by much.

"No," the first man interjected. "You've got ten seconds. Either way, you're coming. Ten..."

Mark's head spun.

"Six..."

It's hilarious. Counting down like that.

"Three..."

Mark snickered.

"One."

One of the men lashed out, striking Mark below the ribs. The air left his lungs in a rush, pain surging through his body. His limbs locked up, paralysing him in place as he fought to draw breath.

He gasped as the men half carried/half led him to a black vehicle that had pulled into his driveway. It was a shiny Rolls Royce SUV and Mark briefly saw the reflection of trees and the sky. He saw another figure standing next to the back door, arms crossed, waiting for them, wearing the same navy attire. His stomach churned.

He was thrust into the back and the man who punched him joined him. The other squeezed into the front passenger seat. The man who had been standing by the car soon occupied the driver's seat. There was a man already seated in the back of the car.

There were no introductions. No pleasantries of any kind. It didn't take long for them to be on their way, wherever that was.

"I hope they weren't too hard on you. Sometimes they get a little... direct."

Mark, still in some pain, turned toward the man who had been waiting in the back of the vehicle. He didn't even bother to look at Mark as he spoke, more interested in his tablet. The sun seeping through the window glinted off the face of his gleaming watch, a stark silver against his black suit. His voice was as deep as his expensive cologne, both of them dominating the small space of the car.

"Sometimes, they find that people need... *encouraging*."

"Where are you taking me?" Mark began. Some of the pain had now subdued and he was breathing almost normally again.

"Not far, about a thirty-minute drive."

"Where?"

The man ignored Mark's question. "How rude of me. I didn't introduce everyone. The two gentlemen you met at your door—the man in the front is Bruno, and the one sitting with us is Hunter."

They both turned toward Mark and nodded.

"They're very thorough. Aren't you, boys?"

"Yes, sir," Mark heard them both say, almost at the same time.

"They're friendly, once you get to know them," the man continued.

"The driver, his name is Jett," he said, pointing to the man that had been waiting for them outside the vehicle.

"And I can't forget about me. You can call me Hendrix."

"What do you want from me?"

"Ah, you ask the wrong questions. I can understand why, of course. But let's enjoy this Sunday afternoon drive. What do you say?"

Mark was in no position to argue. He stayed quiet. Wherever they were headed, it couldn't be good. And this strange Hendrix—someone with more power than he deserved—clearly enjoyed toying with people.

Mark sighed and stared through the window, his nausea a reminder of what would happen if he argued.

They'd been driving for several minutes when Hendrix propped his head up and looked at Mark for the first time.

"I need a favour."

Hendrix's voice came as a surprise. "My daughter, she's not well. She's diabetic, but she's developing ather-osclerosis and non-alcoholic steatohepatitis. It might progress to cirrhosis."

Mark stayed quiet. It was weird that Hendrix requested a favour after forcing him to be there, through violence.

With his fingers, Mark applied pressure where he'd been punched. It was tender and produced a dull ache.

"I need you to cure her," Hendrix finally said.

Mark said nothing and so too did Hendrix for the remainder of the trip.

* * *

They arrived at a large estate, with a long windy driveway that led far off the main road until it entirely disappeared from view behind them. Trees canopied above the asphalt, resembling a tunnel as they neared.

Mark was led through the front door, across tiles that he could see his reflection in. As they walked, Hendrix explained that his otherwise delightful and energetic daughter, Zoey, had been a victim of a sedentary life.

Mark saw lines on Hendrix's face he hadn't noticed earlier.

"She's twelve. It's generally asymptomatic so we didn't know for a while—"

They made their way to her room. It had rose-pink walls, and a large bed in the middle with an off-white, fluffy rug underneath. Some plants occupied the corner and the window looked out onto a calm lake.

Hendrix mentioned blood tests while he woke her but Mark barely heard—he felt her pain in his chest, the same discomfort in his upper right abdomen and his arms momentarily drooped down his sides. Mark went and sat on a chair that had been pushed up against the bed.

"This is the man I was telling you about. Do what he says, okay, sweetheart?" said Hendrix as he spoke to Zoey.

"I'm going to make you better," Mark began. She nodded slowly.

Mark softly grabbed her wrist. For a second, green canvas filled their eyes.

Soon, shapes began to form.

Thick humidity filled the air and sweat quickly coated Mark's skin, damp soaking through his shirt. The moss-scented area was overgrown with trees and vines and insects covered the ground.

A wooden sign of a light-brown shade in front of them said: *Welcome to the Land of the Amazons.*

"What are Amazons?"

"Warriors," Mark replied. "You're an Amazon Princess and we need to find your treasure, using your map."

"Dad said it would be like a dream," she replied. She studied a map she'd found in her pocket.

"It's a treasure hunt," Mark said, and she beamed at him. "Which way do we need to go?"

"That way, I think," she replied, pointing toward a path that led them into thicker plantation.

Zoey walked ahead on the narrow rainforest trail. Some thick branches had fallen across and others hung in their way, but Zoey had no problem climbing over them or ducking. As they walked, the sound of the river flowing and the singing of birds and insects kept them company.

Soft, rhythmic thuds started behind them. Mark held his breath and stopped. He ushered for Zoey to be quiet and peered over his shoulder. He briefly caught sight of the muscular striations on the tiger that was headed their way, with jaws strong enough to crush both of them. Zoey, now a statue, gaped at it.

"Run!" screamed Mark. Ahead was a small stream, and a treehouse just beyond that.

Zoey scampered toward the stream, her long, blonde hair flailing behind her. The thuds grew louder with each aggressive strike—the tiger was quickly gaining on them. When Mark glanced back, bright red eyes glowered at him, set on their target.

"We need to get over this!" Mark shouted, through heavy gasps of air, as they reached the stream. Mark, without hesitation, ran past Zoey and used the large rocks as platforms and within seconds he was on the other side. Zoey had stopped, terror written across her face.

"Zoey, come on!"

She shook her head as her eyes rapidly darted from the tiger to Mark.

"I, I can't do it."

"What? Of course, you can."

"I can't."

It wasn't far between jumps. Maybe a metre or so.

"I can't do this, kids at school make fun of me."

They didn't have much time. "Zoey, you can do anything here. In the real world too."

"No, I'm going to fall in, like I always do, and you'll laugh at me like everyone always does." Words failed to come out of Mark's mouth.

The vicious cat's roars and thumping got louder.

He racked his brain. What would Michael say? He was good with kids—but the pity turned to him gritting his teeth.

"I can't make you jump. But if you don't try, I can't help you."

She stood fixed to the spot with nervous glances over her shoulders. Mark spun around and faced the treehouse.

"I'm turning away. No kids from school and I won't look."

Mark held his breath and soon soft thuds hit the rocks as Zoey made her way across. Seconds later, she stood next to him with a confident grin but their moment was interrupted by a roar, nearby birds launching into the air in fear.

The tiger was only a few car lengths away.

"Up the treehouse!" Mark shouted, but she'd already run past him and began climbing the stairs leading into the canopy.

Their arms were sore, but they eventually made it to the top, and to the safety of the golden-brown wooden structure, high above the ground.

Inside, a wooden chest floated in the centre of the room. Zoey snatched at it. It creaked open and dust filled the room. Inside lay a golden heart and a gold medal with a number *one* on it.

Moments later they were back.

"I feel—wow!"

Mark tilted his head up and for the first time, he saw Hendrix smile.

"Call me Dave. And the way we treated you earlier—I have my ways. Sometimes it's hard for me to separate," he said, after checking on Zoey.

Mark considered that was as good as an apology but didn't respond—he'd done what he came for, it was time for him to leave. Dave led him downstairs to the main entrance.

"I'm sure you'll find that a generous compensation for what you did here today," Dave said. Jett, the driver, handed Mark a small aluminium case.

Mark unclipped it—it was filled with cash, held together by some rubber bands.

"I need to go," Mark started.

"You won't stay for dinner?"

"No."

XVI

In the passenger seat, Mark squinted at the late afternoon sun as it pierced through the windshield. He barely processed the smell of leather which had now invaded his nose.

Although they twisted through the driveway and out onto the main road, the SUV glided over the asphalt as though not bothered by the bends—and the blowing of the air-con on his face soothed him a little. His mind drifted toward Rachel. He hated feeling like he needed something but at that moment—

"How do you do it?"

There was no one else in the car—obviously Jett was talking to him.

"What?"

"Healing. How do you do it?"

Mark sighed and briefly shut out the world by closing his eyes and pinching the bridge of his nose. He wasn't in the mood for conversation with someone who'd kidnapped him.

"I don't know, it just happens."

"What do you mean?"

Please shut up.

"I'm psychic. I use energy for healing and take people to a place I can do that."

Jett seemed satisfied with the answer and didn't say anything else.

Mark didn't thank Jett when they arrived. He just slipped out and headed inside—he switched his work phone on, and sluggishly sifted through emails.

Tension ticked in his jaw, neck clenched as he scrolled through hundreds upon hundreds of emails, countless text messages and voicemails—and he hadn't even gotten to social media yet.

Now engrossed in his work, sweat trickled down his forehead. His shirt clung uncomfortably to his back—even then, the thought of air-con didn't enter his mind.

He stopped and gave one email slightly more attention.

Hi Mark,
Hope you're well.
Thanks again for what you did at the hospital—I feel great! I've never heard of anything like it.
I hate to ask—actually, I tried calling and sent a text but couldn't get through...
But it's my dad. I suspect hyperthyroidism, but he's stubborn and won't go to a doctor and I'm a little worried.
Do you think you could visit him?
Not super urgent, he might come around but if you can, let me know when suits you.
Megan

Hi Megan,
I'm glad you're feeling great.
I've been away, hence the late reply but that's no problem. I'll see him.
Give me another call on my personal number and I'll save it, otherwise feel free to reply to this email.
Mark

He'd just moved Megan's email into a new folder titled 'Megan' when the ringing of his phone echoed through the house—an unknown number took over the screen.

"Hello?"

"Hey, it's Megan—thanks, by the way."

"No problem. Is your dad okay?"

"Well, I suspect hyperthyroidism, or Graves' Disease. He's lost a lot of weight and there's a family history."

"Why won't he go to a doctor?"

"He thinks I'm being paranoid. But I don't know..."

"I can come tomorrow afternoon, or evening. Send me a text to confirm."

"Okay, thanks. I'll talk to him and let you know."

"No problem, speak soon."

Hanging up, Mark exhaled loudly. Bar his heavy breaths in his ears, the only other sound was the faint barking of a dog down the street.

His head hung heavy on his shoulders and there was a dull ache in his lower back but he continued with the emails. At a quarter past nine, the watch on his left wrist vibrated, reminding him that bedtime was in forty-five minutes, and that he should 'wind down'. Seconds later, his eyes drifted to his left where his phone lay as it too, showed the same reminder. Ignoring it, the clicking of his keyboard continued and so too did the faint barking of the dog.

At midnight, as he had moved on to his social media messages, both devices reminded him that bedtime was two hours ago—and that his alarm would go off in just five hours.

He pulled his laptop shut, quenched his thirst with the nearly neglected glass of water on his desk and took himself to bed.

* * *

4:45AM—he was up before the chime of his alarm. As he rolled over to switch the alarm setting off, he felt a tenderness in his lower back—the same ache that had begun the previous night. He dismissed it, changed into some workout clothes and made his way to the gym.

He received the text from Megan over breakfast.

She'd spoken to her Dad and he'd agreed to meet Mark that night. It was just as well—he'd started booking appointments for that afternoon.

He managed to squeeze in several clients before his watch warned that he needed to leave to be on time. Darkness engulfed the garage and for a split second, just before the light came on, Mark froze. A dark fog seeped through and arranged itself into a demonic entity across the white wall. The sensor light flickered on, devouring the darkness, and the entity with it. Sweat dripped down Mark's forehead. He took some deep breaths then slipped into his car.

There was the odd car here and there and the brightness of the full moon almost distracted him. But to avoid thinking about that demonic entity any longer, Mark poked at the car's infotainment screen until the sound of a podcast on emerging technology filled his ears and mind.

He'd barely listened by the time he pulled into a concrete driveway. The moon and Mark's headlights suggested it was a sandy beige, however, it was difficult to make out exactly. Directly in front towered a concrete two-storey, also of a light shade.

He got out, made his way to the door and poked at the doorbell. The ringing echoed inside.

Megan opened the door and wrapped her arms around him—and instantly Mark felt encapsulated in warmth, the same warmth he'd felt with her before. He'd only experienced it with two other people before now: Henry and Apollo.

He became distracted when Megan's dad poked through and held out a slender arm which Mark shook. His lanky body contrasted with his deep, masculine voice.

"It's nice to meet you," Mark started.

"Same. Name's Luke. Come in."

Megan disappeared upstairs as Mark walked on porcelain tiles that led through to an open-plan lounge. The ceilings were high, a cooling breeze whistling through the open space. He sat on a marble, napoleon corner lounge.

"Megan told me what you did. At the hospital."

Mark nodded.

"As long as you're not a doctor," Luke added with a nervous laugh.

"What do you have against doctors?" Mark replied.

"Nothing, I just don't want this to be Megan's way of making me see one. A practical joke."

Mark chuckled, sensing Luke's hesitation.

"You're not one of those twenty-four-hour doctors, are you? Those that visit homes?

Again, Mark chuckled. "No, I'm a healer."

"Okay. And what do you do?" Luke asked.

"How about I show you?"

"Sure, why not," Luke replied with a shrug.

Mark moved across the lounge to sit next to him, and placed his palm on the back of Luke's hand.

In seconds the room disappeared.

Water seeped through Mark's canvas shoes and into his socks—and he nearly slipped on the smooth, hard surface below. His nose burned from the smell of cigarettes although, he couldn't see any smokers through the vast black that surrounded him. A streetlight flickered nearby, but all he could make out was gleaming water, stretching a couple of metres in every direction. Splashes echoed as he walked through the void. He shouldn't be here.

"Luke?"

No reply.

A breeze came from behind him, raising his collar. He twisted but nothing was there. His feet squelched in his shoes as he wandered through the shadows, the only noise coming from the contact of his rubber soles with the inches-deep water.

He shivered as the temperature dropped and he heard a familiar scream ahead—Rachel.

"Mark!"

A light shone on her in the distance—and she was all he could see among the darkness. Her eyes were wide, terror fixed on her face.

"Mark, help!"

Blood rushed to his legs and without thinking, he sprinted across the darkness although his shoes barely gripped the surface below.

Soon, fatigue gripped him, his legs growing heavy, and his heart screamed in pain—but he wasn't getting any closer. The fatigue turned into a burning pain—his leaden legs and the slippery surface below now threatened to topple him over.

At that same moment, Mark nearly staggered at the sound of a horn that matched Rachel's screams. In a split second, a truck screeched on the wet bitumen. Mark's mouth grew wide and so too did his eyes as it crashed into her. The truck's headlights momentarily blinded him and at the same time, the void rippled away and Rachel's screams faded.

He tilted his head upward and recognised the high ceiling. To his right, Luke stared awkwardly.

"Sorry, just give me a minute."

He wondered if Luke could hear the thumping of his chest. *I need to get it together.*

Mark took several deep breaths, allowing his heart to slow—but even though the cool breeze flowed through the room, sweat prickled on his forehead and his palms were clammy.

The heat of his palms absorbed into his thighs as he wiped them on his jeans—the denim texture on his hands a momentary distraction from what he'd just experienced.

He felt the pressure near his eyes as he pinched the bridge of his nose and closed his eyes.

"You okay?" Luke asked. Mark opened his eyes and twisted his neck toward Luke.

"Yeah. Headache. I'm fine now."

"Would you like a glass of water?"

"No, this won't take long."

Mark cleared his thoughts, inhaled deeply and gripped Luke's wrist.

Instantly, the room twisted and morphed into something entirely different.

A boxed room. No objects. And, crucially, no perceivable exit. The room was bare but for a single thick, unlit, white candle sitting on a white saucer in the middle. The ceiling was so low that if Mark looked up, his nose would scrape it. A flickering lightbulb filled the otherwise dark room with intermittent light. And the cream walls—they felt like they were closing in. There were red stains on the dark-grey carpet that indented slightly where Mark stood.

Luke had it worse than Mark; he was taller.

"What is this?"

"An escape room," Mark replied, his voice bouncing off the walls.

"Interesting. I went to one with Megan years ago. She's a smart girl. Basically single-handedly solved the whole thing."

Mark nodded then sat on the floor in the corner of the room—the thin carpet instantly reminded him of the soreness in his lower back. He bent in his knees slightly and leaned backward, the coolness of the wall penetrating his back.

"You're not going to help me?" Luke asked. He'd found the lighter in his pocket and didn't waste time in lighting the candle.

"No," Mark replied, tilting his head into his hand then stroking his mouth as he stared at Luke.

"There's nothing in here. Just this candle."

Mark stayed silent.

The dead silence was broken by Luke's attempts to find an escape.

There was a knocking as Luke investigated the walls for hollowness. Then scratching. Next, Luke dropped to all fours to study the carpet stains. Mark heard heavy breathing and saw Luke's muscles contract as he attempted to pull the carpet from the ground at the corners and edges of the room.

With sweat now flowing down his face and dampening his t-shirt, Luke stopped and scrunched his face as though deep in thought. He scratched the top of his head and Mark saw as the rise and fall of his chest became less frequent and aggressive.

When his breathing steadied, Luke banged at the walls with the outer side of his fists until he was reduced to sweating again.

"Can you give me a clue?" Luke asked, panting.

Mark shook his head. It was hard to know how long they'd been there now but his glute muscles burned on the unforgiving carpet. He'd had to adjust a few times but between the soreness in his lower back and now his backside, he stood and was now leaning into the wall.

"I don't know if I'm enjoying this," Luke muttered, just as the light above made its last flicker and with a soft hiss, turned off.

There was a loud thud. Luke had kicked into the wall with the toe of his shoe but immediately grimaced when his foot swung back.

"I need to get out of here," Luke said, rubbing his foot.

Mark allowed the carpet to capture his attention. Apart from where Luke and he stood, and the candle sat, the entire surface of the room could be seen. The walls were barren. The ceiling, too, was bare, except for the lifeless lightbulb—and their only light now came from the mostly-dead candle which provided a warm light that made Mark's eyes feel heavy.

"Mark?"

Mark had sat back down and he glanced up at Luke but said nothing.

"Mark. I need to get out of here."

Mark shook his head and a disappointed sigh followed. He stared as Luke yanked the lightbulb from the ceiling and looked into the hole with hopeful eyes. Luke quickly shook his head in disgust and sat on the ground, knees bent in just as the candle too went out.

In the pitch-black room, Mark's only sense of awareness was in hearing Luke's heavy breathing.

"Well, this is shit. Should've just gone to the doctors."

The darkness instantly morphed back into Luke's living room and for some seconds Mark's eyes pained as they adjusted to the light.

Mark smirked and looked over at Luke, knowing full well what Luke jokingly wanted to call him.

Mark saw as the edges of Luke's mouth formed into a smile. A slight shake of the head.

Mark chuckled. "You're welcome."

"You bastard," Luke replied, laughing.

Mark peered to his left and noticed Megan at the kitchen counter. She twisted and stared at them.

Mark held his chin, staring at her. "I think you're psychic," he said.

"What?" replied Luke who was still chuckling to himself. But Mark shook his head. He wasn't talking to him.

Megan's attention shifted from Luke to Mark. "Me?"

"Yeah."

"What makes you say that?"

"I can feel it."

Megan's eyes darted across the walls then locked with Mark's before scoffing and shaking her head.

Megan and Luke led Mark to the door and as Megan went in for another hug, Mark felt it again. His heart momentarily swelled—unexplained joy and warmth filling his body. He remembered the feeling. It took him right back to his childhood, and the day before Christmas—and the day before his birthday.

In his car, the podcast on emerging tech had barely resumed when Mark tapped at the car's screen. Eventually, he pressed; *call*.

"Hey, Mark, what's up?"

"I can teach you." Mark barely waited for Megan to respond. "Healing. I'm convinced you're psychic."

"Um."

"If you're interested, meet me at mine tomorrow night. Same time."

He hung up, his attention now on the darkness around him and the low buzz of the car. As he stared ahead he had to squint at a dark mass with a humanlike figure that glitched itself into his vision. It evaporated as soon as he pulled on the high-beam lever.

FLASHBACK #8

Mark and Rachel were submerged in a sea of bright lights as soon as they walked inside the arcade—blues, reds, pinks and greens popped from screens every which way they looked. Chimes, bumper thumps, rolling balls and animated voices invaded their auditory senses. It didn't take long to spot Lauren, Rachel's best friend, and her boyfriend Kyle at the entrance lounge. Brad, Mark's work friend was there too with his partner Chris.

It was game night. The teams they would compete in, and the games played, had been pre-organised by Rachel and Lauren. The rules were simple: the team of three that accumulated the least points would have the burden of purchasing drinks for the remainder of the night. Mark was teamed up with Lauren and Brad, while Rachel teamed up with Chris and Kyle.

A bowl of gin punch was delivered just as the group set up for their first game—bowling. Around them, the sound of bowling bowls knocking down pins rattled through the space. Rachel clapped and cheered. Mark stayed focused and quiet—eyes set on the prize. He barely heard the group when it was his time to bowl. Rachel's gutter balls didn't dampen her mood. Mark looked across at her after her third gutter ball—she pranced back to her seat, a childish grin on her face.

A series of spares and strikes from Mark ensured his team won with ease. Despite Brad's less than average score of seventy (according to Mark), the team led by a full one hundred points.

The second round was a series of shots into an elevated basketball hoop. Each player had thirty shots and their averages were used to tally the teams' performance. Rachel's team won the round.

Darts, table tennis, MotoGP and table soccer followed. By the last round, the teams had equal scores—three victories apiece. Air hockey would round it off. Lauren had beaten Kyle. Chris had beaten Brad in their match. Mark looked across the table. Rachel looked determined—she had a sly smirk. Mark winked.

Mark led five points to nil. He pulled his eyes from the table and stared at Rachel as she placed the puck down to resume the game. He glanced over at his friends watching the game. Although they smiled, Rachel's excitement outmatched any of theirs. Mark chuckled just as Rachel's shot found its way into the goal earning herself her first point. Her arms shot into the air.

"I'm still in this!" she yelled across to the group.

"You got this, Rach!" Kyle shouted over the sound of balls, pucks and screens.

Mark shook his head. His heart steadied and his muscles relaxed for the first time that night.

Rachel won the match by two points.

Grinning, Mark shrugged at the group and made his way to the bar to order a round.

* * *

"Did you let me win?"

Mark and Rachel sat in the back of their Uber—the game night was over.

"What?" Mark replied.

"Air hockey."

"I never let anyone win anything. Ever." Mark replied. An uncontrollable smile formed on his face just as Rachel placed her head on his chest.

XVII

Late night with Jose. He'd just started going through emails and there it was—an email from the producer inviting him to be a guest on the talk show. Expenses paid. A trip to LA.

Without thinking he accepted a video call for the following day.

Mark dragged himself from the computer, pulled some books from the upstairs bookshelf and placed them on the kitchen counter. He smiled as he eyed Dan's *A Peaceful Healer: The Hidden School.*

He picked up his phone and dialled Dan's number. Dan answered almost instantly.

"Mark, how are you? I saw you on TV a few weeks ago—nice work."

"Thanks. Actually, I had a question."

"Shoot."

"Did you know I was a healer when we first met?"

"Sort of. But I ignore it these days. Been wrong more than I've been right." Dan laughed. "Why?"

"Just curious. Someone I met. I felt it. Same with Henry and Apollo."

"Interesting..." replied Dan.

"Can I bring her to meet you?"

"Sure. Just don't forget that there are many types of psychic abilities—and I only work with healers."

"Right," Mark replied.

"Also, sometimes the energy of someone's potential is real. And other times it's non-coding."

Mark went to ask what he meant when he heard the ding of the doorbell down the hall.

"Sorry Dan, have to go but I'll come around soon. With Megan."

He hung up and went to let her in.

Before they headed upstairs to the healing room Mark made them both chamomile teas.

Teas in hands, they made their way to their classroom.

Mellow-soft, ambient melodies resonated throughout the room as Mark went over the basics—terminologies, energy and healing—the extent of his scope.

Teacups empty, Mark looked down at his watch. It had already been two hours. He called it a night and as he took Megan to the front door he grabbed the books on the counter.

"You can borrow these," he said, handing them to her.

"Thanks."

They were at the door when Megan said, "This is all fascinating. Just don't get your hopes up."

"It's okay, but I want you to meet someone. Dan. He taught me how to heal. We'll go next time."

She accepted Dan's business card. Displayed a faint smile, then turned and headed to her car.

* * *

The following day, James, the producer, spoke to Mark during the video call. They organised the travel arrangements—it was two weeks away.

"Jose is a comedian. So, the show's typically light-hearted," James said. "Any preferred topics?"

"What I do best. Healing," Mark replied.

"Perfect. Any guests you'd like to bring?"

"No," Mark replied after a pause.

"Excellent! Well, thanks for accepting our invitation. Our team's excited. You'll receive a confirmation and itinerary of your trip shortly."

"No problem, looking forward to it," Mark replied before the call ended.

* * *

Mark managed to squeeze in the time between appointments to take Megan to Dan's Academy before his trip.

The delicate chimes of soft piano tones drifted through the front lobby as they waited for Dan, momentarily mesmerised by the bobbing blue lights on the walls.

After their introductions, Mark headed to the nearby café. He opened his laptop to work but the chatter nearby distracted him so, instead, sipped at his flat white.

About an hour later he waved to Susan, the barista, as he left.

Mark asked Dan his opinion.

"I don't know. I know I wasn't confident about you at first. But this feels different."

"It's only her first day."

"That's true. We've agreed to weekly lessons, so we'll see."

"Thanks," Mark replied.

Back home, Mark grabbed a suitcase in the hallway cupboard, picked out and folded clothes and placed them neatly inside. He rolled the suitcase near the front door, ready for the following day.

It was a thirteen-hour flight. He didn't mind it too much; he'd done similar trips for Varion. He just had to ignore the tightness in his lower back and the urge to get up and walk around—after a few hours his restlessness kicked in. With eyes wide open, his body insisted he stay awake the entire journey.

Landing. Jelly legs. Uber. New car smell. Hotel. Jet lag. Clean sheets. Hard mattress. Soft pillows. Burgers. Limousine. Black leather. Adrenaline.

Jose was as advertised—a mixture of funny and witty. Mark had to adjust his eyes to the lights and cameras— and he found himself squinting and then scanning the audience. Before long, they were on.

"So, you're kind of a big deal now. Probably made some money. What's your retirement plan?" Jose asked.

"Ha-ha, haven't really thought about it. I just want to help people," Mark replied.

"And they can't help themselves—go to a doctor? It's a lot of pressure to put on yourself isn't it?"

"Well, I do what I can," Mark replied.

"Speaking of doctors. Any come to your house with pitchforks?" Jose said, laughing.

Mark laughed. "No pitchforks—yet. Should I be worried?"

"Well, maybe," Jose replied. "You're braver than I am. I hear you work from home?"

"Yeah, it's easier for me," Mark replied.

"I would've kept it secret. No one would bother me then."

"Fair enough," Mark replied. "But it really doesn't bother me."

"Like I said, braver than I am. And possibly better man too. I'd be looking at retiring, disconnecting my phone, deleting my socials and disappearing—maybe the Himalayas," Jose added with a wink.

Mark couldn't help but laugh. "Why's that?"

"Mostly peace and quiet."

Laughter rippled through the audience.

"It's been great having you on the show," Jose eventually said.

"No, thanks for having me," Mark responded.

* * *

The flight back was similar. His muscular pains and restlessness were relentless. In the next aisle, and behind him, passengers slept. Mark wasn't as lucky. His mind focused on the drone of the plane while his eyes focused on staying wide open.

Eyes heavy, a lethargic and jetlagged Mark made his way through the airport. As he waited for his rideshare, the heat bore down on him, seeping through his long-sleeve shirt and jeans. It didn't take long for his ride to arrive—a black SUV.

He must have dozed off. The sun still shone bright and it took some moments to make out his whereabouts. The driver had taken the long way. Oh well. About ten minutes away. Good. He needed a shower. And to sleep in his own bed. The cabin was quiet except for the low hum of the air-con. And the driver hadn't tried sparking up a conversation. Even better.

They should've turned right back there. Probably adds another three minutes. *Ugh*. Oh well. Mark sighed and checked his phone after a soft vibration in his pocket—a text from Megan. He'd get back to her later.

Again, they should have turned but the driver un-flinchingly drove on.

"You missed the turn," Mark said. Mark stared into the driver's eyes for the first time in the rear-view mirror. The driver stayed quiet. Cold eyes. Blue. Pale skin. "Which way are you going?"

No response. Mark rolled his eyes.

"Hey," Mark started. He caught the driver's gaze again. He noticed the suit. Navy blue with a white shirt underneath, peeking out at his wrists. Eyes locked in the mirror, Mark narrowed his own disapprovingly and shook his head.

The car slowed and then stopped. They were outside an industrial estate. Tyres crunched across the gravel as a black utility van approached and parked next to them.

"Get out." The driver's voice was chilling.

Before Mark could process the demand, the door was wrenched open, exposing bright, natural light. He briefly saw three men before his vision was overtaken by black as a bag was thrown over his head.

The gravel was uncomfortably unsteady beneath his shoes as he fought being dragged toward the van. His head and elbows slammed onto a hard floor, causing him to wince and grunt loudly. The sliding door closed with a loud bang followed by the two front doors. Soon the engine sounded and the van started moving.

As he rolled around with the vehicle's twists and turns, he yelled and shouted until his voice went hoarse. He continued until he was hit on the head with something solid and everything went black.

XVIII

Mark tasted blood in his mouth. Two distorted figures stood in front of him. His head throbbed but his vision gradually cleared. With no bag restricting his sight, he could make out the lightbulb over his head which emitted a warm light. There were no windows, only a black door at the opposite end of the room. The floor was hard beneath his rubber soles.

"I thought we made ourselves clear," the man in front of him, to his left said. The one to Mark's right walked up to Mark and punched him on the side of the face, blood spraying from his mouth. He was tied in a chair and felt his head droop to the side. The throbbing worsened. The ropes tying him to the chair rubbed his ankles and wrists raw, leaving his skin red and sore. Sweat trickled down his arm and his mouth was bloody, yet simultaneously dry.

"You ignored our letters, and then you ignored us," the same voice added.

Mark recognised small circles on the top of their right-breast pockets. They didn't raise their voices but they were pissed—their eyes pierced through Mark. Eyes that stared with darkness and lack of emotion.

"If you don't listen again..." The edges of his lips curled up.

Mark wasn't given the chance to respond. The world turned black just as something long and grey headed straight for him.

* * *

Mark woke up to find that his head was in excruciating pain. He recognised his house in front of him. His eyes had to adjust to the darkness around him.

He'd been left there.

The dampness of the grass seeped through his clothes but he wasn't bothered by it. His eyes felt puffy and his entire body ached. As his elbow dug into the ground, sharp pains surged up his arm. Straightening his back to get off the ground punished his ribs—a reminder of where he had crashed when forced into the van. He pushed into his temples but the pain worsened.

It took some time to get up. Finally, the pounding of his head subsided. He dragged his body off the ground and toward the house. His luggage had been dumped by the front door.

Opening the door caused conflicted emotions. The middle of his chest swelled and felt hot and for a split second he felt the urge to smile—but he wasn't in a positive mood.

He noticed the white envelope on the dining room table almost straight away, his name scrawled in the centre in no handwriting that he recognised.

He tore it open.

Find where the Sun meets the Ocean on Joan Jacobi Lane at 8PM. Tonight. Do what you do best.

He showered and cleaned himself up to distract himself from the note but his curiosity peaked as 8PM drew closer.

At 7:30PM, he grabbed his jacket, jumped in his car and drove toward Joan Jacobi Lane.

He got there right at 8PM. A short street—he could easily see both ends. Mark jumped out of the car half expecting an ambush but none came. It was quiet, except for some distant sirens, the odd car over on the next street and the coughing of a homeless man nearby. The cool breeze made him appreciate his jacket.

It didn't take long to lap the street twice and investigate a few lightless alleyways along the way.

He scowled at the thought of going there for no reason before being drawn to the coughing. He turned toward the homeless person. He was hunched over and vomiting. Some of it sprayed on his green t-shirt.

"Are you okay?" Mark asked.

Great.

He shuddered at the thought of healing after what he'd gone through.

Slowly, he made his way to the man on the ground. He was clutching his chest now. He was a young man. His face was pale and his eyes were puffy.

Mark stopped.

The green t-shirt and the green door behind him. *"When the Sun meets the Ocean"*. Where yellow meets blue.

He made his way past the homeless man and knocked on the door. No answer. The knocks became bangs. He shouted. Nothing. *Serves me right for being so gullible.*

Fuming, he turned away from the door thinking about the note; *'do what you do best'.*

Without thinking, he grabbed the young man by the forearm.

It didn't take long for their surroundings to blur and morph.

They were at an animated racing track. Mark sat in a racing car. The vehicle beneath him rumbled, the aggressive exhaust demanding attention. There were no coverings over the windows. Strong fumes and the acrid smell of burning rubber poured into the car. The bright sun that shone through the car's openings stung his eyes and made the interior feel like an oven. He yelled over to the young man, who was in the car next to him.

"Pick up power-ups on the track to help you win!"

The response was a smile and a thumbs up.

Ahead, red lights flashed, followed by a final green light.

The race was on.

After one lap the young man led the field by some distance. Mark glanced at a screen on his dashboard. He was fifth out of twelve racers. One hundred and twenty metres separated him from first place. Two laps left.

He picked up a grenade by driving over a purple flashing box. He pressed a red button titled 'launch' on the edge of the steering wheel. The grenade flew toward one of the vehicles in front of him. It found its target and the car began spinning out of control and off the track, mulching up grass as Mark drove past.

Fourth.

He drove over another mystery box. A picture of a shooting star appeared on his screen and a hologram hovered above the dashboard. He had no idea what it did, but he didn't care.

His adrenaline pumped as a car zoomed past him, leaving a trail of blazing, multi-coloured lights. He launched the shooting star.

The shooting star glowed bright red, then striking white then finally, a blinding blue before it flung out in front of him and hit every other car in front of him. He quickly reclaimed his fourth position but then gritted his teeth.

In the distance, his shooting star crashed into the young man's car causing it to spin wildly out of control, leaving black tyre Marks on the track. Mark could hear the screeches, even over all the noise of the track. Two cars sped past the young man as he turned his vehicle back in the right direction. Only half a lap to go.

First and second place blazed off in the distance but Mark could still see them. Just.

As the finish line drew closer, the young man remained in third and Mark, fourth. Mark saw the finish line as he drove over the last mystery box. Seconds later, huge boots with wings appeared—a mega turbo boost.

He shook his head in frustration.

Out of desperation, he drove up as close as he could to the young man and started shouting. There was too much wind noise and the roar of the engines didn't help.

With one last attempt and with all his might, he snatched at the mega boost hologram and hurled it from his window. It soared through the air and hit the young man's car.

Seconds later, the young man's car grew wings and launched itself into the air with a loud whoosh. It flew over the other two racers and the finish line, securing a narrow victory.

The track and the sun's rays faded away.

"Wow—wasn't expecting that. Follow me," the young man said.

Mark glanced back onto the street before following him through the green door.

XIX

It was a dark hallway—Mark couldn't see the other end. They passed some worn-down doors with peeling paint and took the last door on the left. As they got closer, Mark could make out the colour of the peeling paint—a washed out green.

The contrast in the new hallway was surprising. Everything was white: the doors, the walls, even the tiled floors. And there were lights now, strips of bright fluorescent lights lining the ceilings. It was free from dirt, dust and markings—and peeling paint was a thing only of the past hallway.

They stopped at a white door halfway down. Mark had to tilt his head to see the top.

"His name's Jamie."

"Who?" Mark replied.

"I was just told to bring you here. It's Castro by the way—in case you were wondering."

Mark nodded but his head turned back toward the door when he noticed the handle move.

"I'm sure we'll see each other again."

As Castro finished speaking, the door opened. Mark turned to say something but Castro had disappeared.

"Mark. Finally. Quick, come in."

Mark expected someone different. Someone older.

A teenager peered out onto the hallway, scanning the area.

"Come in," he reiterated.

White aesthetics dominated the interior here too, the décor built on a skeleton of white walls and polished tiles. A white leather sofa sat slightly atop a fluffy rug of the same shade. There was no TV in the lounge but instead, there was a holographic wall similar to Dan's academy opposite the lounge. A jungle filled the display. The camera glided through the trees—the lens picking up even the raindrops resting on leaves. The white theme continued throughout the apartment—white pillows and beanbags, a marble coffee table and a white bookshelf that nearly reached the ceiling toward the dining room.

"It's Jamie."

Mark nodded and followed the stretched hand pointed at the sofa.

"You've been in contact with *The Establishment*."

"*The Establishment*? Mark asked, sinking into the sofa.

"The Professor wanted me to show you something," Jamie continued.

"Who's that?"

"It's irrelevant."

"They couldn't show me themselves?"

Jamie shook his head. "There's a reason Apollo went off-grid. For safety."

"What do you mean?"

"Humans lived at higher states of consciousness—we all had these psychic abilities once. Everyone did."

"What other—?" The words died on Mark's tongue.

"Abilities are there?" Jamie finished his sentence. Mark nodded. "Energy manipulation through psychokinesis, divination, mind control, astral projection, manifestation, telepathy, time manipulation—can't list them all. Some are more influential than others. Apollo can dive into your mind—so psychotherapy."

"Fair enough," Mark replied.

Jamie continued. "Something happened, years ago. *The Great Fall*, maybe you've heard of it?"

Mark shook his head.

"Our abilities disappeared. Not sure exactly how but I'm sure *they* did something—*The Establishment*. Some sort of DNA manipulation."

Mark nodded. "How do you explain us?"

"Good question," Jamie replied. "Not sure. Maybe a glitch. Error maybe. But some kept their abilities. Important historical people."

"Like who?" Mark asked.

"I don't know everyone right now. But... some were evil, working for *The Establishment*. Others, not so bad. Most just stuck to themselves. Better than being brainwashed."

"Brainwashed?"

Well, it depends. You're not dangerous. Probably not much use to them. Keep to yourself, don't make a scene, don't communicate with their targets, and you'll be left alone."

"They have targets?" Mark asked, incredulous.

Jamie nodded.

"I want to know more about these historical figures," Mark said.

"They're all well-known. Some were killed. Some worked for *The Establishment*. Others fought... and lived. There was one guy. Odysseus. He had twelve abilities."

"How do you know all this?"

"I grew up in their orphanage. *They* raised me with all the other kids that had powers. Until I was ten when The Professor broke me out—"

"Out? Like a prison?"

"If a prison included brainwashing, then yes. I can project into the past. I was seven when I realised that time doesn't exist—so then I would escape the orphanage by projecting. When *they* found out I was using my power *they* told me something was wrong with me. After The Professor got me out, I saw how *The Establishment* killed my parents. They shot my parents then took me with them."

"Sorry," Mark said.

"He saved me—The Professor. He set me up here—got me enrolled at school. When I finish school and save a bit I want to move as far away as possible—get a fresh start somewhere."

Mark nodded. "So you're a time traveller?"

"Sort of, but not really. I can only go into the past. And I can only observe, I can't interact with anything. I saw the file *they* had for me. They called me *The Historian*."

"So time travel is real?"

"Time doesn't really exist. For me, the past, present and future all merge into one. I can synchronise with the past through observation. But the last person who could physically travel through time—they killed her. Alyssa."

Mark swore under his breath.

"If only you knew—ready to go on a trip?"

"Sure," Mark replied.

The room started spinning, the white walls merging into an ivory blur. Soon, the spinning stopped, and the blur was replaced by a dark-grey fog that chilled him to the bone. Mark crossed his arms in his jacket. Over some seconds the fog cleared but Mark still shivered. He turned. Jamie was barely an arm's length away.

They weren't alone. They had intruded on a meeting. Several chairs surrounded a large glass table, covered in tools, gadgets, and various devices. Screens had been built into the walls—they showed diagrams of humans with their limbs spread out. All chairs surrounding the table were sat in and at the head, a hooded figure stood and spoke. He wasn't human and neither were the others. All of them were at least a foot taller than Mark.

"We've gone back five thousand years. We can't stay long—it's a secure meeting. Some I can't even get into," Jamie whispered.

The hooded figure at the front spoke first, his deep voice rumbling. "They'll work for us," he said. "Entertainment, time, money and sexuality—do we agree on the four primary modes of control?"

The figures sitting nodded.

"For secondary—we've got social, medicine, legal, marriage, war, mind-control, schooling, language and food. Do we agree?"

More nods were directed at screens displaying a mixture of words, diagrams and symbols.

"It's crucial they believe they have autonomy. But we will deprive them of their abilities. They'll have no choice but to rely on our vices and protocols to survive."

"We'll use advanced technology—always remaining thousands of years ahead of them—and we can fine-tune if needed," another in the room said.

"And those that oppose?" Mark turned toward the voice—someone in the middle of the room.

"They won't conceptualise another way. For those that do, it's simple. Killed. We will have a strict, zero-contamination policy. Efficiency and smooth transactions are crucial for our survival."

More nods.

"Using synthetic DNA technology, non-coding DNA will make the farm easier to control and harvest. Any questions relating to that can be directed to Akku."

"We need to leave," Jamie whispered.

Mark turned toward him, confused.

The figure at the front put up one arm to hush the others and turned his face, eyes darting across the walls. "I sense—energy."

Mark stared at the figure. His eyes found Mark's. Mark held his breath and froze when the figure looked directly at him with cold, deep-set, blue eyes. Mark shuddered. The figure had pale skin. Mark made out muscles despite his long clothing—vascularity like a map protruded from his skin at the forearms. He made his way toward the back of the room, toward Mark and Jamie.

Nausea set in as the room spun, the meeting place, screen and figures converging into one blur.

The fog cleared and they were back in Jamie's apartment. Jamie's eyes, wide with fear darted around frantically as he chewed on his bottom lip.

"We need to leave."

"Why? Wasn't that five thousand years ago?"

"They can track us. Can't explain right now."

"We'll need to split up—they're after me."

"What was that?" Mark said.

"A meeting to organise the trade deal with the Archons."

"*Archons?*"

"Highest-level malevolent extra-terrestrials. They feed off fear, suffering and sacrifices."

"And those hooded figures?"

"I don't have time to explain—you need to leave."

Mark paced toward the door. He glanced back but Jamie had vanished. He made his way out of the building and to his car. There wasn't a soul to be seen, the only movement a handful of leaves blowing across the bitumen.

He made it home. As he sat in his garage he struggled to breathe. He felt like he was being watched and felt invisible hands wrap themselves around his neck.

He hopped out of the car and heard a footstep behind him as he pressed a button to lower the garage. He spun around—

* * *

The wooden chair burned his glutes, the pressure radiating up to his lower back. His head drooped forward but once his eyes regained focus he tilted it upward and instantly recognised the brick walls of the small room from earlier. The lightbulb above his head provided minimal light, barely illuminating a metal bucket on the floor at his side. His shoulders ached from the strain of his wrists being tied behind his back for so long. He leaned forward in an attempt to alleviate the pain, allowing gravity to pull his head back down—only for the back of his neck to scream in protest at the stretch.

He could just make out the echoes of a voice. The muffle in his ears faded and the voice became clear.

"You're a nuisance."

Mark tilted his head toward the voice, but the leaden weight of his head stopped him from holding the man's gaze for more than a few seconds. It flopped back down and sweat trickled down his forehead and into his eyes, causing them to sting.

"I thought you were harmless..." the man continued. It was the same man from earlier. A rigid body beneath a square face. His short black hair had been fashioned into a buzz cut and sunglasses hid his emotionless eyes. "...annoying, yes—but harmless, like a housefly. You know it's there, and you want to get rid of it, but you'll accept living with it because it flies away. But you? You're worse. If you were a fly, you'd continue to buzz, louder and louder. Each second bearing down on me—the vibrations pounding and hammering at my senses. Until I can't take it anymore and, well, you know how the rest goes."

"We should've gotten rid of him," said another voice. Mark didn't recognise this one. He had sunglasses on too. He was bald. A slim figure wearing a black, tight-fitting suit.

"No, you know the rules," said the first man.

The door burst open and in entered a third figure. He too wore glasses but tore them off as he entered. His footsteps were heavy, vibrating through the floor as the man charged toward him. He shoved the other two out of the way.

"Where is he?" he demanded, hitting Mark across the face.

Mark couldn't muster the strength to speak. He shook his head weakly, now feeling blood dribbling from the side of his mouth.

"We've tried being reasonable with you!" Another strike. The force nearly made him and the chair topple to the side.

* * *

Opening his eyes, it felt as though the room was spinning. It was difficult to stay awake. Head feeling like lead, he glanced down only to find that his blood covered the floor.

"Where are the others? We know you've been *communicating*." The interrogator had brought his face right next to Mark's. Each word was calm but there was no mistaking the fury in the tilt of his eyebrows and the way his eyes twitched. The same fist used to assault Mark was still curled up in a tight ball—the veins in his forearms looking like they would rupture the skin at any second.

Mark shook his head—the motion immediately made him vomit. It sprayed all over the concrete below. The interrogator kicked the bucket in front of Mark, making a loud scraping noise but it was too late. He turned to face the other two.

"He's useless," one of them muttered.

"You're lucky. If it were up to me, you'd be dead," the interrogator said, not even bothering to turn around. Mark recognised him now—it was one of the men who'd visited, the leader.

Mark felt heat in his chest.

The room turned pitch black. Mark heard grunts and saw blurs of people around him, but his eyes were droopy and his hearing faded in and out. It was only when a new figure stepped in front of him did he truly see what was unfolding. Castro was there and was now untying the ropes.

"Get up!" Castro shouted.

Trembling, and with all the strength he could manage, he drove his heels into the ground, instantly relieved when his legs separated him from the wooden chair. Castro punched the leader, who joined the other two on the floor who had been knocked out cold.

Castro grabbed Mark and hoisted him as they made their way to the door.

Once outside the room, Mark noticed a foyer leading to a door. The thirty or so metres seemed far.

"That's the exit," Castro said, reading Mark's mind.

Mark limped, his legs threatening to give way as they made their way toward the door. The throbbing in Mark's head worsened.

Outside, the vomit and blood-soaked jacket was useless against the icy, late-night breeze. He recognised the industrial estate. There was an old sedan pulled up over the same gravel he'd been dragged through. Castro led Mark to the car, tossed him a jacket and towel from the boot and soon gravel crunched under the tyres as they drove away.

XX

Mark slid down the window and allowed the wind to soothe his swollen face. His eyes drifted shut and he focused on the soft polyester beneath him in an effort to distract himself from the images of the past twenty-four hours that tortured his conscious mind.

No such luck.

"How'd you find me?" he asked.

Mark attempted to turn his head toward Castro, but the kink in his neck sent sharp pains surging up to his head and he froze. He slowly raised his hand to his face, gingerly touching where he'd been hit and winced. Eyes still blurry, he turned toward the window, trying to hide his injuries.

"You know that feeling you get, when something doesn't feel right—and so you have to do something?"

Mark nodded and momentarily focused on his chest, ears and forehead. They felt normal. For the first time in hours, he wasn't creeped out by recurring panic in his chest.

"Something told me you weren't okay and The Professor confirmed it. I hope it's okay I take you there, to him?"

"It's fine," Mark replied.

"I'm like you. Well, I can't heal, but I have psychic abilities. It's like having a sense of what's happening. I experience things before they happen—it's hard to explain."

With some effort, Mark twisted his body away from the window.

"They really punished you back there." Castro turned and looked at Mark's beaten face.

"Thank you," Mark said, after some moments.

"Don't mention it."

Buildings blurred past them in the window. It didn't take long to leave the industrial area behind as they headed onto the main road toward the city.

Castro couldn't have been much older than twenty. He reminded Mark of an athlete—lean and muscular.

Castro caught Mark's stare.

"I used to be a spy for them. For years they sent me out killing people—all innocent. They told me it was for the greater good—that was bullshit. I'm glad I grew up and saw through the lies and manipulation."

"Shit," Mark muttered.

"They killed my parents and abducted me as a baby. Said I was a prodigy. Jamie eventually showed me the truth but I didn't believe him. Talk about cognitive dissonance." He laughed awkwardly. "They said my parents died because they were sick and then put me in their orphanage, feeding me their shit my whole life—and as a kid, you don't know any different. You just accept things."

Castro lapsed into silence, but occasionally shook his head and his face would contort into a scowl.

Mark stared out of the window, the half-moon stealing his attention.

The car stopped. They were in Brisbane's inner city, and on a familiar street—Joan Jacobi Lane.

The cool air seeped through the thin jacket as Mark opened his door.

Mark followed Castro toward the green door. Once inside, they took a different door which led to a hallway covered completely in red—the walls, the carpet, the ceiling and even the lighting were in shades of red. Three quarters down and Castro pushed at a red door with 97 on it. This hallway was coloured completely yellow. The door at the end led to a room with rows of seats and an altar at the front. Soft yellow light filled the room. Castro led them to the back where a corridor led to another door, then into a tiny room with only two small, wooden chairs. The room was barely large enough for another person. There were no windows and no other doors.

"Not the fanciest but this is one of our junctions," Castro began. "For now, it's as far as *they* can come. Only we can get through— and, touch wood, we haven't been infiltrated. Yet."

Castro pointed to one of the wooden chairs. Mark sat down. The tenderness in his back as he sat down reminded him of the chair he'd been tortured in—the wood was rigid and dug into him.

"Your signature is your ability. You have to do this weird initiation—I'll see you on the other side. Don't worry, we all had to figure it out by ourselves."

Castro took a seat in the other chair and closed his eyes. Seconds later his head swung back as though he'd fallen asleep.

"Castro?"

No reply.

He went and pushed Castro's shoulder but when there was no response, Mark shook him. Again nothing. Mark sat back in his chair.

The room felt like it was shrinking.

Rachel stood in front of him.

Close your eyes, she whispered.

"You're not real, are you?" She had a ghostlike appearance—a wispy apparition. *Could this test be about Rachel?* He shook his head. *I'm hallucinating again—maybe a lack of oxygen from being in this room.*

He closed his eyes. An open space of all white surrounded him. He didn't have shoes on and his feet were submerged in water. He splashed as he made his way through the canvas. He heard Rachel scream and gargle like she was drowning. He tried following the screams but he wasn't moving.

"Rach?"

He opened his eyes. She was there again, in front of him. *What's going on?*

He took a deep breath, closed his eyes and cleared his mind.

He was surrounded by white. Five numbered, glass doors stood in front of him—the numbers were written in white vinyl at the centre of the doors. Looking through, he saw a person on the other side of each door—they were on white, rolling, hospital beds. From where he stood, Mark could smell cleaning products.

A sixth door appeared near door 5—it was made of solid, brown wood. *Through The Junction* was written on it, in dark bold letters. As he made his way toward it, a seventh door faded in, next to the others. *EXIT* was written in the middle. It was made of solid, black wood.

Mark stroked his chin and scratched at his head. His eyes were locked on *Through The Junction*. He made his way to the door and gripped the handle. At the last second, he changed his mind and went to the *EXIT* door and pushed down on the handle.

His eyes were forced open. He was back in the small room.

He cleared his thoughts and closed his eyes again. There were ten transparent doors now among the two wooden doors.

He went and stood in front of the *Through The Junction* door. He felt the handle's cold metal as he pushed down and made his way through.

His eyes were forced open. Next to him, Castro still slept in the darkened room.

Again, he cleared his thoughts and closed his eyes.

The two wooden doors were now closest to him. Mark couldn't count the number of transparent doors now—there were too many, and they filled the entire plain. He glanced at a transparent door near him—*1108*—but it was anyone's guess how many there were.

He opened it.

A middle-aged man lay in the bed—he was shivering and had the sheets pulled up to his neck. Mark placed his palm on his forehead. He felt heat seep into his arm just as he began healing him.

Once the man was healed, he thanked Mark. Mark left the room and the door vanished. He went to a nearby door—*57*. An elderly lady sat on the bed. Her knees bent in and her head was curled over her knees. She rocked slightly. Mark healed her within seconds.

In the next room—door numbered *708*—Mark found a child. He was curled in the foetal position clutching his stomach and moaning. Mark healed him too.

He continued like this for hours—for days, even. He'd lost track of time—there were too many doors—but he didn't stop.

* * *

The blinding white everywhere stung his eyes. Only one transparent door left now. Mark dragged his feet toward it—his shoulder ached as he lifted his arm and pushed the door open. Mark's eyes widened when he saw the body lying on the bed. The man was lean with a white, long-sleeved shirt and black suit pants. Stubble covered the lower part of his face and thick black hair covered his head. His feet hung over the edge of the bed—eyes closed but even chest movements matched his deep breathing. There was no mistaking who it was.

It was Mark.

Mark grabbed at a wrist that was down by his clone's side.

The room disappeared. Mark was surrounded by white except for a door of a blue shade nearby. It was scratched and faded with a mixture of white and black streaks throughout.

He walked through it.

On the other side, it was a still evening—the air was humid. Castro sat on a metal bench nearby with a grin on his face. They were at a bus stop, but Mark doubted Castro waited for a bus.

There were no limitations to the lucid dream—Mark looked up to see a blue-grey, ringed planet and a bright, blue moon that hung low in the night sky.

"Not bad," said Castro, standing up. "The Professor holds the record I think. Only a few minutes apparently."

"What? That took forever," Mark replied, turning away from the sky.

"To some, maybe five minutes is a long time but don't be too hard on yourself," Castro said as he looked down at his watch.

Mark took some seconds to process the confusion brewing in his mind. His thoughts were interrupted by Castro who led him down a dark, winding, bitumen path toward a stand-alone building some distance away.

"Welcome to *The Sanctuary*, headquarters of *The League*—a group of people who oppose *The Establishment*. The Professor, he's here."

Mark followed Castro, his legs aching slightly from the elevated walk. The grass was kept short on either side of the path—the odd tree here and there lacking in any sort of movement. A still lake nearby reflected the celestial bodies above.

Well-trimmed hedges surrounded the building. Huge totem poles stood out the front among some palm trees and Mark saw the building for what it was. A mixture of thick concrete and light-brown wood covered the exterior. A bright orange light shone on the writing high up on the building: *Sanctuary Cove*. Mark craned his neck, searching for a cross, but none was there.

"How long have you known about this place?" Mark asked.

"A few years. The Professor found me. Well, I found him. I was sent to kill him, but—he saw me coming like he sees everything. He got me away and taught me to resonate with this place."

"There are others here?"

"Yeah, not sure exactly how many though—I've seen Jamie and Apollo here."

"Apollo's here?"

"Sometimes—but I haven't seen him in a while," Castro replied.

"What is this place?"

"It's not a physical place and there are other junctions you can tune in from. It's basically people transmitting the same frequency who meet at the same point, somewhere in the aether. When you resonate here, you send a communication request to be allowed on the same frequency, like a radio."

Although a little confused, Mark nodded. He was too exhausted and in pain to question things.

They walked across grey cement toward a large front door. Castro placed his palm into a hand-shaped indentation in the wood. The door swung open.

The concrete theme flowed through to the interior. The walls were a mixture of white wood and light-grey concrete. Polished concrete floors reflected low-hanging lights from the high ceiling. A wooden staircase ahead led to three higher levels. Beyond the stairs were transparent meeting rooms, pods and clustered tables and chairs.

Castro led Mark to a lift near the entrance.

They went down two floors—his eyes were met with a dark, metallic corridor with blue neon lights lining the walls. As they made their way through, Mark fought the urge to question Castro. *Who's this Professor? Seems like a big deal.*

They stood in front of a door. Neon lights outlined its frame.

"This is as far as I come," Castro said. "Was good to see you again." Castro turned to leave.

"Why do they call him The Professor?"

Castro half turned, chuckled and continued toward the lift.

"Good question. When I started teaching, it was always *The Mystic*. Then it got changed by some students, and it stuck."

Mark's eyes widened and at the same time were drawn to a dark, slim-fitting business suit on the man that stood in front of him. Mark's eyes eventually found their way to the man's eyes—behind aviator reading glasses. His short beard hadn't changed. And his hair had the same balanced, contoured wave to one side. There was no denying it. *But how? How could Henry be The Professor?*

"Just call me Henry." He'd read Mark's mind. "We won't be long."

Mark was led into the office. Opposite, the window took over the entire wall. For a moment Mark admired the blueish lunar glow through the glass. Mark walked across grey tiles and onto a swivel chair across from Henry's desk. Henry sat across from him.

Henry narrowed his eyes. "I'm disappointed."

Mark frowned, confusion brewing in his mind.

"One of my abilities is that I'm a seer. I gave you a chance because I thought there was a cure for your ignorance, recklessness—and arrogance—but I was wrong. You're not so great."

Mark responded by frowning, which turned to frustration. Henry's words stunned him.

"You don't live by our virtues."

Mark rubbed his chin and stared toward the moon outside for a moment. He turned back, holding Henry's gaze. "What do you mean?"

"I saw this moment coming. I wanted you to prove me wrong, but I saw it all. How you treated Rachel, your ability. Not being able to heal yourself—"

Mark scowled. "I don't get it."

"What don't you get? Your selfish desire to mask your remorse by using healing as a distraction, your self-loathing. Your lack of direction—"

Words failed Mark so he resorted to shaking his head, his face scrunched into an angry scowl.

"I haven't seen anything worthy—you're not the person I was hoping to work with."

Mark's temperature rose, his clothes uncomfortably tight. His fists turned into balls of rage. He glared at Henry—but there was a niggling guilt nestling at the back of his neck, causing it to strain.

"You've changed," Mark blurted out. His muscles were shaking. He took deep breaths, trying to calm himself down.

Henry shook his head. "And you haven't."

"You changed my whole life. What was I supposed to do?"

He's expecting a lot. Locked me in a cage and assumed I'd escape. How is he disappointed that I didn't?

Mark forced himself to tamper down the urge to punch Henry.

"You don't deserve what you have," Henry continued. "Do you realise how lucky you are?"

Mark shook his head, his nostrils flaring. *I need to calm down.*

"Seeing into the future isn't so straightforward. The future is fluid, and everything can change in an instant."

Henry slumped back in his chair and took off his glasses.

"When I first saw you. Years ago, at Varion, I didn't believe it. The universe chose you? Someone so self-obsessed, careless and inconsiderate, to be a healer?"

"Are you saying there's something wrong with me?"

"Healers show empathy. I tried proving myself wrong. Told myself the right person had been picked—told myself to give you a chance."

"What do you hate so much about me?"

Henry sighed. "I let myself down. Even Rachel suffered because of your carelessness. You're self-absorbed."

"I'm done here," Mark snapped.

"But you know I'm right. I've been waiting for years for a healer who could change the world. But you—you're not that person."

"And you expected me to know what you wanted from me?"

"I shouldn't have to tell you what to do."

"Some guidance would've helped." Mark furiously stared at Henry but Henry was now looking out the window, muttering to himself.

"Eighteen. That's how many powerful healers have ever lived. It's a shame."

"Are you enjoying this? This another stupid test?"

For the first time, Henry lost his composure. His face twitched and his jaw flexed as he turned his head sharply toward Mark. "This isn't a test." Henry's voice was calm but his nose flared. "Speaking of tests, you failed."

"I failed what?"

"The initiation. You only healed those people because you had to—"

"I could've left at any time."

"Sure. Always with an excuse. You're entitled, ignorant and oblivious to what's going on."

Mark pushed Henry's desk to move his chair back but the force rattled the pen holder, tipping it over and scattering the pens across the desk with a clatter.

"How much do you charge people to heal them?" Henry asked as Mark stood.

Mark felt flustered. *I've got bills to pay, what the fuck am I supposed to do?*

"What do you want from me?"

"You've put us on their radar. And because we've crossed paths, you've recently been a target."

"But you contacted *me*."

"Yes. To save your life." Henry sighed. "We've got a deal. Cut the shit and they'll leave you alone. Your ability isn't something to show off for fame, or to get rich. It's to restore balance."

"And why didn't anyone tell me this?"

"We don't usually need to be told. But listen to me carefully—be careful what you do in public. They've worked hard to build our way of life. Killing you to preserve that won't be an issue for them."

Mark's eyes dropped to the floor.

"That's all I wanted to tell you. I won't doubt my ability in future. But take my warning—or not. I can see that your weakness, selfishness and lack of ability to heal yourself will lead to your downfall."

Mark flinched.

"Castro will take you back."

Henry pointed to the door but Mark was already on his way.

Henry's voice came from behind as Mark made for the exit. "You're not a shit person, Mark. It's just—the good that's in you, it doesn't define you. But really it's my fault for pushing you down this path."

XXI

"What happened?"

Mark turned his head toward Castro as he pulled Henry's door shut. His muscles were tight, his jaw clenched. He didn't reply. Instead, he shook his head and crossed his arms.

They made their way out of the building, Castro not saying a word.

The moon and planet above—and the midnight-blue lake that reflected them—didn't have the same glow they had before. But Mark barely noticed. He felt hot and uncomfortable.

They reached the bus stop. Castro glanced over toward Mark. A nervous look on his face. His lips curved up weakly. "I'll see you around."

Mark said nothing. With one last look at the bright spheres above, he made his way through the blue door.

He opened his eyes. The wood beneath him was painful and his thighs felt numb. Next to him, Castro's head was drooped to the side, still in his slumber.

Exhausted, he made his way through the church-like room and down two familiar hallways coded by their colour—yellow and red. After some minutes of physical perseverance, he stood behind the green door. He swung it open, exposing Joan Jacobi Lane.

Exhaustion turned to relief when he discovered his phone still had life—albeit only eight per cent.

As he stood and waited for his Uber, Mark scowled at the thought of Henry's rejection of him. It was a hard pill to swallow. His thoughts frustrated him. There was a dull ache in his jaw now. *And Megan. Maybe I'm wrong about her. Shit.*

* * *

The Uber arrived. A blue sedan.

Time felt strange. He checked his watch. He'd only waited five minutes. *Why does it feel like I've waited hours? What did Jamie mean about time not being real?*

"How's your night been?"

Mark ignored the question and rolled the window down. The cool breeze was instant relief for his hot face. He massaged his jaw and stretched his neck to one side. He swallowed, attempting to control the onset of his nausea.

The driver peered over every so often. Crinkles formed on his forehead when he did. The bloodstains on his shirt and beaten face probably didn't help but Mark didn't care. He closed his eyes. He longed for his bed and hoped his body would withhold resorting to fainting in order to maintain homeostasis.

The car was still rolling on the driveway's concrete as Mark pushed at the door to open it. His legs and ribs ached as he hopped out. He stumbled toward the house and was relieved to find it deserted. Clinging onto the railing, he dragged himself up the stairs toward the bedroom.

His woes followed him into his sleep. In one dream he was in a state of sleep paralysis, bound to his bed. The windows were open, allowing in an icy wind that stung his skin. He turned his neck toward the wall. *She* was there. Mark tried springing up but his body wouldn't move—he was stuck. He screamed, but nothing came out of his mouth. All Mark could hear was feet sliding on the carpet as the demon dragged itself toward him. The bed indented as *she* jumped on and crawled toward him, knees now either side of his stomach. *She* bowed her neck and brought her face inches from his. Mark's eyes darted away. His muscles were clenched, trying to break free. Unable to move, Demonic Rachel bent further and locked her mouth with his. It felt like a vacuum had been placed over his mouth, sucking everything out of him.

She faded away.

His legs felt like cement. His heart was screaming. He splashed and kicked, trying to tread water but he'd been doing it for too long. And his suit was too heavy—it threatened to drag him down. The muscles across his entire body were on fire.

Eventually, his muscles relaxed as he started drowning. At that moment, Mark saw three blurry figures above him who became clearer—Henry, Castro and Jamie. They floated inches above the water. With the little strength he had left, Mark drove his arm through the water to get their attention.

Why are they laughing?

"Can't even save himself," Mark heard Henry say to the others as he plunged deep into the water. The blue-green turned to black as he continued falling.

* * *

He saw her everywhere now—lurking in the corner of the bedroom as he glanced over, standing over him as he woke up, seated at the dining table as he stepped downstairs.

To make matters worse, his emails had gotten out of control again. There were text messages he hadn't replied to. He ignored people who wanted him outside.

It took some days but the clusters of people died down. And it was just as well, he needed to leave the house—at least go to the gym, get groceries or go for a walk.

There was a knocking at the door, and Mark could no longer ignore it. He looked at the security monitor. Looked like a family. Okay. He sighed as he got up from the lounge.

Even before opening the door, Mark could tell why they'd come—their son was unwell. The man and woman—they'd brought him for Mark to heal.

He was young—maybe five or six—and he was pale and lean. Mark saw sleeping bags and pillows near the door. He ushered the family inside.

They sat across from Mark in the living room.

He knew what the doctors had prescribed before anyone said anything—and he'd been fearing this moment. His muscles spasmed as his heart rate increased but despite his nerves, he knew what he would need to do.

It was always going to be a matter of time.

But this time, it would be different. Because it would be raw. He'd suppressed his dark feelings but Mark feared they'd resurface. Especially now that *she* had a genuine reason to be furious and resentful.

The boy's mother started muttering. Describing her son's condition. Mark had zoned out—lost in his thoughts. But one word stuck out, confirming his fears.

"Leukaemia."

Mark caught her gaze. He sat down next to her son.

"Liam—his name's Liam," she said. "I'm Natalie—and this is Jaxon," pointing to her partner.

"Liam, can you close your eyes for me?"

Liam squeezed his eyes shut.

"Just relax. Take a deep breath."

Mark heard a sigh.

"Think of somewhere you love. Where's your favourite place in the world?" he asked.

"The beach!"

Easy.

Mark pulled his eyelids shut. Soon, he heard waves. The sun coated him in a blanket of warmth. He smelled the sea and sunscreen. People were splashing, surfing and swimming nearby. There was a soft breeze that blew leaves on the golden sand that massaged their feet.

Moments later, the sun disappeared. The gentle breeze turned into something more forceful—and sinister. People nearby struggled with their umbrellas. Soon, the twigs and branches of nearby trees swayed and were completely broken off. Mark's tee flapped aggressively, providing little protection against the now freezing temperature.

"Don't worry, it'll get better." He looked at Liam as he spoke but had no idea if it was true.

It didn't take long for the trees around them to uproot, flinging sand into Mark's eyes. They crashed into one another and the nearby cars with sickening crunches.

"What's happening?" Liam's lip trembled.

Lightning flashed across the sky followed by loud rumbles and booms which made Liam jump. Seconds later, Mark's clothes were drenched.

The beach had become deserted—no more people cheering or ice cream trucks.

Mark saw her. She struggled as she dragged her feet through wet sand toward them. Her body was limp. Her dark hair blew furiously behind her.

"I know what you did," she hissed. "You killed me!"

She started lifting each foot with each stride. She was colourless and moved quickly—resembling a dark grey and white blur.

Just as she closed in, Liam screamed. Mark opened his eyes.

Liam sobbed. His parents stared, confused. Mark shook his head.

"I can't help him," he said, some minutes later.

Their silence added to Mark's discomfort.

There were no objections. Mark wiped his face, looking at them as they made their way to the door. Liam turned his neck before making it outside. Mark stared into his eyes and shook his head.

Never again. Not cancer. It's not worth it.

FLASHBACK #9

George, Michael's assistant, hadn't drawn up the weekly schedule correctly. Mark had five meetings today, not four. And with two presentations, how was he able to work on his pitch— selling NetFlow within a new sector—to legal companies? He had to make the pitch the following day.

He gritted his teeth. He removed his jacket and slung it over his chair. His office felt hot and stuffy. His first presentation started in fifteen minutes. He should probably get going.

He opened his laptop and considered his alternatives. There were none. He'd have to stay back today. He clicked his web browser—multiple tabs were open. He closed them, each closed tab providing some relief to the workload he had ahead. He opened up the presentation he would be giving—on how Varion was responding to the influence of cryptocurrencies, NFTs and the VR/social networking mash-up. It looked fine.

He snapped his laptop shut and made his way to one of the meeting rooms. He heard a chime in his pocket— and felt the soft buzz. He pulled his phone out.

I'm shit scared. Can we talk? Even just a few minutes? x

Mark switched his phone to silent and popped it into his back pocket. As he entered the meeting room it vibrated again, but he didn't check the notification.

XXII

Maybe Henry was right.

Anxiety nestled in his chest when he thought about the family—Liam especially. *Is this guilt?* He launched his laptop. Moments later, he unpublished his site. Next, he deactivated his social media accounts.

The ringing of his work phone stopped him as he went to remove the sim card. He stared at the screen, the phone vibrating in his hand.

"Hello?" He couldn't help himself.

"Hi, is this Mark?"

"Yes."

"I'm outside. I wanted to see you for healing."

Mark allowed him in—a middle-aged man named Bryan. The first thing Mark noticed was redness on the back of his neck. Mark led Bryan upstairs.

It didn't take long for the room to fade away and be replaced by a dark grey—a familiar storm. It was the same beach— and they were surrounded by chaos. Thick, dark clouds covered the sky and palm trees nearby had their branches at nearly ninety degrees. Mark and Bryan struggled to stay upright. Strong winds forced them to grip onto nearby, slippery tree trunks. Sharp raindrops sliced through the air and stung Mark's face. But that wasn't the worst of it. The demon returned, dragging her feet through muddied sand. Her lean body inched closer.

Then she sprinted toward them with long strides, her feet thumping into the sand.

Mark opened his eyes just before she reached them.

* * *

As Bryan left, Mark removed the sim card.

At the same time, a buzz came from his other phone. A text from Megan. He hadn't gotten back to her previous message: *I'm pretty sure Dan doesn't think I'm a healer. Lol.*

Mark poked at the newest notification.

I'll drop your books off tomorrow. Will you be home?

Yes, Mark replied.

He set the phone down and peered outside—he swore he sensed something but there was no one there.

Not long after, a thumping at the door disturbed his ears. Mark rolled his eyes and made his way toward it. He knew it was *them* before he'd even opened the door.

Buzzcut stood to the left. Baldhead on the right. And the leader was in the centre—just as they'd first visited.

"I'm sure you remember us." The leader took a step forward.

Mark frowned. "I thought there was a deal?"

"What deal?" Buzzcut snapped. "We want that fucker—Castro."

"I don't know where he is," Mark responded, crossing his arms.

"We know." This time the leader responded. "But you'll need to come with us."

"Why?" A quick glance at the leader's veiny forehead made Mark quickly add, "I don't want any trouble."

"Come with us and there won't be," the leader responded.

Mark recognised the dark cargo van that had pulled into the driveway. One of the men opened the back and before Mark was able to climb in, he was shoved inside. Despite the force, Mark was able to keep his footing and took a seat. Buzzcut followed him in.

There were no windows—the air was warm and musty. The interior had been painted black. The two front doors slammed as the other two entered the van. Mark was blind to the outside world, but it didn't take long for the vehicle to start moving. He heard passing traffic.

"That Castro—he's a piece of shit. If I ever find him..."

Mark closed his eyes, tuning out Buzzcut and focusing on the motion of the van. They'd been driving a few minutes—had to still be in the area. One right turn so far.

"...if you know where they are, and you're not telling us. We'll kill you—"

It had been about ten minutes. The van was moving fast—Mark's torso was angled toward the back. He jerked sideways when the vehicle turned now. He'd almost rolled off the seat during their last turn. It was impossible to know where they were.

From a standstill, the vehicle accelerated. Must've stopped at a red light. As Mark adjusted to the change in speed, a loud bang came from the right side of the van. The van jerked to the left, throwing Mark across it into thick metal, shoulder first. Somehow, he was able to stay upright. The van came to a halt.

"What the fuck!" Buzzcut yelled. He banged at the van, right behind the driver. "Stay here."

Buzzcut glared at Mark before opening the sliding door and disappearing, the lock clicking shut behind him. There were voices outside but Mark couldn't make out the words. He tried at the handle but the door wouldn't open.

He exhaled deeply and returned to his chair, massaging his shoulder. At the same time, his chest and ears vibrated—he could sense someone on the other side of the door. *What's going on?*

The sliding door opened abruptly, filling the darkened interior with light. He'd never seen her before—the woman who stood just outside.

"Quick, come on."

Mark considered that it was better than being kidnapped so heaved himself off the seat and toward the opened door. He slid the door closed behind him.

They were at a large intersection near a service station on the other side of the road. Cars had piled up behind the van—hostile beeping from drivers rang through the air. Just ahead, the three men were caught up in a heated argument with a man in a blue singlet. The woman ran in the opposite direction—toward the service station. Mark followed. The heat, blaring on the bitumen caused Mark to sweat. Warmth penetrated his jeans as they made their way across the busy road.

Mark was led to a dark muscle car parked near the entrance of the fuel station.

Once inside, the car's engine rumbled. It was anyone's guess how they fled discretely with its aggressive exhaust note—the car roared as it made its way in the opposite direction to the van—and chaotic intersection.

Mark wiped his chin and glanced over at the woman. He struggled to find the right words. "Where's Castro?" He closed his eyes and shook his head. "I mean—thanks."

She peered over at him. "No problem." Then turned her head back toward the road. Her long, curly, black hair swayed over her shoulder as she turned. She smiled but kept her bright, light brown eyes on the road.

Mark's chest swelled. Breathing steadily, he sunk back into his chair—the soft leather of the bucket seat was comforting.

Their drive was totally silent. Mark pretended to be distracted by what was outside, allowing his head to trail buildings, trees and people. Sometimes his head would turn in toward the woman but he'd quickly turn it back in the opposite direction when she looked across.

Driving south and eastward, they eventually reached Cleveland.

They arrived at a tall, multi-storey building that stood behind thick concrete walls. Mark hopped out and followed the woman toward the gate. Among the darkened steel and concrete, tinted glass windows covered most of the building's exterior—but Mark made out some balconies high up. It was impossible to see the top from where they stood. Also, the dark tint made it difficult to make out the interior.

"They shouldn't bother you again," she said as they walked toward the entrance. "It's Grace."

"Mark."

"I know."

Mark chuckled.

"We were worried about you—you're welcome here any time. To be with others like us—and for safety."

"Is Apollo here?" Mark blurted.

"There's a lot going on—you have no idea."

"What do you mean?"

"We'll explain soon," Grace added.

They paced toward the towering structure.

"We finally felt safe enough to bring you here. But, just so you know, I wanted to get you away for a long time," she said. "I'll explain more inside."

Grace entered a code at the gate. The thick steel clunked and opened for them. As they entered, Grace peered over her shoulder and eyed the street behind them. Mark noticed a symbol above the gate—an interlocking square and compass with an eye in the centre. As soon as they made their way through, the gate closed.

As they neared the building, Mark noticed the same symbol perched above the door.

Grace tapped at a touchpad on the door. There was no handle. It glowed and displayed symbols before swinging open.

The interior was reminiscent of a hotel lobby—an expensive one—with a mixture of deep red, gold and white throughout. The walls were coated in gold and red, and white marble covered the floor. The nearby benches and sofas were of red leather. Two giant, Hercules-looking statues made of shiny gold had been erected on either side of the entrance. Mark briefly caught sight of two gold plaques at the foot of the statues. *Strange names.*

They walked past an unaccompanied front desk that had golden lights above.

Grace led them through the lobby and past winding stairs. They came to a door with another touchpad, which also gave way when she placed her palm on it. On the other side were three lifts coated in more gold.

"These two will get you most places here," Grace said, pointing to the ones on the left and right.

"And the middle one?"

Grace smiled.

The same symbol he'd noticed at the entrance had been engraved above each lift.

They stepped into the lift on the left. There were various buttons—going up to one hundred—and many buttons below ground level.

The lift whooshed and feeling like freefall, plunged them downward.

It was difficult to know how far down they'd come. For a moment, Mark found it hard to breathe and his ears popped.

The lift door opened. The walls of the corridor were of a hexagon shape—it looked like a spaceship interior and was coated in blue and silver-grey. Two men stood by the lift.

One had long, brown hair. He was older than Mark, with a dark-brown beard and beady eyes behind rectangle glasses.

"Welcome to *The Alliance*," he said. His arms were open. He had a welcoming smile. "First, let's have a look at you. Grace?"

Grace placed her palm on his head and applied some pressure.

"He's fine," she said, seconds later.

"Get Mark settled then meet us in the Grand Meeting Room—actually, no, the Yellow Room," the same man said.

"Sure," Grace replied.

Mark followed Grace back into the lift, where she handed him an access card.

They reached an upper level and before long, Mark's room—at level seventy-two.

The gold, red and whites of the lobby had made their way up to the apartment. Light brown laminate coated the floor. A fluffy red rug sat beneath a black, leather sofa. Mark walked over to the large window, peering out onto the bay and islands in the distance. He poked his head into the main bedroom—a large bed was placed in the middle, on top of thick, off-white carpet.

"We should get going," Mark heard Grace say from the door, as he pulled back the living room blinds to expose more of the ocean.

"Yeah. Sure."

They used the lift again, up to level eighty-eight. They made their way into a room with high ceilings where art depicted witches, nature and sorcery like a pagan art exhibition. Faint yellow light made it difficult to see clearly but there was a group of people already there—and they wore brown tunics and cowls, like monks. Mark looked up and found the source of the flickering lights— firelit torches that lined up horizontally on the walls.

The head of the group was one of the men he'd met just before—the one who introduced Mark to *The Alliance*. Arms crossed, he splayed his right arm as Grace and Mark approached.

"My name's Kevin," he said as they neared.

They all sat in a circle and shuffled to make room for the pair.

"This is Link," he said, arm pointed to a man Mark also recognised from earlier. "Link can see and interact with things we average people can't perceive."

Link bowed his head. Kevin went around the circle.

Cera was athletic and well built—a warrior in battle, according to Kevin.

Linus, a quiet and frail-looking man, was capable of psychic projection.

Larissa was a master of telepathy.

Hector could synchronise with other realities and dimensions.

Maia was adept at telekinesis.

Damon, like most in the group, could engage with the paranormal.

"And, I can gain insight into a situation using occult means—divination—which is why you're here," Kevin added. "*The Establishment* is trying to control you. Under the false pretence of *The League*, they pretended to save you—to groom you."

"They won't let me go back," Mark responded.

This time Grace spoke. "They're planning to come back for you—first, they'll discard you. It's a form of manipulation."

"Those guys who tortured me—they're with *The League*? Henry, Apollo, Castro, Jamie?" Kevin's eyes lit up, his eyes jerking up to meet Mark's for a split second.

"Yes," Kevin asserted.

"I don't know why though. I'm just a healer."

"I know why," Kevin replied. "You're capable of doing more than you know—and it's a threat to them."

"What do you mean?"

"Do you know that ninety-nine per cent of the average human's DNA is junk DNA, or non-coding DNA—serving no purpose?

Mark shook his head.

Kevin continued. "In the beginning, when *they* manipulated our DNA, that was the plan—and so the genes determining our abilities were turned into junk DNA."

"Wait, what? Who?" Mark looked at the others but they just stared back.

Kevin continued. "—it just sits there, doing nothing. And so, you have to ask yourself, why? Why something so significant with no use?"

Mark shook his head, glancing over at Grace.

"—the answer is, it was modified. Nothing's created to have no purpose. We were manipulated to keep us weak."

Mark replied. "So what's your point?"

"It leads to my hypothesis—your ability. You can rejuvenate junk DNA and I want to test it."

"Me? Are you serious?"

"Imagine the lives you could change—making everyone live in their power again. What do you say?"

Mark frowned. "I don't know. I have to be careful."

"We can't force you—and you're free to leave if you want to," Kevin replied. "Would be a shame though."

Mark looked through the dim lighting and at the faces of the group. There was no panic in his chest. His ears and forehead felt normal.

The room was silent. They all stared. The tension made his neck tighten. He looked over at Grace. She smiled. Her eyes sparkled despite the low lighting. She had a shapely figure, a sweet voice and jet-black, curly hair. Best of all, she had a bubbly personality—and it reminded him of someone. Through her smile, Mark could see shiny, halo-white teeth that lit up the room.

Mark shook his head and his attention shifted back to Kevin. "This is—it's happening too fast."

Kevin smiled. A warm smile. "Then you're free to go. But think it over."

"I'll take you home," Grace added.

* * *

Mark and Grace sat in awkward silence. Mark stared out of his window.

"It's not that I don't want to help," he said.

"It's fine." Grace placed her hand over his wrist. It soothed him, and the tension that had taken up residence in his muscles dissipated.

"I have to be careful. If I go overboard—"

"No—I understand."

They made it home without incident. The front yard was empty. Grace escorted Mark to the door.

"Thanks," Mark said.

As they stood outside, her eyes sparkled. She bit her lower lip.

"Want to come in—for tea?" Mark offered, hoping to ask her more questions.

"Sure!"

Mark led them to his living room and went to prepare their beverages.

"*The Alliance*—how long have you been with them?" Mark asked, handing Grace her tea.

"A while—years. Kevin, he's great. And his vision— he wants everyone to be like us. He hasn't stopped talking about you."

Mark cocked his eyebrows, trying to figure her out.

"What if *they* come after me?"

"You'll be safe with us."

"And how do I know if I should believe you?"

"Easy. Use your psychic ability. Translate the energy that *you* feel," Grace replied. "You'll have to decide for yourself."

Content with her answers, Mark changed the subject. It didn't take long for the both of them to enjoy a late afternoon wine. Soon, another was opened. After some time, Mark ordered sushi.

Grace mentioned to Mark that she enjoyed art. "We should visit the Art Gallery—the Water Exhibition looks amazing!" she said excitedly. Mark grinned.

They spoke about art, books they'd read, Kevin, Henry and even Apollo.

"Oh, shit is that the time?" she exclaimed. Somehow, without either of them noticing, the hours had passed until it was nearly midnight. Mark had gotten grapes from the fridge for them to snack on. She tossed one at Mark. It hit him on the side of the head and bounced off, disappearing somewhere. Mark laughed.

"This is your fault," she said, lifting one hand to brush it against his forearm.

"My fault?"

Earlier, she'd disappeared to his cellar and reappeared with his Wirra Wirra Hiding Champion Sauvignon Blanc. Mark had thought it was a good idea at the time.

"Can we keep this party going?" she had asked.

Grace spoke tenderly. Her words were a little more than a soft murmur, laced with tenderness as she gazed at him. Desire sparked in her dark eyes as she leaned in.

Mark wrapped his arm around her.

Her bright, brown eyes, normally filled with kindness and compassion, searched for assurance. They seemed to twinkle when she was excited—this was no exception.

Mark hadn't expected her to kiss him but he didn't mind. Her lips were soft. Her perfume positively overwhelming.

They headed upstairs to the bedroom.

Even in minimal light, it was easy to make out Grace's athletic silhouette as she undressed. Mark gripped her by the upper arms and pulled her toward him.

On the bed, she pulled off Mark's shirt and unzipped his pants. She yanked at his belt and tossed it across the room. Mark brought his lips to hers and kissed her obsessively while he slid his hand over her body—her arms, her back and legs. He stopped and squeezed her thigh.

The blanket had no chance of staying on the bed—the sex was hot and passionate—and she had pulled his body close. Mark wrapped his arms around her and squeezed her toward him. The bedsheets were in a state of chaos, nearly having joined the blanket on the floor—and their passionate lovemaking was to blame.

Their senses overloaded until they both climaxed. Mark grunted, Grace moaned softly.

Panting, Mark pulled her onto his chest. He could feel her still-racing heartbeat against his skin. He stroked her hair. She propped her head up and stared into his eyes.

"I'll come," Mark said, once he was breathing normally.

"Oh," she said through a cheeky grin. She squeezed Mark's torso and rested her head on his chest.

XXIII

They hadn't wasted any time, a quick breakfast, followed by packing and then they left.

"Who stays here?" Mark asked as they walked into the building.

"People we trust," Grace responded.

In the lift, Mark couldn't ignore the buttons. "A hundred levels?"

"It's actually higher," Grace had said. "But you'd need clearance—and to use the other lift."

"The middle one?" Mark asked.

She didn't respond but her lips curved up into a grin as she glanced sideways at him. Mark shook the question from his mind. He left her in the lift as he made his way to his room.

He pulled his suitcase into the apartment—the morning sun lit up the living room and kitchen.

Mark took his tee off and walked out onto the balcony. The cool breeze was perfectly offset by the sun. Its rays tingled his skin, the warmth soaking in. He took a deep breath and looked out onto some islands in the distance. The blue of the ocean matched the cloudless sky.

"You ready?"

Mark spun around. He hadn't heard Grace come in.

"Yeah, give me a sec."

Mark slipped his tee back on and followed Grace.

In the lift Grace didn't flinch even though it was almost supernaturally fast, Mark feeling like he would fly and hit his head on the ceiling.

As the lift door opened, Mark's gaze spanned across a waiting room and lobby. A large TV with low volume was perched up on the wall to the side. Nurses and doctors in all white walked in various directions, chatting to each other in low voices. Screams, moans and pained grunts seeped through the walls. At the main desk, a keyboard clattered, protesting its misuse by a lady with a tight bun.

"We've been working on this project for years," Grace said, leading him past the waiting room. "Nothing's worked."

"DNA project?"

"Yes."

A glass sliding door gave way as they approached. Empty roller beds in rows had been connected to computers. Opposite, chairs had been turned to face the beds.

"The man we've been waiting for!"

Mark turned as a man with short curly hair made his way toward them. His wide smile showcased perfectly straight, pearl-white teeth, the same brilliant shade as his robe.

"Percy Givens," he said, arm stretched.

Instinctively, Mark pushed out his hand and shook Percy's.

"I'll be running the experiments. First, we need to find out why you can regenerate DNA."

Kevin joined them as Percy spoke.

The hard plastic of the chair Mark was instructed to sit in pained his thigh after some time. Soon after being seated, a needle prick pierced his arm followed by the swipe of strong antiseptic that wafted into his nose.

"This will relax you," Percy said, handing Mark two tablets and a cup of water. Mark swallowed them but moments later felt as though he'd had too much coffee. He stared straight ahead as a camera flashed. "We'll study your brain activity," Percy added.

Percy placed some electrodes over Mark's head. Faint tingles ran over his scalp—it was a strange sensation, though not painful. Next to them, some numbers appeared on a screen.

"We'll give you patients to heal," Percy said. "Korevirus, or K-H-I-P twenty-eight—unfortunately, there's no cure and obviously we don't want an outbreak."

At that same moment, the door slid open. A thin man sat in a wheelchair, and a woman in white rolled him toward them. Mark heard his laboured breathing as he was brought closer and eventually right beside him. The man's head flopped from side to side—his eyes wide.

"No," he moaned.

"Phil, we're here to help you," Percy said.

Phil's head steadied. Mark locked eyes with him and gripped his wrist.

The ward disappeared.

Mark struggled to stay upright on the wooden floorboards beneath him. They were surrounded by choppy waters that splashed onto the ship's deck. Huge sprays of water had already started soaking Mark's tee shirt—and they shouldn't be there.

Skies that were blue only seconds ago now materialised thick, dark clouds. Tee shirt already soaked, Mark's pants followed suit when thick raindrops fell from the sky. Rough waters turned into crashing waves. Mark was thrown onto the ground, hitting both knees on hard wood.

He grabbed at something that splintered his finger. Mark looked across at Phil who held onto the ship's side railing. High winds and the rocking of the vessel nearly tossed the both of them off the edge.

"Hey!" Mark shouted, straining to be heard over the noisy howling of the wind.

Phil glanced over. Legs out straight, Phil sat on the deck, arms still clinging to the railing.

A few centimetres of water and Mark didn't care. But now, the water was above his thigh—and the front half of the ship was angled downward. He could feel it sinking.

Mark allowed the strong winds to pull him to the ledge. He peered over and caught sight of something yellow that floated near the dipping vessel. Silver oars poked over its edges.

"The lifeboat!" Mark shouted as he waved to Phil to come across.

On the other side of the ship, Phil shook his head. It was difficult to make out Phil's face clearly.

Mark took a deep breath and jumped.

He made little contact with the life raft—the inflatable rubber rubbed against his arm as he plunged into freezing water. A strong current pushed him away from it and he struggled to stay above the surface of the water.

As his head dipped, he caught sight of something orange. He grabbed at a ring that had been tossed from the lifeboat. His muscles ached as he and Phil fought the current and after some minutes, Phil managed to pull Mark over the rubber and into the raft. Mark laid on his back, panting. He sat up and watched as the ship submerged and disappeared.

"Surprised you jumped," Mark said when he regained his breath.

Phil stayed quiet. Mark tried taking them back—to the hospital—but nothing happened. The storm cleared. They were surrounded by open water. The raft floated on smooth glass. Soon, the sun returned and all Mark could smell was rubber. He sat up, the heat of the raft's edge piercing through his tee shirt and burning his skin.

"I need to tell you something," Phil began.

Just as Mark glanced up at Phil, the ocean rippled away.

The smell of antiseptic and the dull ache in his arm returned. *What was that?*

"How are you feeling?" Mark asked.

Mark didn't look up but there was no reply.

He raised his head and turned toward Phil. Mark gasped. Phil's eyes were wide—and he was convulsing. His mouth frothed. Percy, nearby, scribbled into a notepad, then tapped at a keyboard on a laptop.

Moments later, Phil's eyes rolled back and then his head drooped back on the top part of his chair.

"Someone help him!" Mark yelled.

Kevin exploded into the room. "Get a paramedic in here, quickly!" His voice boomed.

Frantically, several people poured into the room, their robes creating a temporary sea of white. One pushed at Phil's chair. The others took notes.

"You okay?" It was Grace. She grabbed Mark's shoulder. His breath steadied. "Not working huh?"

"I don't know what happened."

"It's fine," Grace replied. "We'll try again tomorrow—unless...?"

"Unless what? Wait, is Phil okay?" Mark asked.

"He'll be fine."

Mark sighed.

What happened?

Percy removed the electrodes and with Grace, Mark made his way out—through the ward, waiting room and into the lift.

"We'll try again tomorrow," she said when they reached Mark's room. "Don't worry about today."

XXIV

The fan above him grated on his last nerve. He got up, switched it off, and tapped at the air-con's control. Minutes later, he was too cold. He snatched at the air-con's remote on the bedside table. He tapped at it, making the room slightly warmer. But now it was too hot. He tossed and turned, trying to sleep. He closed his eyes only to see Phil's drooped head, with his eyes rolled toward the back of his head.

He tried clearing his mind. But Phil returned.

Frustrated, Mark sat up and slipped on some clothes and shoes.

He grabbed his room access key on the kitchen bench and made his way out.

From where he stood, the gold of the lifts gleamed in the dim lighting. He made his way to the ground level of the building. The lift stopped with a soft thud and the doors opened smoothly.

His feet slapped on marble as he made his way toward the entrance.

"Where are you going?" Mark turned toward the voice. The security guard had on long, dark clothing and despite the time, wore sunglasses.

"For a walk," Mark replied.

"Can't let you do that."

"Why?"

"Safety."

"What?" Mark could feel his head getting hot. He felt the pressure in his jaw.

"I don't make the rules, speak to—"

"What's going on?" Kevin had come around the corner and into the main lobby.

"I'm just going for a walk, I don't know what this is all about," Mark replied, nodding his head upward toward the security guard.

Kevin's eyes narrowed. His eyebrows lowered—frowning and shaking his head. "He's fine," he said to the security guard.

"I didn't know—" the guard replied but Kevin cut in.

"Mind if I tag along? I could do with a walk." Kevin had turned toward Mark.

"I mean, if you want," Mark replied, appreciative of the company.

The two of them made it outside and onto the esplanade. The cool breeze blew some leaves off trees. There were faint sounds of crashing waves.

"Sorry about that."

"It's fine. Just weird," Mark replied, staring at the moon's reflection on the shimmery water.

"Phil's fine, by the way."

Mark exhaled. Relief. "That's good."

"We'll try again tomorrow."

Kevin looked across at Mark. It was an encouraging smile.

"Don't get too excited. I'm not sure what happened with Phil," Mark said.

They turned around at the lighthouse and made their way back. Mark said goodnight to Kevin in the lobby and made his way up to his room.

Even though his head was still hazy, at least he no longer saw Phil's dying face when he shut his eyes. It wasn't long before he drifted off.

* * *

The sun shining through the window woke him. He made his way downstairs for breakfast at the café.

As he munched on toast, Grace walked over to him.

"Thought you'd be here," she said, sitting down next to him. "How are you?"

"Better, I went for a walk with Kevin last night— down the esplanade."

"Really?"

"Yeah. I couldn't sleep. The guard was being weird though. Oh well—all good."

"If you've got time to kill, come to the briefing."

"Briefing?" Mark queried.

"Yeah, basically we talk about the experiments. What we'll to do today—that kind of thing."

"Yeah, why not."

Mark followed Grace to the underground clinic. Several people sat in sturdy plastic chairs watching Percy present various diagrams on a screen. DNA and his own name, among a few other terms, were all Mark fully understood.

The meeting ended and Mark was taken into a familiar room. A child sat in one of the chairs, a teddy bear clutched to her. She rubbed her eyes as Mark entered—a doctor was crouched by her side.

Mark was instructed to keep his head still so they could attach electrodes as soon as he sat beside her.

Muttering, Percy mentioned the virus again. Mark glanced at the girl and smiled weakly.

"Sam, Mark's going to help you feel better, okay?"

Mark didn't wait for a response before cupping her forearm.

It took some moments for Mark's eyes to adjust to the darkness that surrounded him. He felt the cool plastic chair beneath him. His rubber soles gripped onto lino. *What's going on?*

"I want Mummy and Daddy."

Mark shot his head to his right. Sam still sat next to him. Her feet dangled, unable to reach the ground. He scanned the room and quickly recognised it; it was the same room they'd been in just moments ago, but the lights were now off. It was late, and the doctors had disappeared. So too had the sounds of keyboards, rolling beds, squeaky chairs and the TV's low volume. Instead, it brought attention to cries, moans and pained grunts that could be heard through the walls.

"I want Mummy and Daddy!" Sam started sobbing, squeezing her teddy bear and smearing it with tears and snot.

"Let's find them," Mark replied. He shot up from his seat.

"I know where they are but I need your help," Sam replied.

Sam twisted off the chair, out of the room and onto the main corridor. Mark followed. The night lights gave the hallway a dark-grey tinge. Squinting, Mark tried making out the other end.

Their footsteps echoed as they passed closed doors, unable to see what was on the other side—but gasps and pained hisses floated through.

Mark was startled when he caught sight of his reflection in the lino and glass. Staring back at him wasn't himself, but Link. He looked down at his hands. They'd grown. Slightly darker too.

Weird.

Sam came to a door at the end and stopped. "It's locked."

Mark didn't hesitate. He placed his palm on the sensor. There was a click and the glass slid open, revealing a T-junction. He followed Sam toward the left. Mark briefly turned his head to the right. His eyes rested on a sliding glass door with a dark tint.

"This way."

Mark followed the voice, hoping they'd find a light switch. A small amount of light from the hallway behind them reflected on some glass on the walls and the floor but it was difficult to see where they were going.

"We're nearly there. Mummy and Daddy are over there." Mark could just make out the outline of Sam's arm pointed toward pitch black.

Mark's foot scuffed on something.

He ignored it and followed Sam until they reached a door with an inscription on the wood in cursive. *Electi Populi* had been ingrained in the middle. Mark recognised the symbol above it—the square, compass and eye.

"We made it," Sam said, raising her head at Mark.

Something flashed and protruded from the wall beside the door. Mark moved closer—it was a touchpad, the screen faintly glowing blue. Below the screen was an indented circle just big enough for a finger. Without thinking, Mark rested his index finger on it. He pressed down and felt a prick. The door chimed and the touchpad's screen turned to bright green with a number briefly appearing—*60895*. The door swung inward, revealing the faint outline of cloaked figures in the darkened room. Mark squinted, trying to make out what was going on but it was difficult to see clearly. Before the door had fully opened, a force behind him pulled him away. At the same time, the room faded away.

Bright, white lights around him stung his eyes. The familiar squeaking of chairs, the closing and opening of doors and the low voices of doctors and nurses slowly filtered in. He turned his head. Sam adjusted to the light through squinting of her own.

A woman in scrubs rushed into the room and gripped Sam by her sides. Sam was picked up and rushed from the room. Mark watched Sam's tears soak into the woman's coat at the shoulder but she didn't make a sound. As Mark bowed his head he caught sight of the teddy bear she'd had. It had fallen onto the floor, right by his feet.

Mark grabbed the fluffy bear and squeezed its synthetic fur. It was wet and soft, almost soothing—until he glanced up at Kevin. Lines had appeared on Kevin's forehead—and as Kevin frowned, Mark tossed the bear to the floor and brought his hands up to his face.

If only I'd managed to heal her. Fuck.

XXV

Kevin had now been proven wrong twice. Grace and Kevin tried hiding their disappointment but Mark knew, just from their short, tense conversations that they weren't happy. It was easy to interpret forced smiles when their eyes didn't match their strained expressions.

And Grace barely visited Mark now. It had been two days since he'd failed with Sam and she'd barely contacted him. *Did I fuck up that badly? Are Sam and Phil okay?*

Eyes adjusting, Mark sat up in his bed. Arm stretched, he tapped at his phone on the bedside table. No text from Grace. Instead, he was greeted with the dim blue of his cyber wallpaper.

It was too much pressure. So much for fighting *The Establishment.*

What happened with Sam and Phil, Mark kept to himself. In saying that, even he struggled to comprehend what took place. He'd lost control.

He nearly strained his neck as it jerked to the side when his phone flashed and chimed. He snatched at it. She'd texted—Grace.

Come to the clinic.

Mere minutes later, the lift doors hissed as he stepped out. The same lady with the tight bun continued to abuse her keyboard at the desk—the forceful click-clacking of plastic keys overwhelmed the soft murmur of voices.

Sweat and other odours filled the air as he stepped out of the lift. It was a crowded waiting room. Children and adults filled most of the chairs. The only conversations were those between nurses and doctors nearby, who darted in every direction like busy bees.

Among the sea of eyes, Mark noticed an older man seated by the TV who had a brown stain on his ripped shirt. For a second he looked directly at Mark but then shuddered and shifted his attention back to the TV—a daytime talk show. Beside him sat a younger man, who took up nearly two chairs. He had his head bowed, pain written across his face. He scowled when his eyes met Mark's.

Only two other chairs were empty—and it was easy to see, and even *smell* why. Sandwiched between the two chairs sat another large man who filled the room with loud coughs and sniffling. Sweat had soaked through his shirt, creating dark circles on the front and back. Mark could almost see the cloud of body odour wafting off him.

Eyes stared as Mark made his way toward the opposite end of the waiting area.

Grace walked out of a room at the end. He'd nearly mistaken her for a doctor. She had on a white robe and her hair had been tied into a ponytail.

"We'll give it another try," she said to Mark.

Mark nodded and followed her into a room that had a hospital bed and two chairs facing each other.

"First one—name's Pete. You know what you need to do right?" Grace asked, as she attached the electrodes, handed him two pills, and powered up a nearby laptop.

Mark nodded. His hand clenched the edge of the plastic chair he sat in.

Mark glanced over as Kevin and Percy entered. Behind them was the man who'd been sweating profusely in the waiting room. The body odour nearly watered Mark's eyes as he made his way toward the empty chair—and now Mark had to fight the urge to throw up.

Mark closed his eyes.

As soon as his hand made contact with Pete, the room disappeared. It was replaced by another room, with white walls and brown laminate flooring. Mark stood on a thick red rug. There was a light breeze coming through the window.

It was his room.

He turned his head away from the window and toward the frantic shuffling of feet. Pete plodded toward the door.

"Hey, what are you..."

As soon as Pete reached the door, he disappeared. Loud thumps resonated from the hallway.

Mark sprinted after Pete, who was now hurrying toward the lifts. Stomps echoed across the walls.

"Pete, I'm here to help you!" Mark yelled, closing the gap between the two of them.

Pete had made it to the lifts and he jabbed at the buttons. He then twisted and faced Mark. Panting, Pete raised his arms and shouted, "Stay away from me!" He glared at Mark. Mark was forced to stop only metres away.

"What's your problem?" Mark asked.

"Just stay the fuck away from me!"

The lift door opened. Pete entered and the lift made its way down. Mark jumped in the next one and headed to the ground floor. He barely made it in time to watch Pete shove at the front doors and sprint outside—Mark was powerless to stop him.

The lobby vanished. He opened his eyes and looked up. Grace shook her head slightly, staring at the red flashing screen of the computer.

Pete, now hyperventilating, was escorted out by Percy who returned with someone else—a lady he'd seen earlier in the waiting room. She was so thin that Mark could have easily wrapped his hand around her upper arm. Percy assisted her to the chair where she slumped down heavily and then rubbed her hip.

Mark closed his eyes, focusing on the task.

"Mel, Mark will cure you," Mark heard Grace say.

Mark stretched out his arm and placed his hand on Mel's wrist. The white walls rippled away.

Immediately, the hospital room returned. Grace shook her head. Kevin frowned, and Mark bowed his head.

Percy held Mel's hand as he led her out of the room.

Minutes later, Percy returned with a child. "This is Noah," he said, as he lifted him onto the chair. There were dark rings under Noah's eyes. Mark smiled weakly. Noah stared at the floor.

Mark grabbed Noah's wrist and closed his eyes again. Seconds passed. Minutes passed. Nothing happened. No rippling away of the walls, no evaporation of their surroundings, no morphing of the walls, converging into a blur. Nothing. He opened his eyes and scowled.

"You feeling okay?" It was only when Mark looked up and saw Percy's eyes that he realised he was talking to him.

"I'm fine—I don't know what's going on."

"Should we stop—"

"No. Bring in the next one," Kevin snapped before Mark was able to reply to Percy.

Percy carried out Noah and soon returned with Sam from only a couple of days ago. Mark was filled with relief, knowing Sam was okay. She held onto a white bear this time—this one she squeezed by the neck and held tight by her torso.

Mark's eyes had been closed for only seconds before Percy grabbed Sam, unhealed from illness, and took her from the room—her white bear still tightly held, this time by the arm.

Every few minutes a new person was brought into the room. Mark had lost count. At times, when he started to heal, the room began to disappear. But most often, Mark failed to make that happen. Each shake of the head, strained expression and scowl from Kevin, Percy and Grace added further salt to injury and frustration.

Phil was the last to be brought in, in the same wheel-chair as before. His eyes rolled and his head swung from the sides as Percy brought him to Mark.

Mark took a deep breath, wiped his face and wrapped his hand across Phil's forearm. The room faded away.

Mark's body bobbed up and down, and strong rubber had overtaken his sense of smell once more. His skin burned. Looking down, his upper arms and shoulders were pink. There was a searing pain in his back. He looked up. Phil sat lounged with both arms stretched on the edge of the lifeboat.

Mark's eyes scanned across the horizon. No sign of birds. No indication of life. And the clusters of clouds above provided little to no protection against the sun's rays.

At least it's calm.

Minutes passed. Maybe hours. They floated on the life raft. Phil had opened the emergency pack. Mark had refused the rations of dry biscuit. He'd taken a swig of water. But Mark's focus was on taking them back to the hospital. Although still waters surrounded them, Mark knew it was only a matter of time before their supplies ran out.

He slipped his tee shirt back on. It didn't take long for darkness to set it. Cold winds stung his face. Phil wrapped his arms around his body. As water poured into the raft, Mark took to work. He used a plastic bailer, removing the water as quickly as his arms would allow.

As his shoulders began to sting, he saw the hospital dissolve into appearance around them. The winds stopped, his tee shirt dried and before long, he was seated on something sturdy. The relief, however, was short-lived. Opening his eyes, Mark saw Percy crouched by Phil's wheelchair. Phil was unresponsive. There were no chest movements and his head had dropped forward—and his eyes were closed. Percy jerked into action, quickly spinning the wheelchair and half running Phil out of the room. There was shouting in the corridors but Mark couldn't make out the words.

Shit.

Before Grace or Kevin said a word, Mark yanked at the electrodes and made his way out of the room. The waiting room was empty aside from the lady working at the front desk who briefly stopped to look at him as he passed. As he entered a lift to make his way up, he could have sworn he heard screaming through the walls but he didn't care too much—he cared more about the fact that he'd let Kevin down again.

XXVI

Mark hid in his room. It had been days since he'd seen the others—Grace, Percy and Kevin. He'd occasionally go downstairs but luckily he hadn't run into them.

Rain splattered against the window's glass, providing little visual relief. Mark resorted to staring at the wall of the living room. *What the fuck am I doing here?*

He tried comprehending what he'd been through over the last few weeks, but it was difficult. He struggled to structure his thoughts—and even memories. *Should I tell Kevin I'm not who he thinks I am—or does he already know?*

He thought about the previous week—nothing came to mind. Yesterday—he wasn't sure. This morning—*wait, what the fuck happened this morning?*

"Are you okay?"

Mark hoped she hadn't been standing behind him long as he spun to face Grace. "...I don't know," he admitted. "My head feels weird, like I'm forgetting things."

Grace walked over to him and cupped her hand on his forehead. The dull aching in his head disappeared. His muscles relaxed.

"I can influence neurotransmitters, which has an effect on moods."

Mark joined her on the sofa.

"Try and relax. Take some deep breaths."

As he lied on the leather, she applied some pressure on his chest with her hand. His heart rate slowed gradually, dropping from a racing pitter-patter to a steady thump-thump.

He closed his eyes. At first, he felt as though he'd sunk into the sofa but seconds later, the pressure changed. His body floated toward the ceiling. Feeling much more at ease, Mark opened his eyes to thank Grace—only to realise that she wasn't in front of him anymore. Instead, he was greeted by the sight of the ceiling.

He looked down and saw Grace still had her hand on a body. His body. He'd spoken to Dan at The Academy about this, but he'd never thought he'd be capable of astral projection.

From where he floated he could smell the faint scent of Grace's perfume. He felt the chill of the air-con on his skin.

He glided in front of Grace, waving his hand in front of her face. Her face cocked back momentarily and her eyes darted until they found their way to Mark's physical face. For a second she frowned.

He flew to the door. He felt weightless. He peered down, trying to make sense of what he was—and what space he occupied—as he floated in the air. There was nothing there. No outline of a body. No blob of mass. He was nothing more than a pair of eyes.

He flew through the closed door and into the corridor. He recognised Roger, the cleaner. Roger had become a close friend over the last few days. Yesterday they'd debated over...

Mark couldn't remember.

Below him, Roger pushed a cleaning cart and then entered a room before shutting the door behind him.

I wonder how long it'd take me to get home.

As the thought entered his mind, Mark was thrust at a high velocity. High winds whistled past him, his eardrums ringing as his vision blurred. Seconds later, he was inside his house—in his lounge. He flew through the house but found no clues that anyone had entered. The dishes he and Grace had left were still on the drying rack. His bed was still made. He went to close his open laptop but ended up flying through it.

He thought about Henry.

His house dissolved—his kitchen transforming into a different house entirely. Now, he stood outside a closed door. Smooth jazz wafted through the house. There was an abundance of natural light seeping through the glass that separated the interior and exterior. In the distance, ocean waves crashed against the cliffs. He glided through the closed door. He'd entered a home office, with shiny floorboards and a wooden chair and desk. Hanging plants perched on a bookshelf and others in pots sat neatly on a desk among a computer monitor, lamp and books. The man was unmistakable—Henry—and he muttered to himself as he paced back and forth. Mark moved closer so he could hear.

"They're on to us—it's what I saw."

As Mark edged further into the room Henry froze and stared directly at Mark. Mark held his breath. His mind raced, then he thought about Grace and his apartment and Henry instantly dissolved. Instantaneously, his surroundings morphed into his room. At that same moment, Grace was leaving the lounge and headed for the door. Mark shot his eyes open.

"Grace." Mark, reunited with his body, quickly shot up from the couch.

Holding the door, she spun.

"I had an out-of-body experience," Mark said.

"You can astral project?"

"I think so," Mark replied.

"Let's go."

"Where to?"

"Kevin—we need to let him know."

Mark followed Grace into a lift and toward Kevin's office. He hadn't been there before.

"Come in," said a voice before Grace had even knocked. They entered and Grace filled Kevin in. Mark's eyes were glued to the reflective marble flooring and then the bookshelf that ran along the wall with its own strips of golden, ambient lighting.

"I know—and this is perfect. Mark, we need your help." Kevin had barely waited for Grace to finish.

Mark's eyes were torn away from a crystal chandelier hanging above a fancy office desk. "Help? With what?"

"Finding—certain, terrible people. We need to do it now, before they realise," Kevin replied.

"They?"

"*The Establishment.*"

"Oh, of course."

It was the first time Mark had seen Kevin smile since the failures at the hospital. "Yellow Room, ten minutes," Kevin added, placing his hand on Mark's shoulder.

Mark followed Kevin and Grace out of the room. Minutes later they arrived at The Yellow Room; it was distinct with flickering lights from flame-lit torches and pagan art on the walls. Huddled in a group, Kevin explained to Mark what they needed to do.

"He shouldn't suspect your energy. When we try and track him, he disappears. It's because he knows—and sometimes days in advance."

"Who?" Mark asked.

"Henry," Kevin replied. "Lead us to him with your astral projection. Tell us his exact whereabouts and we'll deal with the rest. He's here somewhere, in the city."

Xena, Cera, Linus, Hector, Maia and Damon stood among the group. With one last look at Kevin, Mark closed his eyes. Heat drove through his feet, rising to his forehead. It became hotter as it flowed through his body. He focused on Henry. Everything remained pitch black. He floated in darkness.

"What's happening?" Mark heard Kevin say after some minutes.

"Can't find him," Mark replied.

"Keep trying," came the reply from Kevin.

After some moments, light filled the darkness.

Mark found himself airborne, wind hissing past him once more as he zipped through the air. He saw the ocean in the distance and also some cliffs. Perched on top of them was a glass house that left nothing to the imagination. Even from this distance, Mark could make out the bright lights within, highlighting some of the interior. A magnet pulled him toward it. As he neared, Mark saw the faint figure of a man through the glass. Henry.

"I found him." Mark's voice boomed over the landscape.

"Nice work."

"Mallet Street," Mark added. He'd peeked at the street name as he flew over it.

"We'll be there in twenty," Kevin informed him.

The glass that surrounded the house was the only barrier separating them—and Mark floated just outside the window and watched as Henry sat and typed at his computer. Every so often Henry would glance in his direction, shake his head and continue typing.

He flew into Henry's office and watched from the corner of the room. He felt the uneasiness in the air.

As he floated closer, Henry stood.

"Mark?"

Mark flinched. *How does he know I'm here?*

"I knew it was you—I don't let intruders into my house."

"Keep him distracted," Mark heard someone say in the background. "They're on their way."

"How did you—" Mark began.

"You don't survive as long as I have without learning to protect yourself. What brings you here?"

Mark racked his brain.

"I need you to reconsider." It was the first thing that came to his mind.

"You're lost, Mark. Blind to what's going on. So no, I won't reconsider."

"What do you want from me?"

"I can't tell you that—but maybe your first step should be to wake up."

Despite not having a body, Mark's rage still rose, his face burning up as his anger mounted.

Henry continued. "Your psychological disorder—you have work to do. And as I said, you're not worthy."

Had it not been for the lack of means, Mark may not have been able to stop himself from hitting Henry across the face. Mark hated him. The mocking. The calm arrogance. Mark felt like he was about to explode.

"That's what I'm talking about," replied Henry. "Anyway, I need to tell you—"

But it was too late.

At precisely that moment, the team, led by Kevin, burst through the office door.

"Of course, I should've seen this coming," Henry said with outstretched hands. Even now, seconds before his doom, he hadn't deviated from his demeanour. *What the fuck is with this guy?*

"I knew he was different—but to use him like this?" Henry stared directly at Mark.

Those were his last words. Kevin fired a gun and shot him in the head, the gunshot probably echoing for miles.

As Henry fell, Mark flinched. He'd never seen anyone be killed before. Henry fell in slow motion until he hit the ground with a soft thud, blood seeping from the side of his head. At the same time, Mark's vision blurred, but it only happened for a split second—like a computer screen's static. It didn't take long for his vision to clear.

He'd seen enough.

He preferred to be with his body. He'd helped them find Henry. They could see out the remainder of the job without him.

XXVII

He'd had a headache since the astral projection with Henry, and it had progressively gotten worse. He had opened his eyes but the pressure felt as though his head would explode at any second. He'd fainted soon after and Link had to drag Mark onto a stretcher and then to the clinic.

All Mark saw now were white walls—and he'd been there for hours. He looked up at the digital clock on the wall—10PM. The room felt too small. The air-con made him shiver. Mark had asked for Grace but Link said she was busy, and that she'd come as soon as she could. Mark had little energy to argue. Percy walked in at one stage, asking if Mark was okay and Mark responded by shaking his head and pointing a finger toward his head. Talking made it worse—there would be a throbbing pain in his jaw that went up to his temples.

Percy had brought in some tablets for Mark. "Painkillers," he'd said. Mark didn't argue, taking them all down in one go with a gulp of water. It eased the pain slightly but a soft, dull ache remained. "Stay here tonight. The nurses will check on you," Percy had said. Mark didn't debate. He nodded and rested his head into sleep. That was hours ago.

Mark propped his head up. The dull ache at the top of his head returned. He turned. Beside him on a table were some pills in a paper cup and some water nearby. *Take these*, was written on a small torn-off piece of white paper. Mark didn't hesitate. He sat up, poured some water into the cup and popped them into his mouth.

The dull ache developed into a sharp, burning pain pushing into the sides of his head. It was impossible to ignore and his eyes started watering. He closed his eyes, trying to locate Grace. For some minutes, he floated in darkness. Focusing on both the headache and Grace drained him. He brought himself back into the room— 10:30PM.

He noticed a call button beside his bed. He pressed it. He tossed and turned and squeezed at the sides of his head. The pain worsened. No nurse.

With blurry vision, he staggered to the door. And tried the handle. It had been locked. *What the fuck?* He banged on the wooden portion of the door, then at the glass panel. As his arms began to ache, a figure appeared on the other side. The lock clicked. The door swung open. A gush of warm air seeped into the room. A temperature he would have preferred.

"Mark, are you okay?" *Where was she when I pressed the button?*

"Headache, it's getting worse," Mark ground out.

"Take a seat," she said, ushering Mark back into the claustrophobic's nightmare of a room. Mark shook his head, instantly regretting it when the dizziness got worse.

"I can't go back in there," he said to the nurse.

The nurse led Mark to the waiting area. She handed him some more pills, and more water.

"What are these?" he asked as she handed them over.

"Painkillers," she replied.

"The other ones didn't work."

"These are stronger," she replied.

Mark didn't object. He tossed the pills into his mouth and washed them down with more water. After some moments the searing pain faded but his vision still blurred and at times faded in and out.

"I need to go for a walk," he said to the nurse who had stayed by his side.

"I was told to keep you here."

"I don't care—I'm going for a walk."

"Mark—"

Mark made his way to the lifts. With clouded vision and focus, he pressed at a button. The vision of Henry hitting the ground with blood spraying from his head had branded itself into his mind. He tried shaking it but the throbbing of his head returned, threatening to get worse—and it brought on a familiar migraine. His eyes blurred. He wiped the water from them as the lift ascended. *Anywhere but here.*

The lift stopped and opened. It was difficult to keep his eyes open and so he squinted. He didn't see the level but saw shadows blur past him.

He turned into a hallway. He saw a shadow of a man. *Was that Henry?*

The figure disappeared.

He continued wobbling through dark hallways, lobbies, landings and corridors hoping his vision would clear—or better yet—to find Grace. No such thing happened. *Maybe Kevin's office?* He vaguely remembered the way.

He entered the lift and racked his brain. *What level was it?*

He jabbed at level eighty-two. No, that was wrong. Mark closed the lift door and tried eighty-three.

He recognised the checkerboard pattern on the floor. He walked along the black and white squares and soon recognised the door to Kevin's office. His knocks quickly became bangs but there was no answer. He tried the handle. It turned and the door gave way. The office was empty but still, Mark walked in. He sat at the desk, momentarily drawn to the lights providing a golden glow to the luxuriously, black tabletop. Mark eyed the desk's golden legs and finally what lay on it—a black index folder. On the front was written *Subject 9009 – Mark Pierce.* Mark snatched at it and opened it. It looked like a medical report. He recognised the names on a list. They were the people he'd tried to heal. *Why were all the attempts a success?* Next to each name was a green tick and SUCCESSFUL written in dark bold. And just below that:

Trial experiment(s) with remodelled KHIP-28 have been successful. Subject 9009 NOT found to alter synthetic viral load in patients. Non-coding DNA molecules remained unchanged, leading to a primary and secondary success. Conclusively, subject is NOT considered a threat.

Mark struggled to digest the document. He shook his head, tossed the file back on the desk and made his way out.

The throbbing eased as he lay down. He'd made it back to his room.

It took some time but eventually, he drifted off to sleep.

* * *

The red blotch on his chest matched just how much it stung. Really, it was anyone's guess how long they'd been out there, floating on the water. Mark looked across the yellow life raft. Phil ate a biscuit, but Mark could have sworn most of it crumbled onto his shirt. The contents of the emergency kit lay sprawled untidily among their feet—hooks, a compass, a survival manual, some biscuit rations (possibly soggy), a torch, whistle, first-aid kit, and flares, among other things.

Mark looked out to the horizon. A foggy haze made it difficult to make out clearly.

"Can I trust you?"

Mark's eyes darted over to Phil. The sun forced him to squint and bring his hand up to his eyes like a visor. "What do you mean?"

"Can I trust you?" Phil asked again.

"I guess. Why?" Mark replied.

"You're one of the good guys?"

"What are you getting at?" Mark replied.

"Something I need to tell you."

"What—"

* * *

The blanket scratched his skin. His sweat had soaked into the bedsheets. He pulled the blanket off the bed and onto the floor. He twisted his body and tried getting back to sleep.

* * *

He opened his eyes and lifted his head, looking around. It wasn't his bedroom. He was strapped to a chair, with thin, electrode-like wires connected to his head. *Wasn't I in bed a second ago?* There were also tubes, like worms, running into his veins, nose and mouth.

He struggled to keep his head raised but was able to glimpse at Percy before his head dropped. Percy, who stood in front of him, said something but Mark couldn't make out the words. His head didn't ache but he felt drained. He could barely lift his feet off the ground.

Heavy eyed, he let his eyelids close—and the feeling of leather straps binding his wrists dissipated.

* * *

When he opened them again, he recognised Sam just ahead of him. They stood in front of the same door with the inscription; *Electi Populi*. It opened slowly. Mark held his breath. Faint light broke into the room, illuminating hooded figures—the same ones he'd seen with Jamie. They towered at least a foot above him and they had formed a circle. Inside the circle, Mark made out a naked man and woman, who, facing away from each other had been tied together with ropes at the waist. Their muffled cries barely reached Mark. As Sam screamed, the figures turned their heads toward them. As the nearest twisted his body toward them, Mark made out bulges of muscle at the thighs. He headed toward the door, footsteps pounding on the hard floor.

Mark shot his eyes open. His chest thumped. He recognised his room. He felt Grace's hand on his forehead. He relaxed and sunk further into the leather sofa, the headache fading away. *What the fuck is going on?*

His breath steadied and his head almost felt normal. He filled Grace in on his failing memory, the visions and the lucid dreams.

Mark briefly saw the whites in Grace's eyes as they widened.

"How long was I out, just before?" Mark asked.

"Not sure," she replied. "When I came into your room, you were on the ground, convulsing—you should see Percy."

Mark thought about it for some seconds. "You're probably right. I can't even remember what I did yesterday." He pawed at a bruise near his elbow. He didn't remember it being there before, or how he'd gotten it.

He went with Grace to the clinic. They walked through the familiar waiting area and met Percy in a small office further down than he'd previously been. Percy pulled his glasses off and turned away from his computer as Grace and Mark entered. Percy grinned, dimples showing and eyes twinkling.

"Mark! Grace! What can I do for you?"

Mark filled him in, much the same way he had Grace.

"You're glitching," was Percy's response, cutting Mark off mid explanation.

"What?"

"It happens when you astral project for the first time."

"Why?" Mark asked.

"Everything disconnects—your mind, body and soul—and then when you come back, your consciousness has to stitch everything back together. It's a lot of work; glitching is perfectly normal."

He glanced over at Grace and her soft smile.

"You'll get used to it, and it'll eventually stop," Percy added. He grabbed a medication container from his desk and passed it to Mark. Mark saw his name. "Take those, three times a day—morning, lunch and dinner."

The pills were in a plastic, snow-coloured bottle.

Right then, as Mark shivered from the cool air, Percy's appearance transformed, pixelating for some seconds and turning into a dark blur. He turned toward Grace but the water in his eyes made it difficult to see her clearly.

"Mark?"

Grace had brought him a cup of water. He guzzled down the water with something pea-sized and rigid that Grace handed over. After some seconds of rapid blinking, his vision cleared. Percy was no longer out of focus. The walls around him looked solid. He felt present.

"How long do I need to take these?"

"Until the symptoms stop. We'll assess after a few weeks."

Mark nodded, thanked Percy and left the both of them in the room. It was strange that adjusting would take so long but he wasn't going to question how things worked— as long as the pills helped.

And for the first time in—

Actually, he couldn't remember how many days, or weeks (or maybe even months)—but he could now think, and see, clearly.

XXVIII

"Ben Harrison," Grace said, sliding a tablet across the desk with a photo of a man. Pale skin. He had on a blue, checkered, long-sleeved, button-up shirt—teeth showed through a crooked smile. Mark glanced up at Kevin and the others in the room. The only sound came from the fan whirring overhead.

He shut his eyes. In seconds, darkness turned into a birds-eye view of a cloud-covered inner-city. Motivated by medieval heritage, a combination of Renaissance and Gothic-inspired buildings spanned across the city.

Mark zoomed toward a low-set building, near a river, by the effect of an imaginary magnet—the grass so green and aesthetically contrasted against the river's blue it almost looked like a desktop background. He soared over a main road and entered a room through thick slabs of cement. In the room, he floated behind the same blonde man from the photo. Mark didn't see his face but knew it was him—and he buttoned up a shirt at the foot of a bed. The man turned his head to one side, checking himself in a full-length mirror.

"Krakow, Poland," Mark said after some minutes, opening his eyes.

"You're getting better," Grace said. In the corner of the room, Kevin cracked a smile and ushered Link from the room.

Mark located everyone so quickly now. Even halfway around the world—it only took a minute or so—and he'd helped *The Alliance* uncover the location of many of them—members of *The Establishment*.

"The quicker we find them, the safer we'll be," Kevin had said when Mark met the group in The Yellow Room earlier that day.

Grace pulled the tablet toward her and soon pushed it toward Mark with a photo of another man.

"Bradley Jones," Kevin said. "Investor in the HilderBerf Group. Terrible person."

Kevin described Bradley Jones—as a significant investor of the Group who, involved in human trafficking, also ran a drug cartel and was an influencer of international laws and policies.

Just as Kevin had predicted, Mark found Bradley at a house perched by crystal-clear waters of a pristine beach. Palms trees surrounding the estate held coconuts that would no doubt drop at any moment. The infinity pool in the backyard reflected the home's exterior sharp lines as well as the interior's golden glow. It took Mark only minutes to appreciate where he was—Paradise Island off Nassau of The Bahamas.

By the pool, playboy Bradley, surrounded by lean women in bikinis sparingly sipped at a beverage. Mark got close enough to see the Ray-Ban logo on his sunglasses as well as the condensation on the glass holding his pina colada cocktail.

Mark confirmed the location to Kevin. It didn't take long for people Mark didn't recognise to crash the party. They wore all black, tight clothing and snuck in from the side—Mark saw them before Bradley was able to spring up and escape. A single gunshot echoed as Mark left the tropical island for The Yellow Room.

According to Kevin, Tom Trevers ran a secret group—and Mark believed Tom to be a murderer based on the horrific stories from Kevin. Tom had been lured into the life of a criminal twenty years ago, as a teenager. It was on the coast of California at Santa Maria by a man who promised to give the then young Tom five thousand dollars for killing a woman and bringing her to him. From then, killing was easy for Tom. He had no remorse—and he had become insatiable.

Kevin, with sharp lines on his forehead, explained that now, Tom killed to satisfy a dark ritual as part of a secret club. Mark allowed himself to feel hatred toward Tom. It was a different type of anger—an icy coldness in his heart, rather than the well-acquainted internal rise in body temperature that usually went along with his rage.

Mark found Tom. 7PM—and he was at his home. He sat in the dining room with his family, eating dinner. Mark knew he had two daughters and a son but now saw them in the flesh. Tom smiled across the table where his wife sat. She had on a long, black, shimmery dress that draped down her body. It hugged her lean figure and accentuated her long legs.

"Maddie drew you something today," the wife said. From Tom's profile, Mark knew that her name was Victoria.

Tom turned his head to the left where one of the girls sat. His smile grew and for a second, Mark was able to see his teeth. "Can't wait to see it," he replied.

"Mark, are we clear?"

Mark shoved his thoughts aside.

"Are we clear? Mark?"

"Clear," he replied.

Tom didn't get a chance to finish his meal. Three people Mark vaguely recognised from *The Alliance* boomed through the door. All at once, the family recoiled in their seats as the door came off its hinges and crashed onto the floor, the noise so loud even Mark flinched in mid-air. Tom had barely been able to stand and shield his family. He shouted to Victoria to take the kids but it was too late. The gunshot stung Mark's ears. Tom took a fatal bullet to the chest. He'd waived his arms in the air, trying to form some sort of protection between *The Alliance* and his children, and wife—but it made little difference. As he fell, his head hit the edge of the wooden table. Utensils flung to the floor and screams filled the house.

Surely not.

One of the men aimed a gun at the youngest daughter. Her name was Mia. Mark remembered from the profile. Without thinking, Mark swooped toward the assassin's arm as the bullet sounded, nearly making him deaf. It was useless. He just flew through the outstretched limb. "What the fuck are you doing?" Mark shouted—but of course, the man couldn't hear him.

Mark witnessed it all. How *The Alliance* killed the entire family. Stiff bodies lay on the dining room floor. The cream-coloured carpet had become blood-soaked. It was a murder scene. Five shots—all synchronised perfectly one after the other. On the floor, Tom's tee shirt was stained red and his legacy was no more. And on the table, their meals remained half-eaten.

Mark opened his eyes. He could feel himself shaking. He tried speaking but nothing came out. He was sur-rounded by fuzzy lines and blurs—another glitch.

His breath steadied and his vision cleared—but everything looked different. He glanced over at where he knew Kevin had been standing. Kevin was taller than Mark remembered. He had tough, dry-looking skin. Mark resisted the urge to scream at him. He took a deep breath, trying to calm himself down. His head spun. It felt like it was being squeezed at the sides. The pressure nearly made him lose his balance and fall onto the desk in front of him.

Frowning, Mark peered over at Link. He looked unusual—and he glared at Mark. *Why is he looking at me like that? I didn't fucking do anything wrong.* Link's eyes looked darker than Mark remembered.

Rachel. For a split second, she entered his mind.

* * *

"You okay?"

He was beneath thin sheets, pulled up to his shoulders. He looked across the room. It was Grace. Electrodes had been attached to his head. *How'd I get here?*

"What happened?"

"You fainted—then had a seizure," Grace replied. "You been glitching again?"

Mark bit his lower lip.

"Not really, why's that?

"Your blood tests—doesn't look like you've been taking your medication."

It was true. Mark had stopped taking them. But it had been weeks since he'd started taking them. *Why do I still need them?*

Grace rolled her eyes and left the room. The door slammed behind her. After some time, Mark pressed the call button by the bed. He waited for a nurse who didn't appear. He yanked the electrodes and tossed them by his side. He hopped off the bed and toward the door. This time, the handle turned. He made his way out and through the waiting room. It was deserted.

It didn't take long to reach his room.

He felt lightheaded, his mind fuzzy, and so he sat down on the sofa with a heavy thump. But his vision still swam, blurry around the edges, and he laid down, stretching out in the hopes he would still feel better. A dull ache reverberated through his mind, and he squirmed, trying to find any position that would alleviate the pressure—but no such luck.

His head rotated toward the door as it opened.

He sat up as Grace entered. Vivid, harsh lines filled his view, akin to a static television screen. Then the lines turned into a vision, intertwined with the sight of Grace at the entrance. The vision beneath became more vivid, becoming more dominant in his sight. Grace looked different. Her eyes were a different shade—much lighter, more of an amber colour.

Then, his sight became dominated by a vision, as though astral projecting.

Phil was opposite him. The top part of his tee shirt was covered in biscuit crumbs.

Mark's forearms burned red-hot under the sun.

"They're lying to you," Phil began.

"What?"

"Something is going on. The lifts—go to the top. You'll see."

Before Mark could ask Phil what he meant, the yellow and blue of the lifeboat and open water surrounding them faded into a grey fog. Blaring heat dropped away, replaced by the coolness of the hotel lobby. Mark observed the area. It was empty. No one accompanied the front desk. His reflection blurred in the gold of the three lifts ahead.

The middle lift gave way as he neared. Hissing filled Mark's ears. Inside, there was one button. One with the same, now familiar symbol—with the compass and square with the eye in the middle. The lift rose, picking up speed as it made its climb. The pressure drove Mark's body into the floor. The bright, gold trim lighting brought attention to the infinity mirror effect created by the gold mirrors on each side of the lift.

After an audible thud, the lift slowly opened. More hissing accompanied it.

In front of him was a penthouse with large windows opposite the lifts looking out onto the ocean. The walls and ceilings were a deep-set gold, matching the thick pillars. The floor was a white-gold marble.

Indistinct voices came from the far right. Mark couldn't see who they belonged to, but it sounded like two men in a debate. He made his way through the opening and veered toward the right.

"Why did you call me here—and why are you upset?"

"This wasn't our plan, Akku. They may be harmless, but in numbers, they could be a threat," the other said.

Mark made his way around the corner and saw who had been speaking. Two familiar figures—like he'd seen with Jamie—sat across from each other on gold chairs with a gold-coated coffee table between them. Their muscular bodies—like Greek gods—reminded Mark of the statues in the lobby.

The one that wasn't Akku froze mid-sentence and stared directly at Mark.

"I sense energy that's not ours."

Mark froze.

How could they possibly know he was there?

XXIX

"Mattu, brother—you're letting your paranoia get to you. First, you worry they're getting out of control, now you worry they spy on us."

"Don't give me that, Akku. This was *your* fault. You were the chief scientist. I knew what you were up to—you liberated them, giving them free will in that *garden* of yours, for reasons I'll never understand."

"They were my creation."

"You went soft Akku, that's why you were cast out. Love is a weak, human emotion, especially loving a thing created to be a slave," Mattu snarled.

"I believe in the balance of all things," Akku replied quickly, raising his voice and speaking over Mattu.

"So did *The Mystic*—and see where that got him. You'd best be careful brother, otherwise, you'll join him," said the brother, using his fingers as quotation marks when he said, *The Mystic*.

"Is that a threat, Mattu?"

"A warning."

"What about the man Kevin predicted? The healer? Is he soon to die?" asked Mattu.

"No need. He failed to cure the synthetic virus—and his ability to regenerate DNA has been proved wrong. Terror for the next harvest will proceed as planned," Akku replied.

"So, what of him now?"

"He's working for us. He's no threat—twenty assassinations in three weeks because of him."

"Good," said the one that was called Mattu.

Eyes wide and frozen, Mark held his breath.

Just as Mattu turned and faced Mark directly for a second time, the penthouse slipped away. He found himself laying on something hard and furry. As his palm brushed against it, he realised it was the carpet of his room. Grace had crouched down beside him. He shielded his face as she went to place her hand on his forehead.

He heaved himself off the ground. He felt lightheaded and the humidity made him feel hot and bothered. He nearly fainted.

Vision blurring, he left Grace and without looking back, rushed from the room, frantically trying to get to the exit.

The walls in the hallway spun and waved. His shoulders bumped into doors as he stumbled toward the lifts. He tripped on something, falling to the ground. His arms prevented his head from hitting the hard ground but they ached under his weight. He pushed at the floor and brought himself to his feet again, rocking unsteadily. He bent over, clutching at the wall as his breathing returned to normal. He vomited. It sprayed onto the white walls and ran down onto the carpet.

He made it to the main foyer. Sweat ran down his forehead as he sprinted through. His legs felt as though they'd give way at any minute. He felt eyes on him— glances in his direction as he darted through the main opening.

He ran toward large, metal doors and jerked them aggressively toward him. He groaned, the metal of the handle digging into his palm.

It didn't take long to realise it wasn't the way out.

Instead, it was a darkened corridor leading to shadows. He quickly glanced behind him. More eyes looked his way. The polished tiles of the floor contrasted with the darkness only some metres ahead.

Mostly blinded to what lay ahead, he made his way through the dimly-lit passageway until he reached the end—a lift with only one button—and the same interlocking compass and square symbol. He jabbed at it until his finger ached.

The lift plunged for a few seconds, the jerky motion making him feel nauseous again.

As it opened, a gust of cold air cooled him, granting instant relief from all the running.

He walked through the corridor where flame-lit torches along the walls provided the only source of light. His shadow flickered. Despite walking on a smooth, and bright, hard surface, dark smears coated his white shoes. His legs felt heavy as he continued toward something black and rectangular.

Heavy legs turned to exhaustion as he reached it.

In the middle of the door written in fancy, gold writing was: *Bibliotheca.*

He pushed down on the handle.

The room, soaked in a warm glow from golden lights hanging from the ceiling, had its walls lined with books. They ran from the ground to the beginning of a domed ceiling. In the centre, a blue ambient floor lamp showcased a glass cabinet housing a selection of even more books. Toward the back, black table cloths covered small tables displaying tools, artefacts and gold bars—reminiscent of a museum.

It was only then that he noticed the golden statues that nearly reached the room's ceiling on either side of the entrance. It was easy to recognise them now—and Mark knew before his eyes even passed over the plaques at their feet. They were the brothers. Akku and Mattu.

Akku, with chest muscles bulging over the top of golden cloth covering the rest of his body, held a shield in one hand, and in the other, a rod.

Mattu's veiny and contracted bicep squeezed one of the necks of a three-headed dog. Little was left to the imagination as his linen draped over his thigh, barely concealing his genitals.

Mark made his way toward the cabinet in the centre of the room, the floor squeaking beneath soft carpet.

He grabbed a book perched on a slight angle with soft blue light from the lamp amplifying its title—*The Amended Human Genetic Code*.

Fact or fiction, it made Mark feel uneasy.

The book adored a *superior* race that came to Earth in search of gold, and explained how a scientist among them created a hybrid race through experiments and DNA manipulation—creating a slave race. How *The Scientist*, in an act of unlawful affection toward what he'd created, later committed *The Great Sin*—and granted *his* hybrids the ability to think freely, and for themselves in *The Garden*— causing disagreements among *them*.

Mark's uneasiness peaked—especially when he read about an arrangement involving the trade of energy. Human energy—to the Archons.

He would have read more had it not been for increasingly loud footsteps on tiles nearby.

He snapped the book shut. Arm shaking, he struggled to place it back into the cabinet without making a noise.

So, he held onto it and crouched behind a pillar at the back of the room.

The door opened. Two people he instantly recognised—Kevin and Grace.

"Kevin, it's not working."

"He's not a priority right now."

"We've never had this many issues keeping someone stable."

"It's fine, Grace—have the rest of the afternoon off. Link and I will handle this."

"I don't think he's here," Grace said, both turning back toward the door.

Astral projecting, Mark followed them, some metres behind, through hallways and rooms. At a junction, Grace veered to the left, and Kevin, to the right.

Mark followed Grace.

At a sliding door, Grace placed her palm on the touch-pad. It came to life and gave way. The white inside was blinding, and Mark blinked until the rigid lines and blocks in the living room clarified—a quadrangular, uncomfort-able-looking leather lounge and thick, metallic, rectangular pillars only suitable in a futuristic movie, or maybe a spaceship. The sofa barely sunk when Grace sat on it. She tapped forcefully at her phone.

Mark floated past her, and into another room—a bedroom—in which the white inspiration continued but for a thick, black rug beneath a white, low-set bed. The large window allowed the sun to reflect itself on the white tiles.

On a nearby desk lay a clipboard. *Patient 9009* was written on the top.

Mark's eyes made their way down the report.

Engagement One: Failed
Engagement Two: Failed
Engagement Three: Successful
Engagement Four: Successful
Ongoing: TBD

Notes: Initial engagements; patient found to be resistant to thought reform and hypnosis.

Ongoing engagements find patient is at times resistant, or immune to psychic driving, intravenous therapy (IV), barbiturate, amphetamine, thought reform, psychedelic drugs, hypnosis and electroconvulsive therapy (ECT).

Patient NOT considered dangerous.

He attempted to turn the page but was reminded he was without a body. He brought his attention to the library when he heard a faint siren. In the living room, Grace was on her feet, quickly shuffling her way toward the door.

For a second, Mark saw blurs before being flung out of the room, unable to control the force that pushed him up, down and sideways like a rollercoaster.

Back in the library, Mark zoomed toward his body. The siren pierced his ears.

As he approached the back of the room he observed his crumpled body—now angled to the side and sliding down toward the floor. His eyes were open with a blank, unfocused gaze and the book was still tightly clutched in one hand.

Mark entered his body and searched for an exit. There was only one—the way he'd come in.

Book still in his grasp, he rushed out of the room and toward the lifts. Red lights on the walls that pulsated in time with the siren provided some light as he made his way through a mostly-dark passageway.

He entered the lift. It jerked and soared him upward.

His heart sank as it opened.

Kevin, on the other side, eyed the book in Mark's hand before regaining eye contact. Link was by his side.

"Going somewhere?" Kevin's jaw tensed.

Mark shook his head, backing away. He bumped into something hard and cold—the closed door of the lift he'd just exited.

"Who the fuck are you people?" he demanded, his voice shaking despite his agitation. His fist tightened, threatening to crush the book in his hand.

Kevin took a step toward Mark. "We're here to help you."

Mark pushed his back into the golden doors behind him. Link stepped forward.

"Get away from me!" Mark yelled.

"Don't make us use force," said Kevin, taking another step. "We don't like doing that to our patients."

The book barely made a noise as it fell onto the carpet. In a split second, Mark clenched his fist and jabbed it toward the side of Kevin's face. He made contact, then brought his fist back, cocked and hooked—hitting Kevin again. The last thing he remembered was a hard baton-like object hitting against the back of his head as he tried sprinting past Kevin and Link, and the prick of a needle into his arm.

XXX

He was cocooned inside tight sheets and his throat felt dry. He looked down at his wrist, dangling over the edge of the bed. The sharp pain there came from a tight handcuff that had created red lines. It had been attached to the bed's railing.

The woman in the room peered over at him as he struggled to sit up. With his free hand, he applied some pressure to the back of his head. He flinched, a sharp pain surging from the base of his neck to the top of his head. Standing from her chair, she grinned and made her way toward him. Mark tried smiling back but the pain in his head was all he could focus on.

He felt fatigued and he struggled to make sense of what was going on. The room. The woman. *How'd I get here? Who is she?*

The air-con was powerful, goosebumps rippling across his skin. He looked for a blanket but found none. He attempted to speak but his voice failed him. His vision constantly came in and out of focus. He saw rigid, white walls but seconds later he would see blurs of white.

"How are you feeling?" asked the woman, now cupping his head.

Now he remembered. It was Grace.

He had feelings for her.

"There he is!" It was another voice. Loud. Too excited.

Mark concentrated, trying to figure out the man who'd walked into the room. He beamed—seemed kind. Helpful. Yes, Percy.

xxx

"How are you feeling?" Grace asked again.

It was difficult to speak. His voice was hoarse.

"What's going on?" he began.

"Another seizure," Grace said. His vision returned, clearer. He appreciated her.

And Percy, he just wanted to help.

"We're worried about you." This time Percy spoke.

"I'm fine," he said, his brain struggling to string words together and when it did, the words stuck in the back of his throat.

"You're not fine," said Grace, cupping his wrist. "You're suffering from trauma-induced psychosis—and you're having seizures and breakdowns because you can't face the truth."

"What?"

Grace glanced at Percy and then left the room.

"Mark, your wife. We've tried telling you so many times—you need to accept that you killed her."

Mark struggled to process what Percy said. *I don't even have a—*

Then he remembered. What was her name? *Why is it so hard to remember?*

"Rachel, Mark. You've living in denial—but you have to face the truth—and accept it."

Mark tried responding but instead shook his head furiously. His head ached but he couldn't stop. Soon, his whole body trembled uncontrollably.

The handcuff rattling against the bed's metal railing invaded his ears.

How?

As the convulsions worsened, he felt his eyes roll to the back of his head.

233

XXXI

Somewhere in the darkness, he heard a voice.

"Mark. Mark. Mark?"

It was familiar.

His shoes were soaked. Mould irritated his nose.

He wandered in pitch black, puddles of water rising up to his ankles and wetting the bottom of his jeans. He raised his arms and held them out in front of his face.

"Mediumship is never as exciting as you'd expect, is it?"

The voice came from behind him. Mark turned.

Henry sat on a battered Chesterfield sofa—some of its brown shade had faded. A single, hanging lamp showered the sofa with warm light.

Mark cautiously dragged his feet through pools of water as he made his way toward the couch.

This fucker, who ran The Establishment. How is he not dead?

"Is that what they told you?" asked Henry, as soon as the thought entered Mark's mind.

Mark looked away, only to see darkness.

"Odysseus, the King of Kings—he had twelve psychic abilities."

Mark's eyes drifted away from the black that surrounded them and back to Henry, who'd started listing things.

"—and you're up to what now? Two? Three? Impressive."

Mark sat on a leather chair opposite Henry, cradled in a one-seater.

'They're controlling you Mark. You've helped them murder, and terrorise. The medication, the electrodes—you don't see what's going on?"

"What?" Mark replied. For a second he flashed Henry a sulky look. He turned his head, trying his best to concentrate on the past few weeks. The shadows provided no answers.

"And you've forgotten about Rachel. Isn't that strange?"

Mark held his breath.

"And those episodes... Tell me that you know you're living a lie."

Mark's head trembled. "I don't believe you. No way."

"You don't have to. But the truth is the truth—which you suspect—and that's why you're here, for confirmation."

"I have no control over this," Mark snapped.

Henry's lips curved upward. He snickered. "You saw the extraterrestrial beings—two of the deities that rule the modern world. You can't deny what you saw, right?"

Mark was too occupied trying to gather his memories. *Who was Rachel?*

"Mark?"

Then it happened—a blockage in his mind shattered. Memories of Rachel flooded his mind. He hadn't murdered her. *But what happened?*

He desperately searched for an answer until his head ached. Henry stared.

He regained his ability to verbalise his thoughts. "What's going on?" he muttered.

"You tell me."

"But, you're dead," he stammered.

Henry grinned. "It's time you learnt the truth."

Without warning, light seeped into the darkness. Shapes began to form.

A waterfall nearby crashed onto rocks, the stream flowing past where Mark and Henry stood. Mark's shoes were muddied, sinking slightly into uneven ground. Henry stood, perched on a large rock above head height. Mark joined him, nearly slipping on some dislodged stones as he made his way up. It didn't take long for his hands to be completely covered in red soil. From there, the view was mostly green, with thick shrubs, blowing leaves and the canopy of a healthy rainforest below.

Henry pointed at a clearing in the distance in the forest where a tribe of people congregated around a fire and village—the smell of flame-grilled meat wafting up to Mark and Henry. For a second Mark mistook them for children because of their height. They had flat faces, large noses, dark and shaggy hair to match their olive to brown skin, and wore sheets of fur and leaves wrapped around their waists. Some banged at drums made of animal skin. Few walked toward the village on muddied paths with woven baskets carrying fruit, where they headed into grass huts. Others had dead animals slung over their shoulders. A few walked away from the community with spears. Mark heard playful squeals from the younger ones who ran through the village and out to the nearby river.

"We didn't need much to be happy. Early humans lived with the earth," Henry said, finger still pointed at them.

Mark watched a fisherman pull his spear from the river, a wriggling fish on the other end. He tossed it into a shallow, wooden vessel and yelled to someone nearby who ran over and clapped and danced.

"This was our life before the Akkadians came. Those two brothers, Akku and Mattu came with others—and they came thousands of years ago, looking for gold."

The two men by the river had called others over to appreciate their catch. Children now splashed in the river.

"They'd destroyed their planet—and they needed the gold to repair their atmosphere," Henry continued.

Mark became distracted by someone painting on a large, flat rock. After some moments he made out the drawing—a multi-coloured fish and a spear.

The rainforest disappeared. Mark and Henry were on flat grasslands, the smell instantly reminding him of a football field. His head rotated upward toward a loud groan of a turbine in the distance. A silver ship far larger than any tree nearby hovered above the ground, the metal reflecting so much sun it nearly blinded him. Blades of grass parted as it neared the land. It touched down, ending the loud, high-pitched whirring.

The spacecraft's lowered, rear ramp, with bright green neon lights thumped as Akku, Mattu and others exited.

Henry continued. "Mattu planned to originally use them as slaves—but they didn't want to be slaves. And so Mattu punished them—but they never gave in. They didn't know *how* to be *a slave*."

The grasslands dissolved. Mark recognised the village, but only just. Cracks of whips drew Mark's attention, only for his stomach to turn in revolt at the sight before him. Thick, black smoke drifted toward them as teepees burnt to the ground. Mark coughed. His nose stung. The natives sprinted in all directions, like confused ants. The unlucky ones were on the receiving end of whips being cracked by the Akkadians, ripe, red slashes appearing on their dark skin as they fell to the ground. Gunshots rang out, echoing across the landscape. Children and women screamed. Men threw spears, sticks and rocks but they were no match for bullets. The soil had been devastated by blood, some of it seeping into the river. Bodies floated on the water.

Henry, seemingly unbothered by the massacre, continued. "What's ironic is that it was Akku's idea to develop non-coding DNA to create the slave race. He regrets it to this day. Infusing the hybrid race with a gene specifically formulated to make us worship *them*—and we lost all our abilities. We were no longer one with the earth. We couldn't engage with the energy around us, and so we could be easily manipulated."

The screams faded as the village vanished. Mark felt the soft chair beneath him once more.

"But Akku, he fell in love with us. I guess I don't blame him—like a father loves his children." Henry bit his lower lip. "But the so-called *Gods*, they had other ideas. When they were done with us mining their gold, they decided to trade human energy, like currency—"

The darkness around them morphed. They were surrounded by hills and mountains, a calm stream flowing through the centre. Birds racketed above. Ripe fruits hung from nearby trees, the soft breeze threatening to pluck them from their branches at any second. Pale, naked humans bathed in the river. Some ran along the grasslands, chasing each other, and others, chasing scurrying animals. They shouted in a language unknown to Mark. Mark saw a man pluck an apple from a tree—his munching so loud Mark heard it from where he stood. Rays of sunlight seeped through thick branches, gleaming on a waterfall that led to a stream flowing over smooth rocks.

"—which is why Akku has secretly helped us ever since. He gave us free will here, in this garden, thousands of years ago. That same man and woman who were cast out as a result, went out and bred, giving birth to more humans that could think for themselves—humans that had knowledge and wisdom. But best of all—some of us kept our abilities."

Mark's head spun.

"You know why they imprisoned you here, don't you?" asked Henry.

"What? Imprisoned? I can leave any time I want— what do you mean?"

"Can you?" Henry asked. "You tried going for a walk—remember the guard?"

"No. It can't be true."

"Think about everything that's happened. The drugs, the monitoring, the files, the experiments—"

Mark went to reply but bit his tongue, scowling as he considered Henry's words. He felt uncomfortable. He adjusted in the seat. He felt hot, and his shirt was damp, drenched with sweat. IIis pants stuck to the leather beneath his thighs. He shook his head, trying to connect the dots.

He already knew what Henry was going to say next.

"Kevin's theory. They trapped you here because if it was true—if you could restore human DNA, they were going to kill you."

"No."

"You're alive because you failed their experiments."

Henry went silent. Mark heard his own heavy breathing.

"But I know, and you know, that you can do it. Accept what happened with Rachel. Heal yourself—then you can heal everyone."

Although Mark's breathing steadied, sweat ran down his forehead. His soaking feet barely cooled him—instead his saturated socks clung uncomfortably, making his skin crawl.

"They're saying I killed her." Mark eyed his soggy shoes, his words barely loud enough for even himself to hear.

"What?"

"Rachel, they're saying I killed her. Tell me what happened."

"But you know what happened."

"I need you to say the words—so I know. For sure."

"You want me to tell you something you already know—"

Mark flinched.

"—that she died of cancer?"

Mark jerked his head, raising his eyes to meet Henry's. He slumped back into his chair, the soft leather on his back providing close to no relief.

"Isn't it time you set yourself free?"

Everything went silent.

Mark knew it was true. Everything came back to him.

FLASHBACK #10

Mark stopped typing and focused on the noise in the next room. It was 11PM. He could probably afford to stop working. He left the office and made his way toward the sound.

The light was dimmed. Rachel had her face in her hands, seated on the edge of the sofa. Her shoulders shook as she sobbed, totally unaware of Mark's presence. Mark went and wrapped his arm around her shoulders. Her sobs grew even louder as she turned her head into Mark's chest. Her tears soaked into Mark's shirt. Mark hadn't put much thought into the diagnosis—Stage II Soft Tissue Sarcoma. The doctor said the tumour hadn't spread to her lymph nodes or even distant sites. Even so, Mark felt his own guilt coursing through him as she cried and wrapped her arms around him.

Rachel had mentioned minor stomach pain months ago—he'd convinced himself it was nothing. At the time, she'd said she felt fine.

He'd barely spoken to her about it. He'd been busy with work—but he'd done some research on what it would mean if things took a turn for the worst.

He was plagued with thoughts of his own dad—lying stiff at the edge of his bed—all those years ago. He couldn't go through that again. Not with Rachel.

Everything was okay. It had to be.

XXXII

Slowly, he became more conscious. He made out voices and faint beeps. He was lying on a sturdy mattress, the pressure causing discomfort in his lower back. His arms were by his side, his entire body wrapped tightly in sheets. He tried spreading his arms but had little energy to do so. He focused on a voice, unsure who it belonged to.

"They're not effective anymore."

He kept his eyes closed.

"Completely or partly?" said another voice.

"Not sure, but they said there's no need for lethal injection."

Mark squinted, barely making out a figure who left the room.

The beeping got noisier, and more repetitive. He opened his eyes and looked across at a nurse who was still in the room. Electrodes had been attached to his head. Something had been glued to his chest.

"How are you feeling?" she asked, when their eyes met.

Although her hair had lost its shine and there was no longer a twinkle in her eyes—or even the same level of attraction, Mark knew it was Grace.

He stayed quiet.

The figure who'd left the room returned—Percy. He picked out a needlestick in a cabinet before making his way toward Mark. Louder and more frantic beeping from the screen by the bed caused Mark to quickly glance over at it.

Grace had her hand on his head. With some difficulty, he twisted his arm out of the sheets and pushed her arm away.

"Mark," she began. She smiled, attempting to look encouraging. "You're suffering from a severe psychological condition."

"She's right." Percy sat on the edge of the bed. Needle ready in hand, thumb on the plunger. "Your hallucinations are getting worse—especially when you refuse to take your medication."

The beeping close by grew in pitch, the intervals between each beep becoming shorter and shorter.

"What is this?" Mark hissed, tearing the sheets off himself.

"Mark, it's me—one of the nurses. I've been helping since you arrived," Grace said. She attempted to place her hand on Mark's head. Mark raised his arms, blocking his face.

His head throbbed. His thoughts were scrambled, jumping around from one to the other with no apparent logic or pattern.

Grace turned her head toward Percy with a slight nod of the head.

Mark shoved Percy as he grabbed Mark's arm, bringing the needle closer to Mark's skin. Mark tore the cords connected to his chest and pulled away the electrodes on his head. The beeping stopped. He sprung up from the bed and scrambled toward the door.

A security guard outside the room in long-sleeved, navy-blue attire grabbed Mark's shoulders as he exited.

"Leave him—he'll come to his senses," came Percy's voice from inside the room he'd just escaped. The guard's grip loosened, and Mark shrugged him off.

Ignoring stares, his bare feet slapped on the cold floor as he sprinted down the corridor in his hospital robe.

"I need to get out of here!" Mark shouted, desperate and panicked, half hoping someone would come and help. More stares. People edged away. Not a single one offered any assistance. The woman at the front desk peered across momentarily before dropping her head back to the computer.

"This place—they're lying to us!" Mark yelled. Some people in the waiting area fidgeted in their seats but no one stood. There was barely even a shuffle of feet.

As he neared the end, he ran into someone coming around the corner—the last person he'd hoped to run into. Kevin. It wasn't difficult to recognise the long hair, the glasses and the gold watch but his eyes were darker, yet simultaneously calm. His body wasn't rigid. He smiled weakly at Mark.

"Mark, you need to trust us. You're sick. Let us help you."

Mark shook his head abruptly.

"You're not well—if you leave, you won't get better."

Mark pushed Kevin into the wall. Kevin's eyes narrowed and he gripped Mark's arm, fingers digging in. Mark grunted, trying to break free.

Kevin loosened his grip.

Kevin's faint voice followed as he raced away. "You're making a mistake, Mark. Let us help you get better."

He continued to run, trying to ignore the aching in his legs and the dizziness in his head. He raced toward the lifts—gusts of wind rode up his robe.

He knew where he wanted to go to confirm he wasn't insane.

He racked his brain, trying to recall the room he'd seen with Sam.

He made his way into the ward he'd first met her. The plastic chairs were unchanged. Confused stares pointed his way. Nurses, patients—even children. The ward fell silent. No soft murmurs, no clacking of a keyboard. Not even a cough.

He retraced their steps.

He proceeded down a corridor. Trolley wheels squeaked on the floor until they abruptly halted. Staff stopped in their tracks, eyeing Mark as he passed them.

Mark barely noticed.

"Where are you going?"

Mark turned. Kevin spoke quietly. He kept his distance from Mark.

"You can't keep lying to me," Mark replied.

Kevin took a deep breath. "Mark, we don't have the resources to keep going along with your *healer fantasy*. We hoped you'd come out of your psychosis, but enough is enough. You have to accept reality."

"No," Mark started, eyes darting across the walls.

"You stopped taking your medication, you're getting worse. I've had to exert force—I don't like doing that to our patients." Kevin shook his head, slowly making his way toward Mark."

"Stay right there!" Mark yelled, eyes wide.

Kevin flinched and took a step back. "Mark, I'm trying to help you. I'm your chief doctor. You've been here for months—for rehabilitation."

Mark shook his head aggressively. "No, I don't believe you. That room—I saw it with Sam."

"You were hallucinating. Mark, please."

Mark's breathing steadied, but he continued to shake his head. There was a sharp pain in his head. "I don't—I don't believe you."

As Mark considered sprinting away, Kevin spoke, interrupting his thoughts.

"Take me to that room—but this is the last time. No more wild goose chases, no more trying to convince us you're a healer, and no more claims of having visions about people—dead or alive—and other things that don't exist."

Mark nodded. He stared intently at Kevin—at his face.

There was no crack of a smile. No smirk. No upward slip of the lips. Nothing.

Retracing his steps, Mark led Kevin through brightly-lit corridors. They evaded nurses who rushed in and out of rooms. Some patients were moved on roller beds into rooms as they passed. Groans drifted out of slightly-ajar doors. He nearly slipped on something wet on the floor but Mark didn't stop. He remembered the way now.

They reached the door. He peered over his shoulder. Kevin had maintained his distance and had stopped some metres behind him.

Mark nodded.

Kevin walked to the door, his face still expression-less—eyes level, with a slight squint but his mouth showcased no emotion. If anything, there were subtle lines on his forehead.

Mark shoved the door—instantly frustrated that it had been locked. As he shook his head, Kevin placed his hand on a nearby sensor. It swung, allowing cool air out of the room.

Mark scowled. "I don't—it was right here. I saw it, with Sam," he started.

Although a bright light was on, he squinted his eyes, hoping to see something else in the otherwise empty room. The soft carpet provided some relief as he made his way across the room with Kevin at his tail. "I don't get it."

The room was completely empty. White walls, soft flooring that massaged Mark's feet—and that was it. No tables, no chairs—and no huddled group performing a bizarre ritual.

Mark turned toward Kevin who was now by his side. His shoulders dropped. He slouched. "It was right here— I saw—"

"You've been having hallucinations, Mark—this is why we're worried. You're seeing things that don't exist."

The edge of Kevin's mouth twitched. *Is he annoyed?*

"What about the lift—the middle one that goes up to the penthouse? I saw them—very tall—and the gold—"

"Mark, we've been over this. We've been there already."

"No, we haven't—" The words died at Mark's tongue. *Have I been there—with Kevin?*

Kevin sighed. "Okay Mark, let's go to the penthouse— but this is the last time."

Kevin pointed his arm toward the door. Mark took one last look throughout the room as they made their way out.

They reached the foyer and made their way into the lift in the centre. Kevin tapped the highest button—125. It shot upward, Mark grabbing onto the lift's side railing.

Mark jerked as it came to a halt. His ears felt funny.

The doors opened. Mark's heart sank. His head dropped into his palm. He wiped his face, forcefully pinching the bridge of his nose as he scrunched it.

"Mark, it's time you stop this and come to your senses."

Mark stayed quiet. He looked out onto a deserted outdoor recreational area as the lift doors closed. He made out some sun-bleached deck chairs and weathered wooden tables. Some cushions sat lonely on sofas in an undercover area. Pot plants, hedges and fountains provided some temporary visual relief.

Back against the wall, Mark slid down toward the floor of the lift until his knees were bent in. He brought his head between his knees and put his hands on his head. As he stared at the floor, he saw his tears fall and streak against the metal surface below.

FLASHBACK #11

It had been weeks since Mark had read it—the Cancer Caregiver Guide. He'd saved the PDF to his devices. His printed copy probably lay in among his files at home— strategically misplaced—and forgotten.

Doctor Parker slid a freshly printed copy across the table, its strong toner and warm paper scent instantly transporting Mark to his office—and its one hundred and fifty odd pages caused Mark to frown as he grabbed it. He pretended to show interest in the cover depicting inter-locking fingers of '*loved ones*'. He felt nauseous.

"I know it's not easy."

Mark tore his eyes from the guide's front page and directed them at Doctor Parker.

"She's fine," Mark muttered, searching for anything in his mind that would allow him to persist with the belief.

"Mark, Rachel asked me to meet with you. She's worried you don't understand the severity of her illness—"

"Severity?"

Mark dropped his head, flipping through the guide. He slid his thumb over the paper's edge, searching for a papercut.

"Her cancer—it's progressed to stage four. Tell me you know what that means."

"She's okay—"

"Mark, I know this is hard—no one wants to know someone they love is—well, is in this situation—"

"She's not sick," Mark mumbled, his mouth barely moving. "She's okay."

"I had a meeting with both you and Rachel, months ago. Do you remember?"

Mark nodded. His eyes struggled to meet Parker's.

"I explained to both of you—especially you—how strenuous being a caregiver is—the sacrifices you would need to make—"

"I remember—"

Parker took a deep breath. A short pause.

"We're not sure—well, she's not sure—if you're the best person to be her caregiver."

"She said that?"

"I'm not here to judge your life Mark, I can only imagine what you're going through—but she needs full-time care—"

"—She's not sick—and my job, I can't just..." He eyed his leather boots as his sentence trailed off. He needed to be back at work in forty-five minutes to present to the board regarding the acquisition of cloud-based technology giants, MikroTek—it involved a five hundred-million-dollar deal. He didn't need unjustified negativity.

Parker bit his lower lip. He dipped his head, scratching his forehead.

"I'm not sure you understand what this means for Rachel, Mark."

Mark went to say something but his mouth was dry. The last few months were fuzzy but one thing he knew was that Rachel was okay. And for the sake of half-a-billion dollars, she had to be.

XXXIII

In a daze, it was difficult to know how long he'd been in the chair—or even what time, or day it was. The air in the room was icy cold against his skin. Even worse, the metal cuffs anchoring him to the chair at the wrists and ankles dug into him—and they felt raw.

Grey concrete walls surrounded him. A thin, white robe covered his body, falling just below the knees. He shivered.

He clenched his fists but it was little use against the cold steel holding him in place.

"Why are you so difficult?"

Mark raised his head, trying to make out a man seated directly opposite him on a wooden chair. Mark smelled the mint on his breath.

The man stood and bent down so his head was a tiny distance away from Mark's. Mark flinched. A droplet of something drooped from his mouth and onto his leg. It took some moments to realise it was dribble—gooped down to his thigh. He couldn't wipe his mouth, or slurp it back up. He blinked slowly, allowing his eyes to refocus on the room.

"Going to cooperate now?" The man's warm breath ghosted over his face.

This man. He couldn't be trusted. *Ken? Kayden?*

Through the fuzzy haze of his mind, memories began to form.

With the little energy he had, Mark groaned and writhed violently but it was useless. The chair barely did as much as rock.

The door slammed, making Mark quickly turn his head. A woman entered. He went to say something but his voice was raspy and strained—and he had a sore throat.

The man stepped aside as she neared.

"Oh, Mark," she said, crouching down next to him. Her black hair had been tied into a tight bun. "I wish it didn't have to be like this—I really do."

She sighed and pulled something from her pocket.

She pushed it into his arm. The room faded to black.

* * *

Two blurry figures in white came into focus: one female, one male. They both had light-brown eyes behind square reading glasses. Their white robes hung to their shins. One held a clipboard. Lanyards hung from both their pockets.

Despite low lighting, he recognised the room—the grey concrete walls. His bare feet soaked in the cold from the concrete floor.

"Mark, do you know why you're here?" the woman asked, placing her hand on his arm. Mark turned his head toward her. He struggled to keep his eyes open, let alone answer. "You need to understand the reason you're having these episodes."

What episodes?

He saw flashes in his head. He didn't know how he'd gotten there. The room felt too cold. His mouth was dry. He needed water. His head ached and he struggled to maintain eye contact with the two people in front of him.

The man spoke. "You're experiencing trauma-induced psychosis and post-traumatic stress disorder. It's to be expected—given you killed your wife."

The man sounded serious but sincere. Mark racked his brain but nothing came to mind. He couldn't remember.

Who are these people?

Another man walked in. Mark briefly saw blurry figures on the other side of the door. Faint voices drifted into the room. He didn't know who any of these people were. But the woman...

Think. Think, Mark, think!

Grace, Kevin, and Link.

"Get away from me!" he growled. No ropes and no shackles. He tried standing but his legs gave way, instantly dropping back into the seat. He gripped onto the chair's steel arms and tried propping himself up. His arms shook under his weight, his legs providing little assistance.

"I know who you people are!" He nearly stood but his arms ached and failed him. He collapsed back into the chair, its metal seat thumping hard on him, the penetration running up his spine and causing him to moan.

"Mark, you're suffering a serious psychological condition as a result of killing your wife, Rachel—"

Mark looked up at Kevin. Mark's eyes were wet but the fury inside him caused him to squeeze his fists tightly. His arms trembled.

"—you tried suppressing it, creating an elaborate story that she died of cancer and that you're a healer. It's not true."

Mark froze. His tight fists loosened. The trembling stopped. He felt guilt. It was like a weight pushing down on him. His neck muscles tightened. *Is that why she's always angry—angry at me?*

Memories flooded his mind—the nightmares, the hallucinations and memories of *her* being so furious. *Could they be right?*

"Mark, this is our final intervention—otherwise we'll need to take more aggressive measures," Kevin said. They sat in a semi-circle around him. Mark found it difficult to breathe. Kevin looked over and nodded at Link. Link bowed his head. "You've been here six months and we've hardly made progress. You struggle to accept the truth—"

"No," Mark muttered. He pushed his feet into the ground, attempting to lift himself from the chair. His thighs strained. He was glued to the seat.

"—it wasn't cancer. You made that up. It was you. You created this fantasy that you're a healer to cope. You lied, telling people you would cure them. But no one got better. You ignored letters and phone calls from everyone that told you to stop, and eventually you were admitted here. Your lawyer pleaded insanity."

"No," Mark mumbled. "No way."

"Everything you believe is a lie, Mark." Kevin paused and stared directly at Mark. There were dark shadows beneath his eyes. His face was drained, his skin pale. His hand wobbled as he removed his glasses, placing them in the front pocket of his robe.

Faint voices were coming from outside the room. It was impossible to know what was being said.

"We need you to say it."

Mark's eyes darted over to Grace. *Say what?* The door opened, then slammed shut. A woman entered, a clipboard tucked under one arm. She carried a small camera in the other. In moments she stood in front of Mark, the camera pointed at him. There was a beep.

"Say it, Mark," Grace said again. "I made all of this up. I'm not a healer—and I, Mark Pierce, killed my wife, Rachel Pierce, in an act of rage. Say it, *now*."

He stared into the camera's lens, jaw clenched. His muscles locked up, tension sitting low on his back.

It took effort to stabilise his breathing. His anxiety dissolved and so did the dull ache in his head. He became hyperfocused on Grace's scrawling on her clipboard, the scratching grating on his last nerve. He studied the room, allowing his attention to become absorbed in other things. Kevin's chair squeaked as he adjusted. Link's knee jerked to the left. Grace blinked slowly.

His muscles relaxed.

He fought the urge to smirk. He raised his head, then locked eyes with Kevin. "I didn't kill Rachel." His voice went from a mumble to something more assertive. "She died of cancer—fuck you."

He grabbed the edges of the seat. He groaned, thrusting with everything he had. Arms and legs trembling violently, he began to rise. But before he was able to fully stand, he felt a searing hot flush burn into his arm. He collapsed. The floor rushed toward his face before the world fell away into darkness.

* * *

His face was flattened against a cold and hard surface. He opened his eyes, only to be greeted by grey, ugly concrete. He wiped his mouth. Dribble had accumulated on the floor, creating a small puddle. The single bed by his side had its metal slats close to the ground, a thin mattress atop the short-legged metal frame. Crumpled sheets lay on it. A single pillow leaned against one of the bed's legs on the floor. A filthy blanket was scrunched on the ground near the pillow.

The dark walls didn't help—they made the room seem even colder.

A few steps and he'd be on the other side of the room.

Mark sat up. He wiped some of the floor's grime that had built up on his arms and hands onto his thin, white pants. His white top had been blackened at the front— near his chin, it was slightly damp.

There was a foul stench coming from the toilet near his head. The dripping from a tap behind him irritated his ears—the frustration made him want to wrench it from the wall.

He rose from the floor. His legs swayed. He rocked. He used the bed to hoist himself up.

He staggered to the entrance. His hands clamped around steel bars. The coolness penetrated his skin, seeping through to his shoulders. He rattled the bars until sweat formed on his forehead and upper arms.

"Help!"

He gazed down a dark hallway. There was a clock ticking. *Was that a shadow?*

He eyed a touchpad near the exit.

Despite feeling cold only seconds ago, a warm bubble grew inside of him.

"You're best just cooperating with them."

Mark spun toward the voice.

He made out a faint outline of a figure—almost a ghostlike appearance. Even then, he knew who it was— Akku. Mark turned his head upward, staring into Akku's eyes—bright and blue against a mostly-pale body. "Don't fight them. They'll win—every time."

Akku hovered some inches above the ground.

"I knew it was you—you visited Mattu and me. I didn't want to provoke his paranoia, so I said nothing."

"What do you want?" Mark asked.

"Humans ask that a lot—what do you want from me? What is the meaning of my life? Ugh."

Mark's legs gave way. He held onto the parallel bars as he lowered himself to the ground. The thin pants didn't prevent the nippy floor from trickling through.

"We created you as a hybrid to labour and do our work—our obedient, little slaves—to mine gold—"

"What?"

"Well, I say 'we'—but as chief scientist it was mostly my effort—but Mattu would have you believe otherwise."

"All that, just to mine gold?" Mark asked.

"We needed a lot of gold—and what can I say? We were lazy—we still are."

"I read something about using our energy—the Archons?"

"Yes, after The Gold Mine, there was no use for you. But my brother created an animal farm—a true masterpiece by the way, even to this day."

"How?"

"Human suffering creates a certain type of energy—and everything is supply and demand—so when we found ourselves in the possession of something the Archons feed off, we used it as leverage."

"And they can't just come and claim it for themselves?"

"I'm sure they think we're doing *their* dirty work."

"How?"

"The suffering? Wars, illness, death, confusion, disasters—you get the idea."

"No, how do you gather up the energy?"

"Don't need to. We make it available to *them* and in return, the interlocking chain of command stays intact."

"Why are you telling me all this?"

Akku smirked.

"Always had a soft spot for you—your kind—like you would your pet I'm sure—"

Mark scowled.

"—the main reason I don't often see eye to eye with my brother."

"Mattu?"

"It's complicated—"

"Why's that?"

"I allowed some of you to possess less non-coding DNA—and gave you all free will and the ability to think for yourselves, knowing full well that you may challenge us one day."

Mark heaved himself off the ground. He leant his back into the railing. "Why though?"

"I believe in balance and giving the underdog a chance"—Akku stood rigid, barely swaying—"because where's the fun in not having a fair fight?"

Akku rotated his head, looking around the room. He scrunched his face when his eyes met the toilet. "And now I'm too old to challenge Mattu and the others—and Henry, well, he's gone—so it has to be you."

"What do you get out of this?"

"Such simple creatures. Sometimes I forget I'm talking to humans."

Mark frowned, giving Akku a dirty look. "What's that supposed to mean?"

"You're all so self-obsessed—completely unaware of the bigger picture beyond your own meaningless lives."

"Then why me?"

"Most likely my addiction to controversy—but also, a small part of me wants to entertain the idea that you can do it."

"Do what?"

"Spare me Mark, you're not that stupid."

Mark eyed the floor.

"—I forget how simple you all are. It's really anyone's guess how you've managed to stay alive this long. Imagine, pets, and you leave them to their own devices hoping they don't die or kill each other—that's been me."

Mark shook his head. He dropped his head into his palm. "No, I'm done. Leave me alone." His voice got louder, he started shouting. "Get the fuck out of my head!"

"Very well," came Akku's reply.

Mark raised his head, going to say something else but Akku had vanished.

"Akku?"

All he could hear was the dripping of the tap and the faint ticking of a clock down the hall.

Fuck.

He heard footsteps—and they were getting louder. *Someone must be coming.*

As Mark turned, he made out a familiar face—Roger, the cleaner.

Roger slid a plastic tray across the concrete floor toward Mark. Mark turned up his nose at it—water, a single, hard-boiled egg, brown, dry-looking bread and something white and mushy. He grabbed the cup of water and drank it down in one go.

"Roger, I need your help," Mark said as Roger started walking away. Roger stopped. He spun and dipped his head toward the ground where Mark sat.

XXXIV

"Involuntary commitment?"

"Yes, voluntary manslaughter."

Mark's stomach grumbled as he listened on. They'd woken him up and brought him here—Kevin and another man he didn't know.

His own body odour made his nose wrinkle in disgust. It was as though he was enveloped in filth. His clothes were barely white anymore. Such was life in solitary confinement. Even now, he could still smell the pungent hellhole that had been difficult to breathe in. The toilet refused to flush. He hadn't bathed in days. Cockroaches and mice had made themselves at home—with access to generous amounts of Mark's tasteless, and uninviting leftover food.

It was difficult to know how long he'd been in there. If he'd been brought in three meals a day then possibly just over a week. But his brain had refused to work like a dark haze clouded his judgement. He found himself staring at the walls as they suffocated him, all the while losing all sense of what was happening around him, let alone time.

And even though he now wore shoes, the feeling of cold concrete had etched itself inside his brain—freezing him to his core. The thought of blackened feet with toes nearing frostbite haunted him.

He shuddered.

The chair's cushioning did little to provide comfort. He sat up straight but it only emphasised the pain in his lower back. Even worse, eyes in the room stared, digging into him with barely concealed judgement.

Mark raised his head. He turned toward the front. Kevin was speaking with the man who'd also come to Mark's cell. The sound of the metal door slamming had woken him and he'd shot up from the bed. He was tossed a pair of thin, canvas shoes and told to follow them. He had scrambled to the shoes, bowing at their feet in the process. The man Kevin was with had contorted his face, especially when his eyes met the obscenities of the toilet.

That was thirty minutes ago.

Mark observed the room. He recognised others from *The Alliance.*

The man with Kevin wore a dark suit that bulged at the midsection. His voice was deep. He occasionally looked at Mark with contempt, like somehow Mark wasn't worthy—or even smart enough to be there.

"A full rehabilitation?" he asked, the question directed at Kevin.

"Yes," replied Kevin.

They both turned toward Mark.

Kevin addressed him. "Mark, can you state for the record, what you told Roger that night—and what you subsequently told us after our collaboration-strategy intervention."

Mark took a deep breath. He fought the urge to punch the unknown man's face whose sneer agitated him. *I need to calm down.*

He pushed his foot into the floor. He cleared his thoughts. Another deep inhale and exhale. He counted to five in his head.

"I killed my wife—Rachel."

"How did you kill her?" asked the man in the suit. His mocking had been replaced by narrow eyes and pursed lips.

Mark searched the room for comfort. Grace was over to the far right—a familiar dark, curly bun on her head. Link, two seats down, wore a smart, long-sleeved shirt with long pants above shiny dress shoes. Percy, toward the back, wore a memorable coat of white.

"How, Mark?" Kevin said.

Mark emptied his thoughts. With a slight rattle of the head, he glanced back toward the front.

"I poisoned her."

"Why?"

"I was angry at the cancer—I hated seeing her like that." Mark's voice trembled. He needed something for his sore throat. It was difficult to swallow.

"But she didn't have cancer, Mark—did she?" asked the suited man.

The room felt hot.

"No," Mark replied, eyeing the floor in front of him.

"—and you know that for sure?" the same man asked.

Mark wiped his face and clenched his fist. His jaw followed.

"You have to tell Darius, Mark. This will help your case—and others like you," Kevin said.

"Yes, I know that for sure."

Darius nodded at Mark. His harsh demeanour still lingered. His narrow-eyed expression had shifted to a look of disapproval, like the room reeked of the repulsive toilet—or perhaps Mark was a representation of the toilet itself.

"You've done a great thing, Mark. The system wants to keep you here—with years of mandatory treatment—but we believe we can fast-track the process with a collaborative approach. You should be proud," Kevin said, grinning.

Mark nodded and glanced over at Grace. He felt sick to look at her, betrayal sitting heavy on his shoulders.

"What does this mean?" he asked, keeping his head level, eyes to the front.

"You'll be reintroduced into gen pop—and we'll work on having you out of here as soon as possible," Kevin said, grinning at Darius.

"When will that be?" Mark asked. He swallowed built-up saliva, hoping to dissolve some of the pain in his throat. It only worsened.

"At this stage we don't know for sure—"

Mark bit his lower lip. He rubbed his hand on prickly stubble.

"—that concludes the hearing, Mark. You'll be taken to your room," Kevin said, as he stood. "Grace?"

Mark followed Grace from the room in silence. His mind was filled with thoughts of a warm shower, and finding something for his throat's irritation. He walked some paces behind her, the occasional glance at others in white clothing he hadn't noticed before. Some pointed at him. Some chuckled as he walked past. Others ran along the corridors, chasing each other. Squeals and screams, sometimes laughter, echoed from behind closed doors.

Mark focused on the floors and carpet as they made their way to his room.

"How are you?" Grace asked.

Mark stayed silent. She peered over her shoulder at him. With a slight shake of his head, he looked away. His frustration was that of a hornet's nest angrily buzzing around his skull.

He ignored the security guard by his door who bowed his head. His dark clothing, only a couple of shades darker than his skin, hugged his broad muscles. He didn't smile. Although his head bowed a little, the rest of his body remained dead straight. Mark walked right past him with not as much as a sideward glance.

His room had been cleaned. Folded clothes sat on his bed, the rubbish removed, and dishes washed. The room's recognisable citrusy scent had been replaced by lavender.

Grace ducked her head in to say bye but Mark zoned her out. The door closed.

He made his way to the bedroom.

He found the note in the top drawer. On its other side were disorganised lines indented forcefully into the paper.

I booked for one and was given a suite that could fit four. I have zero complaints about the hospitality here. The food was great with a classy three-course meal. Thanks for giving me six drinks and only charging me for three. The play, Nine-Tails, was amazing, I'll be back for part two—probably for my birthday on the sixth of April. I might bring my partner too next time!

His phone was missing.

He tore back the blanket on the bed.

He searched the bedroom, tossing pillows and linen to the floor. The bedside drawers were wrenched open, their contents flung onto the bed. Some items found themselves on the floor.

He rushed into the living room. Soon, cushions lay on the ground. In the kitchen, drawers were emptied. Utensils lay scattered on the bench.

He pulled a glass jar from an overhead cupboard and filled it with water. Back in the lounge, he tipped the entire amount on the laminate floor and threw the jug toward the ground—with so much force it immediately shattered to pieces.

The door swung open. The security guard shoved his head inside. "What's going on?" His voice was hollow.

"Broken glass—and a spill," Mark replied.

"We'll send a cleaner." The door slammed much louder than when Grace had left.

Mark returned to the bedroom. He sluggishly made his bed and placed some clothes into a backpack. He chucked random items inside the bedside drawers, not caring about any particular order.

A knock came.

"Come in!" he yelled.

He looked through to the front door. His heart sank. A lady he didn't recognise.

He paced through the room, hand on chin while she got to cleaning—the noise of the vacuum cleaner made it difficult to think.

The vacuum stopped and a knock followed almost as soon as he shut the bedroom door.

He sighed, making his way toward it.

"I'm done," the woman said, when he opened the door.

"Okay, thanks."

"This is for you," she said. She reached into her pocket and pulled out a smartphone.

Mark's chest swelled. "Thank you, he replied, going to take it from her. "I would pay you but..."

She cut him off. "No." She placed her palm over his hand as she handed over the phone.

The tension that had been building up over the last few minutes dissolved.

He wasted no time. He brought the phone to life and jabbed at it impatiently, entering the code from the note—14036392642.

He grinned ear to ear and set the alarm for 2AM.

XXXV

He jerked his arm, snatching the phone and switching off the alarm nearly as soon as it started chiming. He lay on a bed that was already made. In the silence of the room his heavy breathing echoed, and Mark had to make a conscious effort to calm it.

He slipped his shoes on and used the phone's torch to make his way into the lounge. He neared the front door.

He sent a message from the phone.

We need you in the lobby.

He moved his head until his ear was inches from the door. Torch off. Darkness and complete silence.

The door's lock clicked. Mark jolted up and raced into the kitchen. He quickly turned the phone's torch back on.

"What are you doing?"

The hallway's light was dim but the guard was easy to make out. His silhouette took over a substantial amount of the door's width. Faint light seeped into the lounge, casting his long shadow over the carpet.

"Thirsty, just getting a drink of water," Mark replied, grabbing a glass from the counter and running it under the tap.

"Okay," the guard responded. After staring at Mark for some seconds the guard turned and pulled the door behind him. Mark stayed on his toes. He rushed to the door. He could hear footsteps heading further away, down the hall.

He wiped sweat from his forehead. His body trembled.

He waited some minutes then stuck his head out of the room. He looked the hallway up and down. Clear.

He started the timer on the phone—exactly five minutes before he planned on outing the power. By then, the guard would realise he was called to the lobby for no reason. Then, he would have about thirty seconds before the emergency generators took over—fifteen seconds for them to kick in, then fifteen seconds for them to fully power up the building.

Roger had given Mark the idea. And Roger had helped install CyberGuard onto the building's mainframe computer—a hacking prototype that Mark had developed years ago.

"You'll need full control of the system—the cameras, security, the lights—everything," Roger had said that night he'd agreed to help Mark. "Unless you're a hacker, good luck."

Mark had to hide in the corner of his tiny prison cell, as far away from the security camera as he could—the offensive smells making his eyes water—as he instructed Roger how to download a CyberGuard Trojan onto a USB.

He'd used a burner phone that Roger had brought him with his meal the following day—taped to the bottom of his meal tray.

Mark asked Roger to leave a coded message with the master code generated when CyberGuard entered the USB—which would give Mark access from any device. All Roger had to do when cleaning the server room was plug the USB into the main computer—and Mark would have full, external control of the building's computer system.

Mark jabbed at the phone to enable pre-recorded footage to replace security footage for the next ten minutes.

He grabbed his backpack by the door and headed into the hallway. Although he stayed on the balls of his feet, his footsteps still echoed—each echo making him clench his jaw. He made his way to the stairs at the end of the hallway.

He heaved the heavy door toward him.

He peered over the railing's edge. It was a long way down.

He interpreted the lines on the reverse side of Roger's note. Two downstrokes followed by a ninety-degree line.

Leaping over two steps at a time, Mark made his way down two floors. He entered a door to the right. Two lifts—unfamiliar in that they were black. *Staff Only Lifts* was written in bold on a pillar between them.

Numerous lines ran downward on the paper in his hand.

Mark pressed level fifty, then hid around a corner. The lift opened. Empty.

He entered. It hauled him downward.

He exited.

Four minutes until the power outage.

He sprinted across the corridor, not caring as much for the noise he made. He came to another door. He found more lifts on the other side, also dedicated to staff based on a similar sign.

Mark jumped to the side as the lift opened but the coast was clear. It was empty.

He reached the first floor.

His eyes widened with panic as the lift doors opened.

A bald man with a white, short-sleeved gown a few paces from the lift stared directly at Mark. Deep-purple, circular patches stood out on his scrawny upper arms. The man's arms shot into the air. His high-pitched voice pierced through the foyer. "You shouldn't be here! Need to tell Kevin!"

"Shh!" Mark hissed, but it was little use.

"Kevin!" the man screamed. His bellowing punctured through the night's dead silence.

"Kevin sent me," Mark said, putting his arm on the man's shoulder.

"No he didn't! Kevin! Someone has escaped! Kevin!" The man pushed Mark's arm off his shoulder.

"Shh!"

"Kevin!"

"Kevin told me to give you this," Mark said, shoving the sheet of paper in his hand toward the man. He stopped shouting and frowned. "It's secret, you can't let anyone get this, understand?"

The man snatched it from Mark's grip.

Sixty seconds until the power outage.

The shouting stopped.

Mark sprinted toward a door on the other side of the floor. He'd left the man frowning at the paper as he flipped it from side to side.

"Eddy, what's going on?"

Mark peered over his shoulder. He saw a faint figure heading toward the man who'd been screaming. Obviously Eddy.

Mark vaguely heard Eddy's reply. "... escaped—he gave me this secret note. He went that way."

Mark had no choice. The power outage would have to be premature. He launched CyberGuard and pressed at the phone's screen, momentarily disarming all doors on the floor. There was a faint clicking of doors.

"Hey!" The voice came from behind him.

He sprinted toward the exit. He jabbed the phone's screen. Everything went dark.

Pain shot up his legs. His feet ached—but his adrenaline surged.

His arm bumped into something solid. He searched for the handle. He gripped onto it.

He swung the door open.

He was met with a cool breeze. Light rain tapped his skin.

He ran down some stairs, nearly losing his footing and collapsing on the landing. He stayed on his feet—just.

Fifteen seconds before the backup generators would lock the front gate.

He rushed toward it, nearly slipping on wet rocks.

He pushed down on a metal handle. It gave. He shoved it open.

He bolted down the street and onto the esplanade.

He bent over and grabbed a tree branch. Panting, he searched for a number plate among parked cars. *He's not here.*

Soon, high revs sounded. Bright headlights headed his way. Rain streaked across his vision.

He squinted. It was only when it was metres away that he saw the number plate. A sigh of relief. The car stopped right by him.

"Quick, get in," said Roger, through the lowered window.

Mark hurried inside.

He slumped into the passenger seat. He rocked his head back, allowing it to lean on the headrest. He placed his hand over his chest. He took some deep breaths.

"I just assumed you got the phone. I was expecting a confirmation," Roger said, gazing at the phone in Mark's hand.

"Oh yeah, sorry. And thanks," Mark replied, placing the phone in the centre console.

Mark wound up his window. He pulled a jacket from his backpack and slipped it on.

He gazed into the car's side-view mirror. Some distance away, lights throughout the building flickered on—all the while the building continued to shrink as they drove away.

XXXVI

Mark's eyes were glued to the side mirror. He occasionally rotated his neck toward the back, at cars that came up behind them. Rolling chunks of metal that caused his heart to speed up each time they neared.

Roger barely flinched. He stared straight ahead. His breathing was normal.

The car slowed. They stopped at roadworks. Mark's arm was tense. He grabbed the edge of the seat, crushing it. A cramp rippled through his limbs, and he hissed through his teeth. They'd been waiting for a truck ahead of them to move for at least a minute. *Why are they working in the rain?*

A car behind them gleamed as it got closer. Then another. Dark sedans blending into the darkened and rain-soaked evening. The drivers couldn't be made out. All they were, were dark lines and shadows. *Why are there so many cars on the road at this time?*

Roger turned his head toward Mark. "You okay?"

Mark raised his head. A quick sideward glance. Then a subtle nod—but his thighs tensed. There was heat building up there.

The car started moving. Ahead, a roadworker waived her arm for them to pass. She'd flipped her sign. Droplets rolled down her yellow jacket.

Mark's neck muscles stiffened. The same two cars trailed them. *That's not enough distance.*

They came to an intersection. Mark gazed across at the service station—where Grace had driven off with him, fleeing from *those men*.

He shook the thought off and exhaled slowly. The car immediately behind them veered to the left. *But why is the other one still following?*

He didn't realise he'd clenched his fists until his fingers started going numb from the force.

Mark twisted his neck toward Roger. "You see that car behind us?"

Roger peered into the rear-view mirror.

"They're fine," Roger responded.

"How do you know?"

"They came from the opposite direction."

Mark bobbed his head and shrugged—but everything still felt tight. He pulled off his jacket.

He closed his eyes, zoning everything out but it all came to him—the nightmares, Rachel, everyone and everything he'd met and done.

Finally, the car behind them pulled into another street. Roger kept his head straight. A brief smirk.

The car came to a halt. Mark recognised his house. Solar-powered lights glistened on the wet pavement. Raindrops bounced off cement and ran down the driveway.

He shoved the car's door open. He went to say something but was lost for words. Roger nodded and smiled. "All the best, Mark."

"Thanks."

As Mark evaded puddles, jogging across the driveway, he made out something dark by the front door.

He turned but Roger was already pulling out. He made his way toward it—a large clump on a slippery outdoor area by the front door.

Mark bit his lip. He recognised him—Jaxon, who'd brought his family, and Liam, who had Leukaemia.

Mark gripped Jaxon's shoulder to shake him. Jaxon jumped, his muscles temporarily seizing, before slowly sitting up. Dark, wet patches spread across his pillow, with matching pools of water littering the sleeping bag hiding his legs. The rain had soaked straight through.

"You can't stay here," Mark said. "You need to leave."

Jaxon rubbed his eyes. He squinted up at Mark. "We've been waiting—for days. It's Liam, we're worried."

"I already told you, I can't help," Mark replied.

"Please—"

Mark looked out toward the street. No sign of approaching cars. A faint bark of a dog, the whooshing of branches in nearby trees, and the soft sound of rain on grass and bitumen—but that was about it. He turned back to Jaxon. He delayed, eyeing his reflection in the window.

"Where is he?"

"The car—"

Mark cut him off. "Go and get him, quickly."

He tore his eyes away from Jaxon's face as it broke into a broad grin.

Mark unlocked the door, switched on some lights and marched into the lounge. Moments later, the family's trail of wet footprints made their way to Mark's lounge room. Liam's bony figure sparked an uncomfortable twinge for Mark. He rushed into the kitchen to prepare warm beverages.

"Liam," Mark began, after joining him on the sofa.

"Yeah?" Liam replied. Mark stared into sunken eyes.

"How are you feeling?"

"I don't feel good," he replied, sipping on hot chocolate.

"We'll try again, okay?" Mark said.

"Okay."

"Put your drink here," Mark said pointing to the coffee table. Mark, worried that Liam's thin arms would fail, grabbed the cup, placing it gently on the table with a soft knock on the glass. "Close your eyes."

He grabbed Liam by the wrist. The faint sound of rain faded.

The late night shifted into darkness of a different kind.

Golden sand had turned to grey, thick clouds blanketing the sky. Heavy winds blasted into them—and streaks of lightning flashed right before their eyes.

Loud crashes and booms took over—challenged by high-pitched howls. Liam gripped Mark's arm.

In the distance, beach tents were airborne. Branches collided with light poles. Trees were no longer straight, instead forced bent like dangerously unstable slingshots.

"Over there!" Mark shouted, even though Liam was right beside him, hand tightly bound to his. Mark pointed across the beach at some multi-coloured, wooden huts, shielding his face from the rogue sand with the other arm. The wind threatened to flick Mark off the ground and he crouched, shuffling his feet toward the huts. He pulled a now sobbing Liam with him.

"Liam, we have to get to the hut, okay!" Mark shouted.

Liam shook his head. Mark shoved his feet into the ground. To his left, a car's bumper flew out over the ocean. Loud crackling close by pained his ears as bright lights lit up the sky.

"Come on, Liam!" Mark shouted.

They were halfway there.

Mark's clothes were drenched, weighing him down. His back ached.

He endured, placing one foot in front of the other, and patiently propelling his lower limbs, ignoring the pain.

They were getting closer. But at times they were thrown backward and Mark would lose his footing. It was difficult to grip the wet sand with bare feet. Strong winds forced them back.

Only a few metres now.

But a familiar sound overwhelmed the storm around them. A shriek—and it came from the hut just ahead of them.

Mark stretched out his arm, trying to grip the handle. He was still too far. He raised his back foot to move forward. He slipped and flung backward. Liam fell and screamed. He'd fallen on something hard—a rock by the looks of it. Mark strained his arm, dragging Liam toward him. Liam's squeals got louder.

Mark got back onto his feet. Holding onto Liam, he forced his legs toward the hut. He made contact with metal. He looked back. His right-hand gripped Liam's arm.

"Come on, Liam!" Mark shouted.

Liam's eyes were wet. Mark dragged Liam toward the door. He groaned.

He twisted the handle and heaved them both inside. The door slammed. The sounds of thunder, rain and the storm ended. But one sound persisted, growing ever louder—the shriek of a furious, and well acquainted, demonic entity.

Liam's whimper took Mark's attention away from the eerie sound. Liam clutched his left arm, tears streaming down his face.

"Are you okay?" Mark asked.

Liam shook his head. His tears had found their way to his chin. "It hurts," he sniffled.

"It'll stop hurting soon, I promise."

"I want Mum and Dad," Liam complained.

Mark went to respond but his attention was stolen by a dim light that flickered on above them, illuminating the space ahead. At the sides, light seeped from opened doors and onto the hallway's wooden floorboards. Mark made out a door at the other end before it was overtaken by a woman's figure—Natalie, Liam's mum.

"Mummy!" Liam called.

"Liam! Don't move!" Mark barked. He eyed the woman. Her flowy sundress shimmered, filling the area around her with light.

"But I want Mummy," Liam whimpered and took a step forward.

"Yes, Liam—come here," she said. She grinned, a twinkle in her eye.

"Liam, stop!" Mark shouted.

The floorboard's creaking stopped. Liam turned to face Mark.

"Liam, sweetheart, come here."

"Liam, stay still—that's not your mum," Mark said.

"What do you mean?"

"Trust me. When I say, I want you to run as fast as you can to that door. Your mum and dad are on the other side."

Liam nodded. He still held his left elbow with his right hand.

"Liam, come to mummy. He wants to hurt you. Show mummy your arm," she said, now arms outstretched.

"No, Liam, stay right there," Mark snapped.

Mark went to tell Liam to face the demon but it was too late.

She bolted across the floorboards, so fast it looked like a series of blurs coming in and out of focus. With little reaction time, Mark shoved Liam from her path, knocking him to the ground. There was a loud thud, then a scream. More sobbing followed.

Mark propelled himself at the demon and tackled it. She fell on his arm—searing pain rippled from his shoulders to his fingertips.

She shrieked and began to morph.

Her eyes narrowed. Natalie's brown skin faded to a washed-out, pale complexion. Wild and dark streaks of hair hung from her head—but only moments ago she was Natalie, with shiny, and straight, brown hair.

"Liam, run! Through the door!" Mark groaned, squeezing his arms around the squirming and contorted figure who threatened to break free. Her skin was slimy under his hands, and he had to fight the urge to throw up at the smell of rotten eggs pouring off her. Liam scurried toward the door.

By the time Mark managed to get on top of her, his arms burned. Fatigue pulled at his limbs, making him weak.

She punched his chest. The force pushed him off the ground, sending him flying backward—straight through the wall. Pieces of wood stabbed him.

She rose to her feet and sped toward Liam. Mark grabbed onto the wall, ignoring the sharp pains in his arm. He hoisted himself up. His back stung. Ignoring his heavy legs, he legged it toward the demon.

Liam had nearly reached the door. As Liam grabbed the door's handle, Mark leapt into the air. He dove and grabbed the demon by the waist. She screamed.

"I want Liam!" Her screeching pierced Mark's ears.

But it was too late. Liam had vanished.

Mark rolled onto his back. He was out of breath. Every part of his body was in agony. There was strong sulphur in the air. He was sure something in his back was broken.

The demon rose to her feet, cracking her bones. The floor squeaked underfoot as it neared Mark. Squeaks turned to thumps. Slimy feet made their way toward him, leaving wet footprints. Her long and blackened toenails were probably sharp enough to slit Mark's throat.

It was as though Mark was cemented to the floor. He tried raising his arm, but a strong imaginary magnet forced it down. He attempted to lift his head, straining against the non-existent rope around his neck, pinning him to the floor.

"You'll have to do," she said in a high-pitched melody.

She got down on all fours at Mark's feet. Her face peeled. She snarled, showing blackened teeth.

Mark's fighting and intense wriggling had left him fatigued. He stared into dark eyes at the reflection of the dome light. Something dark and oily oozed from her mouth. It dribbled down her chin and onto her chest. Dark droplets stained the bottom of Mark's jeans.

She slapped her hands on his thighs—bit by bit inching toward Mark's face. Cold palms smacked his chest as she crawled on him. The pressure penetrated through to his back, causing sharp pains. A trail of sticky slime seeped through Mark's shirt and onto his skin. Mark froze. Eyes wide. Any closer and her nose would've touched his.

Before he opened his eyes, the demon locked its mouth onto his and tunnelled something icy-cold and gunky into him. It trickled down his throat. A slimy discharge that tasted, and smelled like death.

XXXVII

It would have been dead silent had it not been for the rain's pitter-patter on the roof and windows. No foul stench or life-threatening storm in sight but Mark still felt nauseated and dizzy. He found himself lying on the hard floor. His palms were damp, and his elbows throbbed.

He grabbed onto the sofa and propped himself up. He peered across at Liam who had his arms wrapped around Natalie on the lounge. Liam turned his head in Mark's direction—and grinned. Mark forced his face into a weak smile as he stood.

"You need to leave," Mark mumbled. He didn't mean for his voice to be so shaky. "Now!" he grunted.

The family rose to their feet.

"Do we need to—"

"You need to get out of here, now," Mark said, staring at Jaxon.

Mark dragged his feet, following them to the door. He felt drowsy. He poked his head outside as they left.

Jaxon crouched, picking up his sleeping bag by the door. He raised his head. "Thank you," he muttered.

Mark nodded.

He watched them hurry across the driveway and toward a white car on the opposite side of the street. It was impossible to know if the other cars belonged to anyone he should be worried about.

He shoved the door closed.

He scrambled up the stairs and found a suitcase. He didn't bother to switch the light on. He snatched at clothes and shoved them inside, not caring for specifics. The ensuite received a similar treatment. He found his passport in the bedside table's drawer.

His arm strained as he dragged the suitcase to the top of the stairs. Shaky legged, he lifted it. He felt lightheaded and cold. His arms trembled.

Even before he made it down the stairs he knew someone was there. He turned into the lounge. He shook his head at the three people that sat there.

"Are you running away?"

"Get out." Mark's voice was weak. He scuffled past them—Apollo—who'd spoken—and Jamie and Castro.

"We need you."

Mark didn't bother to look at Jamie. His feet stomped on tiles as he headed toward the door.

"Get out of my head!" His voice was hoarse. It bounced off the walls.

He saw red flashes. Blood rushed to his head. His legs felt heavy, like they welded into the floor with each step, heavy as lead.

"What did they do to you?"

Mark's breathing was heavy. He wanted to tell Castro to fuck off but his body was sore. His grip around the suitcase's handle loosened—and it crashed onto the tiles.

The walls blurred. Mark's eyes crinkled—they felt swollen.

He swallowed, trying to avoid throwing up.

His legs gave way first. He collapsed down to his knees. They collided with the tiles with some force. His kneecaps tingled with soreness. He tried fighting the exhaustion and perched himself up by holding onto the suitcase. The room blurred—then became dark. On the way down, his head hit something soft. He heard footsteps and soft murmurs before everything went black.

* * *

Clean sheets—and a faint beeping. A heavy head prevented him from turning toward it. Faraway voices seeped through the walls. Conversations among doctors and nurses. Possibly other patients. Artificial fragrances of eucalyptus drifted into Mark's nose. Even then, the unnatural scents couldn't mask what they really were— antiseptics, cleaners, disinfectants and soaps.

Dampened linen stuck to him and made him shiver. He struggled, attempting to roll over. He felt drowsy. His body wouldn't register.

The room came into focus. Harsh fluorescents. His eyes had nowhere to hide—he stared directly at a bright, white ceiling. A blurry figure beside him sharpened and came into focus.

Megan.

A slight tilt of his head. His brain wanted to smile but his facial muscles objected. His lips barely moved.

Her face was red. A worried expression. Mark shook his head as though to say: 'it's going to be okay'. Her expression lingered.

She gripped Mark's upper arm. The warmth was soothing. She squeezed her eyes shut.

"What happened?" she asked after some moments. Eyes open.

There was a scratchiness in Mark's throat. It felt dry.

"It's fine," Mark mumbled, his dry lips barely parting—but she shook her head.

"Mark—" Her expression changed to one of distress. Then frustration. Her eyes narrowed. Her head shaking became a little more aggressive. She flashed him a dirty look. "I asked the doctor why you're here—"

Something warm trickled down Mark's nose. He wiped his fingers across prickly skin. It was blood. He smeared it across the sheets.

He went to say something but she stood. Her head trembled and quaked—her jaw clenched so tight it had to hurt. Mark sighed.

For a second or two, she closed her eyes while gripping Mark's wrist. She let go, took one last look at Mark and rushed from the room—pulling the door lightly behind her.

* * *

Mark looked across the room when he felt the warmth in his chest. He must have dosed off. Darkness filled the room—the only source of light was now a thin strip of low-ambient fluorescent behind his head. It just highlighted a faint outline, difficult to distinguish from the rest of the room. Discussions and chatter in other rooms had ended but there was the occasional slapping of feet on lino and a shadow here and there, passing on the other side of frosted glass.

Mark tilted his head—and promptly winced. He pawed at his swollen neck. It was difficult to swallow. Akku's form, although mostly see through, became more pronounced the more Mark concentrated. He fixated on the floating figure in the corner of the room.

Akku shook his head, although it may have been a jiggle—or tremble. Flustered, Mark's eyes widened. Then he shuddered—or was it a shiver?

Mark was exhausted, his bulging eyes growing more pained the longer he kept them open—but he kept his eyes on Akku, hoping it was just a jiggle, or maybe a tremble. But Akku avoided eye contact—he pressed his lips together and rubbed his chin. He had a pale, saggy face and a frown like someone who'd just been ghosted— or on the receiving end of a flake.

Mark's eyes found his own chest. They rested there for a while—until he decided to raise them and flick them back to the corner.

Akku had vanished.

Mark's eyes fell shut, and the room drifted away.

FLASHBACK #12

Everything was fucked. Fuck cancer.

She was gone.

Mark heard sobbing. His thighs felt sore but his chest felt worse. Someone gripped his shoulder but his eyes were glued to the ground. He'd have to go up and speak soon. His body felt bulky. The few steps to the front seemed laborious.

It finally sunk in. The falsification of Rachel's condition unravelled itself into an ugly truth. One he'd been too afraid to face—or acknowledge.

Mark remembered the first time she'd said she loved him—her broad smile, the twinkle in her eye. They'd been seeing each other for six months. They were in the car on the way home from dinner. She blushed and held Mark's gaze, waiting nervously for a response. She'd stared like a puppy when Mark verbally reciprocated. Her face glowed.

They'd made out in the car.

She was vulnerable—and he was too when he said he loved her too. But Mark was filled with uncertainty—and memories. His dad had loved him too—and he'd left. At the time Mark's fear nauseated him. His stomach churned, butterflies going wild—but not the nervous kind one would generally experience in that situation. No, this was sheer terror.

Feelings were for the weak. That's what he'd told himself—and he'd suppressed them for years. Things were less painful that way.

"You okay?" Rachel had said, kissing his cheek.

Mark had nodded.

But now here he was, all his fears unfolding. History was re-writing itself.

Fuck Varion.

Mark opened up his phone to type a resignation letter. The Cancer Caregiver Guide was open. His stomach churned. She probably hated him for never being there but in his head, it was never going to come to this. But it did—and she died—and unlike Mark's dad, it was entirely his fault.

He hadn't taken it seriously. He'd worked harder than ever for Varion throughout the last year. And during that time, he'd convinced himself she was okay.

And everyone else had been left overwhelmed—the doctors, the nurses, and Rachel's family—while he carried on with his life.

Sweat trickled down his forehead. His heart throbbed. He rose to his feet and made his way to the front, hoping the dryness in his throat would go away.

XXXVIII

Stabbing pains shot through Mark's back. The floor was icy and unfriendly beneath him. His body trembled, his muscles vibrating in response to the chilly air.

Dark sludge trickled from his mouth and down to his chin. Some of it had made its way onto the concrete floor.

He took a deep breath—then turned his head. Shooting pains ran down his spine.

Dismissing the throbbing in his arm, Mark pushed his palms into the floor and rose. The muscles in his back spasmed as he stood. His legs wobbled, like a foal's first steps.

He vomited.

Thick sludge sprayed onto the floor, discolouring it with black gunk.

He wiped his mouth—then staggered toward the middle of the room—toward a chair made of the same stained, grey concrete coating the room. Mark felt a chill even before he sat down—and there was little comfort to be found on the seat. It was cold and clammy, and his thighs complained as they pushed onto the hard surface. The only thing separating it from his skin were his thin, white pants.

Eyes partially squeezed, he tried focusing on the walls. They spiralled and waved. His eyes felt sore—and heavy.

There were two doors on either end of the room: one of white timber and the other of black. The one of white was slightly open—and a bright white shone through and lit up some of the concrete room.

Mark peered through the white door. It was impossible to make anything out except for the glowing white canvas. He eyed the black door on the other side of the room. It was shut.

He stood, his back and legs instantly mollified by the motion, and made his way toward the white door. Warm air soothed him as he neared—but still, white was all he could see. He pulled the door further open and made out a feminine figure in a slim, white dress.

His heartbeat kicked into double time.

He glanced over his shoulder before taking a step forward.

Footsteps echoed behind him. He froze.

"Don't do it."

Even before he rotated his head, he knew who the voice belonged to. *But how?*

Megan had made her way past the chair, the tapping of her feet getting louder. Mark avoided eye contact. He changed course, and re-entered the freezing room—but not before glancing out at Rachel in the white canvas. The door remained half open.

He eyed the floor before locking eyes with Megan.

Her body was animated. She almost skipped toward him. Mark attempted a smile. He hoped it wouldn't let him down and look more fake than real.

"I did it!" she exclaimed. Mark's fraudulent smile broadened. He knew why she'd come. At that moment he knew he'd been right about her.

She reached him. Her grin vanished, replaced with a stuttering, "I—I'm—"

She flushed—but her eyes were still bright.

Her face contorted from a wide smile to accusatory frown. "I know what you did with Liam. You didn't have to—" she said, eyes narrowed.

Mark scratched the side of his neck, eyes falling to the floor.

"You need to..."

Her eyes scanned the walls before falling to the floor—then back at Mark. "...come back."

Mark's darting gaze found Megan's eyes. He crossed his arms over his chest, rigidity present in every element of his posture. His neck ached as he shook his head. The door she'd come through was slightly open—but Mark couldn't see what was on the other side. Only shadows.

"I can't force you, but—" she began.

Mark bit his lower lip. He glanced over his shoulder and out through the door of white. He wiped his face with his hands. The roughness irritated him. He scowled.

"I came to..." Megan said. Her mouth scrunched to the side.

Mark finished her sentence. "To heal me?"

She nodded. "You've helped a lot of people..."

Her sentence trailed off but she held Mark's gaze. Even in low lighting her eyes glistened. Her bottom lip quivered.

"You miss her, don't you?"

Megan nodded her head past Mark—and behind him—through the white door. Mark bowed his head. He eyeballed the walls then spotted two full-length mirrors only some metres away. He stared into one of them—at his reflection—and the reflection of the white door behind him. As Mark moved closer to it, zeroing in on the mirror's gold edge, his reflection blurred—then transformed entirely. It mutated and shrunk. Then his arms thinned. The whites of his eyes became black. The room snapped to an even colder temperature as dark, long hair protruded from his head in the mirror. Mark felt queasy at the sound of bones cracking as his reflection contorted into a monster. Next, came the sludge that trickled from *her* mouth—through inky teeth. Then the snarls. She slammed her fist into the mirror's glass. A crack. Then several more. Queasiness turned to fear. Mark twisted his head.

Megan's piercing stare sent a chill down his spine.

Mark's attention was stolen by a cracking sound as the demon kinked its arms out of shape. She banged her head into the glass. Mark flinched. More cracks.

She tried again. And again. Thumping her skull against the glass. And finally, she crashed through it. Glass shattered all over the concrete floor.

With no glass membrane separating them, she leapt into the air—and toward Mark. Megan screamed. "Mark!"

Cool air gushed onto Mark's face.

Icy hands wrapped themselves around Mark's neck. He fell backward onto the hard floor. He grunted. The demon writhed, squeezing harder. The cracking of bones became more aggressive as it twisted its arms, holding Mark down.

Megan yelled. Mark couldn't make out what she was saying. His eyes bulged as the demon pushed into his windpipe. Mark's arms ached as he attempted to push away slimy arms—trying to get her off him. He wrestled and squirmed. She hung on tightly as he struggled for air. He knocked his elbow on the concrete. His eyes watered. He wriggled, attempting to get free.

She inched her face closer to Mark. He stared into pitch-black eyes, surrounded by pale skin. At that moment he knew.

It wasn't Rachel.

She lowered her face—closer to his. Black gunk oozed onto his cheeks. His stomach churned at the foul stench.

Mark's lips curved up. His muscles relaxed.

She shuddered and froze—with an unfocused gaze. Mark grinned, mocking the demon. Her body seized and her eyes bulged. Her limbs fell limp and she collapsed, the pressure sinking into Mark's chest. She was lifeless, but her eyes were wide open and she'd turned to the side. Black slime dribbled from her mouth and onto Mark's shirt. He shoved her off him as she started vomiting—but some of it ended up on his face.

Panting, he brought his arm up to his face, wiping himself clean of the sticky mucus. He glanced over at Megan. Her dimples stood out as she grinned at him, eyes wide and chin up.

He brought himself to his feet. His legs cramped. He rubbed his elbow, wincing when he applied pressure on the slowly forming bruise.

There was nothing out of the ordinary with the other mirror. As one would expect—his reflection. It mirrored him. No evil entity trying to put him to death. He pushed into his neck with his fingers. He flinched at the tenderness. He tiptoed over glass, making his way to it. It was full length and directly opposite the one that was smashed.

He brought his face right up to the mirror. His reflection impersonated his movements. He searched for a clue, a quick look across at Megan. Nothing. He brought his attention back to the mirror. His reflection had its eyes closed. Mark's eyes expanded. He took a step back when the closed eyes snapped open but it was too late. A tensed arm protruded through the glass. A rough hand found its way around Mark's neck, crushing it. Eyes watering, Mark stared at flared nostrils and a clenched jaw. The man in the mirror's eyes narrowed, teeth gnashing as he tightened his grip. Mark tried making a sound but all he did was squeal. It was difficult to breathe. His arms were fatigued. The room started going black. His throat would crush at any moment. Megan's words were unintelligible, coming to him through a fog.

Mark brought up both arms and wrapped them around the man in the mirror's veiny forearms. Mark could barely breathe. He wheezed, gasping for air. He was choking—and losing consciousness.

He found it near on impossible to inhale oxygen, let alone utter a word. The room was murky and fuzzy. Through laboured breathing, memories came to him—everything—but most importantly, Rachel—and the meeting he'd had with Dr Parker. The Cancer Caregiver Guide came to mind.

He hated Varion.

Mark scrunched his face. He tensed his arms, pushing into the man in the mirror's outstretched limb. It made no difference. His reflection suffocated him—through the membrane of the glass. The grip too strong. Unmovable.

"Mark!"

Megan's scream brought the room back into focus. For a moment, Mark saw a fist flying toward him. It found its target—the side of Mark's face. He tasted blood. His face felt hot. His eyes watered.

I accept.

Mark fixed his eyes on his evil counterpart's. His reflection's fist was scrunched, ready for another punch—arm cocked.

Mark's grip around his reflection's forearm loosened. He squeezed his eyes shut and took a deep breath. He braced himself—ready for the punch.

It never came.

The calloused hands wrapped around his neck relaxed. Then slid off entirely.

He blinked. His reflection was no longer tense. His hands weren't balled up into fists. He didn't stare daggers at Mark—or frown or scowl. He mirrored Mark. Mark raised his arm. "Ouch," he said, pawing his face.

Megan had vanished—probably through the black door where she came. It was slightly open but still, all he could see was darkness.

Mark hobbled to the white door. He pushed it further open. Warm air hit him. It soaked into his skin. A white sofa sat on the all-white canvas. Long, blonde hair hung over the chair's backrest. Mark's skin tingled. He limped, making his way across to it.

Mark caught a glimpse of her face—a shy face, with a mixture of optimism. She twisted as he approached. Mark sat next to her. He gazed into her eyes—bright, hazel-green eyes. He crossed his arms.

"You did it," she said with an adoring gaze.

Mark's nose twitched. He shuffled his feet. She held eye contact as she spoke. "I missed you."

Mark tapped his foot. He bowed his head, clamping his teeth on his upper lip. "Are you going to stay?" she continued.

He shrugged, then rubbed his chin. Hands clammy. He wiped them on the sofa's polyester and took a deep breath before saying, "You're not really her, are you?"

"You already know the answer to that."

"But I need you to say it, so I know for sure."

Rachel said nothing but continued to smile. He managed to pull his eyes away. Looked around him.

His foot stopped tapping.

He locked eyes with her again and held her gaze for some moments.

Although every part of his body was in pain, and for the most part, it distracted him, at that moment, he made sense of what was really going on.

He stood, and made his way back into the concrete room. He walked around shattered glass and to the black door. He reached it and gripped the handle. He saw only darkness but still, he made his way through.

Moving on. A new plan in place. Exploring options.

I accept.

ABOUT THE AUTHOR

Born in Mombasa, Kenya, Brown moved to Brisbane, Australia at the age of seven where he's lived ever since (with family, he was too young to live alone). His interest in books and literature developed from a young age although, it was shared with sporting achievements through soccer (football, depending on where you live) and track & field athletics.

He believes humans were born to create.

Ideas, planning and thoughtful action can create things previously thought impossible and he wants to share that idea with others.

The Healer started with a random idea.

Most days you'll probably find him in the gym—if he's not out exploring nature, thinking of new (and often ridiculous) business ideas, reading, riding his motorbike, or playing the guitar (not that he considers himself any good!).

Brown enjoys provoking the mind, transporting readers to a place where they can challenge their thoughts and ideas with an underlying psychological tone.

Some consider him to be an athlete, a daredevil, a go-getter, an entertainer, a friend, a jokester, a little weird, and a man of action who isn't afraid to give anything a go. He simply considers himself a friend you can rely on. You can visit Brown online at brownmohamed.com or on Instagram (@beerown).